CW00520523

The Clock Chimed Midnight

By **Irene Lebeter**

Published by Author Way Limited through KDP
Copyright 2018 author

This book has been brought to you by -

Discover other Author Way Limited titles at -
http://www.authorway.net
Or to contact the author mailto:info@authorway.net

ISBN-13:   9781980234180

In memory of my dearly missed friend, Isabel,

and with love to her daughters, my special nieces,

Linda and Wendy

.

Acknowledgements

With thanks to

Gerry and Elaine, Author Way Publishing.

Mary Edward, for her very helpful feedback on the story.

Pat Feehan, for his time spent in proofreading the story.

All members of Strathkelvin Writers' Group, for their constant inspiration and encouragement.

All members of Kelvingrove Writers' Group, for their valuable feedback on my work.

Betty Duncan, for advice re midwifery issues.

Janette Martin, for reminding me about Sir Roger the elephant in Kelvingrove Art Gallery.

Betty Paton, Ann Barnwell and Agnes Morton, for going down memory lane with me in order to recall the names of local Rutherglen businesses in the 1950s/60s.

Rutherglen Reformer, for making old copies of the newspaper available on the web.

Centenary Celebration Brochure of the The Boys' Brigade 1983, presented by 195th Glasgow Company, Founded 1914.

Alma Ross, for her questions about the town hall clock which inspired the story and for her advice on Australian flora.

Alison and Giff Hatfield, for information about the Doncaster suburb in Melbourne.

Eryl Morris, Senior Librarian, East Dunbartonshire, for providing the photograph on back cover.

Elinor Ross, for providing me with the name of my main character.

Helen Hodge, for her unceasing interest in and encouragement with my writing. Also for accompanying me on research visits.

THE CLOCK CHIMED MIDNIGHT
PART I

Irene Lebeter

Chapter One

Tuesday, 8th November, 1955

They were halfway across the Indian Ocean when the bleeding started.

Elinor Bonnington awoke in pain and switched on the night-light on the wall above her head. A dark red stain was extending across her cotton nightdress and the sheet below her was blood-stained. She groaned as she got out of her bunk, glad that her cabin mate had disembarked at Fremantle and she now had the cabin to herself.

Hugging her stomach, Elinor dragged herself into the shower compartment. She pulled her nightdress over her head and stood under the shower, allowing the warm water to soothe her throbbing body. She stared in horror at the chunks of bloodied matter that were coming away from her. Once the bleeding had stopped and the pain eased a little, she put on a clean nightdress. With shaking hands she tried to rub the marks off the sheet. 'What's happening to me?' The words were wrung out of her; the teenager had never felt so alone or so scared in her life before.

Elinor crept back into her bunk and lay on the other side of the mattress away from the damp patch, with her face almost touching the cabin wall. She sent up a silent prayer of thanks that her parents were occupying a separate cabin on the deck below.

It was only after she'd been on the ship for a couple of days that Elinor had begun to suspect she might be pregnant. Her first bout of morning sickness had been on the day the ship docked in Fremantle, its last port of call before leaving the Australian mainland, and the sickness had continued since then.

She'd been terrified at the prospect of being pregnant and dreaded to think how her parents would respond to hearing that she was going to have a baby out of wedlock. Dad would be the more understanding of the two but Elinor had little doubt that Mum would blow a fuse. She loved both her parents dearly but found Mum a very strict disciplinarian. Lying there in the darkness, in her head she heard Mum's voice saying, 'I'm only doing it for your own good, darling.' This was always the reply when she challenged Mum's rules.

Yet now that she'd been bleeding, she was distraught at the thought that she might have lost the baby. It would be another link with Michael gone. If she had indeed miscarried then Mum and Dad would never know that they'd been denied their first grandchild tonight.

With sleep still evading her, Elinor's thoughts went back to the day in the middle of September when it must have happened. Michael's parents had flown up to Queensland and Elinor and Michael had his family home to themselves. With Elinor's November departure looming ever closer, she and Michael had been unable to resist the temptation. They both thought that she couldn't become pregnant the first time they had sex; how naïve they'd been.

She remembered clearly her first meeting with Michael Lynch. They were both pupils at Symonds High School in Brighton, one of the early coastal towns to spring up in Melbourne. At the time they met, she was in the middle grade and Michael was in the year above her.

'Hi gorgeous,' he'd said, winking at her when they drew level in the school corridor.

'Hello,' she'd replied, smiling shyly. She decided he must be well over 6' tall; even at her 5'7" height she had to look up to him. The silence between them lengthened, with Michael still smiling at her, and a blush rising up on Elinor's cheeks. Then, unable to think of anything else to say, she'd turned away from him and hurried along the corridor to catch up with her group of classmates on their way to the gym hall.

One of her classmates later told her that Michael lived in Seaview Road, round the corner from Elinor's home in Lansdowne Street. After that, she seemed to keep bumping into him on the way to and from school. When Michael left school to begin a plastering apprenticeship, he and Elinor still met as often as they could and shortly after her seventeenth birthday in June they had begun serious dating.

Sleep eventually overtook Elinor. She drifted off, still trying to decide how to give her parents the slip tomorrow to let her visit the ship's doctor. It felt like she'd scarcely closed her eyes when John, the cabin steward, knocked on the door and brought in her morning tea tray.

'Good morning, Elinor.' Through half opened eyes she saw his smile, his teeth gleaming white against his dark skin. When she'd first boarded the vessel, John told her that he came from Ghana. He addressed her as Miss Bonnington until she asked him to call her Elinor.

Elinor yawned, rubbing her eyes. 'Morning, John,' she murmured, as he placed the tray on top of the chest of drawers. By the time she was fully awake he was disappearing out of the cabin door.

'Are you alright, love? You've been looking a bit peaky the last few days,' Susan Bonnington said an hour later, when Elinor joined her parents for breakfast on D Deck.

'I'm fine Mum. I read in bed quite late last night and I'm tired this morning.'

Susan said no more but Elinor didn't think she looked convinced.

On entering the dining room, they were hit by a wall of chatter. Susan put her fingers into her ears and pointed over to a window table in the far corner of the room. Elinor took her seat at the table beside her mother and facing her dad.

'You really don't look well, Elinor,' Susan persisted. 'I hope you're not coming down with a virus.'

Aware that she was useless at lying, Elinor was glad the waiter chose that moment to come and take their order. 'I'll just have tea and toast this morning,' she said, moving the small vase of flowers on the middle of the table to one side. 'I've eaten so much since I came on board that I'll be a fat slob when I get to Scotland,' she said to her parents by way of explanation.

Andrew Bonnington laughed and looked over the top of his specs at his daughter. 'Don't worry, you'll need some beef on you to offset the winter weather that we're going into.'

After breakfast Elinor made the excuse to her parents that she wanted to attend Keep Fit on the Games Deck. She knew Mum's arthritic knee would stop her from doing Keep Fit and Dad was unlikely to leave Mum on her own.

Elinor didn't have to wait long at the surgery to be seen. 'I'm afraid you've lost the baby,' Dr Harrison said, once he'd finished his internal examination. He looked at Elinor as he was speaking, his eyes moist behind the lenses of his glasses. 'I'm so sorry, you've had what we call a spontaneous abortion.'

Elinor lay on the examination couch and stared at the white painted ceiling, tears sparkling in her dark hazel eyes. 'Will I be able to have more children?' she asked Dr Harrison, her voice a frightened whisper.

'There's no reason why you shouldn't,' he assured her, laying his hand on her shoulder for a moment. 'I'll give you some tablets to take over the next few days to help keep you calm. Your periods might take a few weeks to settle down but they should be regular again soon.' He went to his desk to write up his notes and the nurse helped Elinor down off the couch to allow her to sort out her clothing.

Before returning to her cabin, Elinor called into the Keep Fit class on the Games Deck. Fortunately the class was almost finished when she got there as she didn't think exercise would be best for her right now. But, having dropped in for the last few minutes of the class, it would be easier to answer, without blushing, the questions Mum was bound to ask.

Chapter Two

Friday, 9th December, 1955

The rain battered against the train window. Elinor peered out between the rivulets at the bleak landscape they were passing on their journey north. Everywhere she looked it was grey, with nothing to break the vast unbroken swathes of drabness. How she yearned for the Melbourne sunshine instead of this brooding early December sky which only served to send her already low spirits in a downward spiral.

They had the compartment to themselves. With Dad snoozing in his corner seat and Mum engrossed in the People's Friend magazine, Elinor didn't have to make the effort of carrying on a conversation. She listened to the train wheels clattering over the line, taking her ever further northwards, all the while thinking of her beloved Michael in Melbourne. It had been heartbreaking saying farewell to him when she and her parents had boarded the ship at Port Melbourne almost five weeks ago. As she'd agreed with Michael before the journey, he turned away abruptly once they'd climbed the gangway, unable to stand and watch the ship bear her away from the Australian shores and from him.

Elinor still couldn't understand why her parents had been crazy enough to leave Australia. The family's rented weatherboard bungalow in Brighton was luxury compared to the cramped room and kitchen tenement flat they'd occupied when they lived in Scotland. Dad was brought up in that house in Rosebank Street, Cambuslang, and when his parents died, shortly before his marriage to Mum in 1937, the council allocated the flat to the young couple. A year later Elinor was born in that flat.

Feeling stiff from sitting so long, Elinor got up and went to the toilet. Afterwards, she stood at the corridor window for a while, her thoughts drifting back to the evening, a month after her seventeenth birthday in June, when Mum and Dad had sprung the surprise on her. She was in the middle of school tests at the time and was already wound up about trying to gain high grades. After their meal that night, they sat down to listen to the ABC evening news. At the end of the broadcast, Mum switched off the radio.

She sat on the arm of Elinor's chair. 'Dad and I have something to tell you, darling. We've decided to return to Scotland. We're so sorry to disrupt your education, but your main exams will be over before we leave in November.'

Elinor didn't move a muscle at first but stared from one parent to the other, her features frozen with shock.

Andrew knelt down beside Elinor's chair and he laid his hand over hers. 'Yes, love, with our sailing not being until November then at least you'll be able to complete most of your school year by the time we leave Melbourne.'

'Why didn't you tell me about your plans earlier?' Elinor almost choked on the words.

'I'm sorry, love,' her dad apologised. 'I know we should have discussed things with you but when the travel agent found there were berths available on the 'S.S. Sydney' leaving in November, it seemed to be fate and before we knew it we had booked three passages.'

Elinor resented being forced to go back to cold, wet and windy Scotland. Once the shocking news had sunk in, she'd finally found her voice. 'I'm not coming back with you. I love it here in Melbourne and I want to stay.'

'But Elinor, have some sense, darling,' Susan told her daughter, not unkindly. 'How on earth would you rent a house and feed and clothe yourself if Dad and I weren't here with you?'

'This is all your fault,' Elinor yelled, glaring at her mum, who'd been the one fighting homesickness ever since their arrival in Australia two years previously.

Susan began to weep. 'I'm sorry, but I miss your Aunt Muriel so much Elinor. She's my only sister and we're so far apart.'

Mum was barely 5'4" and of slight build but as Elinor looked at her that evening she'd seemed even smaller and more vulnerable as her sobbing became louder. Despite being angry at what she saw was Mum's selfishness in taking her away from Michael and all she loved in Melbourne, Elinor ran her fingers down her mother's curly hair. 'I'm sorry Mum, I just hate the idea of leaving Melbourne and all my friends.'

Andrew cupped Elinor's face in his hands and kissed her on the forehead like he'd always done when she was small. 'But you wouldn't manage here on your own, love, you have to come back with us. You're still only 17 and we all need to be together.'

'Then can't Michael come with us?' she pleaded, her tears starting afresh.

'But Michael hasn't finished his apprenticeship yet. Anyway, what would his parents say about him coming over to the other side of the world and giving it up?'

'Think about it, Elinor,' Susan put in, her sobs abated a little, 'far better for Michael to get established in a trade and then he could join us in Scotland later.'

The train took a tight curve at that moment and Elinor grabbed on to the corridor rail to steady herself. Her thoughts then rolled backwards to their arrival in Melbourne in 1953. While they were staying in a migrants' hostel, which accommodation was admittedly basic in the extreme, Dad had found work as a painter and decorator. Shortly afterwards they'd rented the house in Brighton. Her parents had chosen Brighton for two reasons; Symonds High School had been recommended by Dad's boss as offering a high standard of education and Brighton was only a half hour tram journey from the centre of Melbourne. The fact that the house was located close to the beach was an added lure to rent the property.

Over the two years Dad had been employed by Garland and Son, the firm had secured contract work in the Melbourne Hospitals and he was earning three times what he'd have done back in Scotland. Because of his high wages, it wouldn't have been long until they could afford to buy a house of their own in Brighton. Like her dad, Elinor had settled well into her adopted country and had formed strong friendships at school.

With such a bright future beckoning, her parents' decision to return to Scotland had come as a real shock to Elinor. When she told Michael of the plan, he couldn't take it in. 'But why do you have to go with them?'

'That's what I said. But Mum and Dad feel I'm too young to look after myself. I wanted you to come with us but they said you need to stay and qualify in your trade first.'

'Yeah, right enough, I think my folks would be wild if I threw away my apprenticeship.' He drew Elinor into his arms. 'Oh my darling, it'll be years until we meet again.'

'We can write to one another while we're apart,' she said, desperation in her voice.

'But Elinor I'm useless at writing letters. I was fine on the maths side at school but I was hopeless at English. I can't spell properly either.'

'I won't mind about the spelling,' she'd insisted. 'Just to get a letter would be enough.'

Standing here now, that same sadness engulfed Elinor

once more. She looked down at her watch; it was almost two o'clock in the afternoon so Michael would be in bed asleep right now.

She made her way back to the compartment, staggering slightly when the train lurched. She slid the compartment door open and went inside. Her dad awoke as she sat down. 'Where are we?' he asked, rubbing the sleep from his eyes.

'We're in the Lake District,' her mum replied, glancing up from her magazine. 'Not long to go. It's going to be a wonderful Christmas.' She smiled and clapped her hands.

A couple of hours later, her mum followed her dad down the steep step from the train on to Platform 2 at Glasgow Central Station. 'Home at last,' Susan said to her husband, beaming as she looked around the platform and heard the familiar accents of the passengers walking past her.

In contrast to her mum's eager anticipation, Elinor's eyes were downcast and her footsteps heavy as she emerged from the train. The station looked even grubbier than she remembered and the humid, steamy smells permeating around her made her nauseous. She couldn't help comparing Glasgow Central to the bright, clean entrance hall of Flinders Street, Melbourne's main railway station.

Her mum let out a squeal of delight when she spotted Aunt Muriel and Uncle George waving to her from where they stood beside the ticket collector. Susan tore along the platform, leaving Elinor and her dad to deal with the luggage. Elinor watched the two sisters clinging together in a tight hug, Aunt Muriel's silvery hair contrasting against her mum's darker tresses.

Uncle George stepped forward to relieve Elinor of one of the cases. 'Hello Elinor, lovely to see you again.' He kissed his niece on her cheek, his moustache tickling her skin.

'Good journey?' he asked Andrew as the two men shook hands. Taking off his specs, Andrew pulled a handkerchief out of his pocket and rubbed streaks of soot off the lenses. 'Yes, we were pretty well up to time all the way from leaving the ship.'

'Did you come direct from Southampton?'

'No, we had to break our journey in London and make our way to Euston to get on the Glasgow train.' Andrew replaced his specs and picked up the remaining two cases, carrying one in each hand.

Uncle George led the way across the station concourse, past the massive clock suspended from the roof and the shell sculpture positioned on the ground, a well-used meeting place for Glaswegians. They followed George out via the Gordon Street exit. He piled the luggage into the boot and ushered them all into the car. Elinor was in awe of Uncle George's car; they were the only family members who could afford to run one. She couldn't remember the make of the greeny/grey car but its shape reminded her of an upside down bath tub on wheels.

With her dad in the front passenger seat beside Uncle George, Elinor sat in the back, wedged between her mum and Aunt Muriel. The two sisters talked non-stop on the journey back to Aunt Muriel's home in Rutherglen.

Aunt Muriel had insisted that the three of them stay with her and Uncle George until they found a house of their own in the Burgh. 'After all,' she'd told them in a recent letter, 'we've plenty of room now that our two have moved out.'

Elinor's two cousins were a few years her senior. Rita now worked in London where she shared a flat with two other girls and Brian was studying at Newcastle University.

'It's really kind of you to do this for us, Sis,' Susan told her older sibling, once they were in the house. 'I hope we won't be too much of a nuisance.'

Muriel hugged her again. 'Of course you won't. Where else would you come but to us until you find suitable accommodation? It's been so hard these past two years not having you live nearby. I take it you will be staying here in Rutherglen and not returning to Cambuslang?'

'No, not Cambuslang,' Susan assured her. 'Although we were very lucky to have excellent neighbours in Rosebank Street, I've always yearned to get back to good old Ru'glen.'

'Great. George is putting your luggage upstairs so once you freshen up we can have a catch up session before we eat.'

Chapter Three

Saturday, 17th December, 1955

'What's wrong, Sis?' Muriel stood in the middle of the kitchen that Saturday morning, when she saw Susan sitting with her arms folded on the table, weeping. Susan, Andrew and Elinor had arrived in Rutherglen just over a week ago and everything appeared to have gone well.

Dropping the bundle of used bed linen on to the kitchen floor, Muriel rushed over to comfort her sister. She pulled a chair up beside Susan and gave her a cuddle. 'Why are you crying? Are you unwell?'

Susan shook her head, remaining mute until her sobbing eased. 'It's Elinor,' she said through her tears, 'she's behaving so differently from the old Elinor. I can't seem to get through to her, she challenges everything I say ….' She stopped speaking and once more laid her head on top of her folded arms.

'Come on now, Sis, I'm sure it isn't as bad as you're imagining. Elinor's a normal teenager, they all get a bit difficult around her age. I remember the rows I used to have with Rita, sometimes it sounded like World War III was starting.'

Susan looked up at her sister and smiled despite her misery. 'I do recall you telling me about Rita at that time. Elinor was still doing as she was told back then.'

'Exactly, but now she's grown into a woman with a mind of her own and very often that will clash with your ideas. Take it slowly, Sis, and things will settle down. I know teenagers can be impossible but, to be fair, Elinor didn't want to leave Melbourne and the friends she'd made there and she must be angry that she was forced to do so.'

'I know she blames me for causing us to return to Scotland. But I was so homesick, Sis. I missed you and George and all the people I'd grown up with. Andrew liked it in Melbourne, as did Elinor, and they had to come back because of me. I feel so guilty about that.'

Noticing that Susan was on the verge of tears once more, Muriel got to her feet. 'You've no need to feel guilty and, from what I can see, Elinor is beginning to settle in here. She loves it in Rutherglen, she told me so the other day.' She picked up the washing from the floor. 'I'll leave these soaking and then I'll switch on the kettle. You know what they say about a cup of tea curing all ills.'

A short time later, the two sisters were laughing about some childhood memories, with Susan's worries about her relationship with her daughter temporarily put to the back of her mind.

***

'It's great to be back,' Susan whispered to her sister the following day, as they settled themselves down on their pew in the gallery of Wardlawhill Church. The pews nearby were gradually filling up with worshippers. All Susan's memories flooded back of the two of them, with their mum and dad, sitting in this pew each Sunday, looking directly down to the magnificent stained glass windows in the transept. The family had used this pew since Muriel and Susan were small children, when they lived in a tenement flat in Hamilton Road, close to the church. Both girls had been christened in Wardlawhill by Mr Wilkes, who'd been ministering to this congregation in Rutherglen for over three decades.

'You okay, Elinor?' Aunt Muriel turned to her niece who was sitting on her other side.

'I like it up here,' Elinor told her. 'You can see

everything that's going on down below.' Being the third Sunday in Advent, they were in a vantage spot to view the Sunday School children acting in the Nativity play.

Elinor was still angry with her mum for bringing the family back to Scotland. It was Mum's fault that she'd been separated from Michael and all her other friends. She glanced along the pew at her mother's profile and guilt washed over her. Elinor knew she'd acted badly in the past eight days since they'd arrived in Rutherglen, and constantly argued with Mum. But she felt cheated and needed to lash out at somebody and Mum was the one in the firing line. She closed her eyes and sighed deeply, praying that she'd soon receive another letter from Michael.

A hush came over the congregation when Mr Wilkes came into church, wearing his black robes with the white clerical collar. When the bible had been brought into the sanctuary, he climbed the stairs to the pulpit and the service began.

'Yes, it's lovely to be home again,' Susan was saying to Mrs Wilkes, the minister's wife, when the two ladies were having a cup of tea in the hall after the service. 'I loved the Australian weather of course but it's the people at home I missed. Andrew and I hated dragging Elinor away from all her friends in Melbourne but hopefully she's still young enough to adjust back here.'

'I'm sure she will,' Mrs Wilkes agreed, while Susan savoured the last piece of her sponge cake; like most churches, Wardlawhill's congregation included many talented home bakers.

Elinor was standing at the opposite side of the hall with her dad and Mr Gray, Aunt Muriel's elder, when she felt a tap on her arm. 'Elinor, is it really you?' a voice behind her said and she turned to face her old school friend, Joanne Scott.

'Joanne.' The two girls hugged and jumped up and down in excitement.

Joanne, her blonde curls shining with health, took Elinor's hands in her own. 'It's wonderful to see you again, Elinor. Are you back for good or on holiday?'

'For good. Mum was very homesick in Australia. We're staying with Aunt Muriel in Parkhill Drive at the moment until we get a house of our own.'

A shadow crossed Elinor's face. 'I'm sorry we lost touch, Joanne. I missed getting your letters once you stopped writing.'

'I'm sorry too but you had so much to tell me about what you were doing in Australia and my letters seemed so dull and boring in comparison. But it's fantastic you're back.'

'We're hoping to buy a house in Rutherglen.'

'That's great.' Joanne had been born and raised in Rutherglen but she remembered Elinor had lived in Cambuslang before leaving for her new life in Australia. The girls had met at Rutherglen Academy, where they were in the same class. Joanne was unable to keep the smile off her face at meeting her old friend once more. 'Why don't you come round to ours some evening next week so that I can hear about your years in Melbourne? Would Wednesday suit?'

'That would be super. And what about you, Joanne, what are you doing these days?'

'I work in the Burgh Chamberlain's office in the Main Street.'

'I remember you were always keen to go to University to study languages and work as an air hostess.'

Joanne shrugged and raised her hands in the air. 'I decided against that. I did stay on at the academy for a year after you went to Australia but I wanted to earn some money. So when an opening came up in the Chamberlain's office last year, I applied for it.'

'Is that in the red sandstone building next to the library? The one with the date 1890 something on the front?'

'1893. Yes, the Council Chambers. Our office is in there and also the Town Clerk's office.'

Their conversation was cut short when it was time for Elinor to return to Aunt Muriel's house for lunch. 'See you on Wednesday night,' Joanne called after her when they were leaving.

Chapter Four

Wednesday, 20th December, 1955

After a heavy overnight fall on Tuesday evening, the snow was still hugging thickly to the streets on Wednesday.

'Maybe you should phone Joanne to cancel tonight's visit,' Susan suggested to her daughter in the late afternoon.

'Oh, Mum, don't be such a spoilsport. It's only a few minutes' walk to Johnstone Drive from here. I can go down Belmont Drive to get there.'

'Do Joanne's parents have a phone?'

'I think so.'

'Well ask Mrs Scott if you can use the phone and ring Aunt Muriel when you're ready to come home. Dad will come down and meet you.'

'Okay,' Elinor said. She hated the way Mum always fussed about things but decided that it was best to agree rather than start an argument.

After dinner she pulled on a pair of sturdy, fur-lined boots. Aunt Muriel lent her a heavy, wool coat that had belonged to her cousin Rita. The road was illuminated by overhead street lights and, as she plodded through the snow, she thought back over the twelve days that had elapsed since her return to Rutherglen. She admitted to herself that she was content to be here. Her good health had returned by now following the miscarriage and Mum and Dad had no inkling of what had happened on the ship that night. As a normally truthful and open person, lying didn't sit well on Elinor's shoulders but she convinced herself that it was in a good cause.

Thinking of how shocked her parents would have

been to know that she'd been pregnant made Elinor wonder if having a baby before marriage would ever become acceptable in society. She didn't think so, at least not in her lifetime anyway.

Halfway down Belmont Drive she slipped on an icy patch but got up quickly, unhurt, and brushed the soft snow off the back of her coat. She loved the crunching sound of the snow beneath her feet and looked back at the footprints she'd left behind. She smiled to herself. I guess we never really grow up, she thought. Walking in the snow was one thing she'd missed during her years in Melbourne.

The storm doors to Joanne's house were open, the lamp standard outside the gate throwing a swathe of light across the front porch. 'Come away in,' Joanne said in answer to Elinor's ring, standing back behind the inside door to allow her friend space. Once inside, Elinor gave her coat to Joanne, while she slipped off her boots. The pale green carpet felt soft and springy beneath her stocking soles as she followed Joanne into the front room, where Mr and Mrs Scott and Joanne's young brother, Hector, were listening to the wireless.

Mrs Scott got up and switched off the radio set. 'Hello, Elinor, and how are you, my dear?' she greeted their guest.

'I'm very well, thank you, Mrs Scott.'

'Hello, Elinor, nice to see you,' Mr Scott said.

'Thanks.' Elinor didn't think he meant it because he looked aggrieved that she'd interrupted the programme he'd been listening to.

'Have a seat over there where it's warm.' Mrs Scott pointed to the armchair at the side of the fireplace, which she had just vacated.

'Thank you,' Elinor said politely and sat down.

Mrs Scott squeezed in between Joanne and Hector on

the sofa.

'Hello Hector.' Elinor smiled at him and he smiled back. At least she thought he did; it was hard to tell because his mouth was barely visible under the long hair that fell over one side of his face.

The flames from the fire hissed and spat against the lumps of coal, their lively movements reflected on the back of the grate. Despite the size of the fire, most of the heat went up the chimney, very little of it spreading to the far corners of the room. The front of Elinor's body was roasted but she felt the chill from behind and was glad of the red polo-necked jumper Aunt Muriel had knitted for her.

'How are you finding our cold weather?' Mrs Scott asked, as if reading Elinor's mind.

Elinor hunched her shoulders up in a shiver. 'It was a shock to arrive to this weather after leaving temperatures in the high 90s in Melbourne.'

Joanne turned to her old school friend. 'What was life like over there?'

'I loved it. It was nearly always sunny and warm although we did get some colder weather around June/July time.'

Joanne laughed. 'It sounds strange to think of winter in June.'

'Yes, I felt a bit cheated as Christmas and summer holidays came at the same time. I didn't really like Christmas in hot weather.'

'And how was school?' Mrs Scott wanted to know.

'I attended Symonds High School in Brighton and made lots of friends there. The Aussies are easy to be with and I was accepted very quickly at the school.'

Mrs Scott continued with her questions. 'Was it Brighton you went to when you arrived in Australia? Or did you move about?'

'Brighton was the only place we stayed in. Apart from the Migrants' hostel when we first arrived in the country. Everyone who emigrates by the ten pound scheme is put into a hostel until they find a house of their own.'

It was Joanne's turn to ask a question. 'What was the hostel like?'

'Very basic with few home comforts but we were only there for a few weeks. They don't encourage you to stay there too long. Then Dad got a job and we rented the house in Brighton. We stayed there until we returned to Scotland.' She went on to tell them about the places of interest in the city and described the sort of lifestyle they'd enjoyed at the weekends, with the beach being so close to their Brighton home.

'It sounds wonderful,' Joanne said, when Elinor drew to a halt. 'I'd love to go there.'

'I'll show you some photographs. Once we get properly unpacked, that is.'

'It's the thought of insects that would put me off living in Australia,' Mrs Scott said.

'They can be a problem, right enough. We lived close to the beach and our windows were long, with the sills close to the ground level, so insects could get in. We had screens over the windows but, even although we were careful to close the screens when the windows were open, the insects still got in. I always checked my sheets before I got into bed.'

Mrs Scott grimaced. 'Do you think you'll ever go back to Australia?'

'I'd go back in a minute but I don't think Mum would return, at least not for good, maybe for a holiday.'

Hector got to his feet. 'Excuse me,' he apologised, 'I need to do my homework.'

'You should have done that earlier,' his mother called

after him. When he'd left the room, she shook her head. 'That boy, he always leaves everything till the last minute. He's adamant he doesn't have any homework and then remembers when he's getting into bed.'

'I've given up on him long ago. He's a lost cause,' Mr Scott muttered, stubbing out his cigarette in the ashtray that sat on the small table at the side of his chair.

Mrs Scott nodded. 'The children of today certainly don't have the respect that we did for parents and teachers. They think they know it all.'

Fearing that her parents were going to continue in this boring vein, Joanne looked over at her friend. 'Elinor, do you want to come up to my room and we can play records?'

'Sure.' Elinor followed Joanne upstairs and into her friend's bedroom, which she knew overlooked the back garden, although there was nothing to see in the darkness outside. The room was decorated in soft pink and lilac shades. Elinor sprawled herself across Joanne's bed, half-sitting, half-lying on it. 'So do you like your work in the Chamberlain's office?'

'Yes, my boss, Mr North, he's the Burgh Chamberlain, is a real gentleman.'

'And are you Mr North's secretary?'

'Oh no, Miss Prentice is his secretary,' Joanne told her, looking through a pile of records as she was speaking. 'According to Stella, the girl I share the main office with, Miss Prentice has worked there for years. My job could be described as general dogsbody but the staff are lovely people and I'm getting a good training there. Did you work in Melbourne?' she asked, as she finally located the disc she was searching for and held it up triumphantly.

'No, I was in the top grade at school and, if I hadn't returned to Scotland, I would like to have gone to college to study journalism.'

Detecting the note of regret in her friend's tone, Joanne tried to reassure her. 'You could still study that here.' She slipped the disc out of its cover and placed it on the metal prong on the record player and secured it with the arm. 'I know you said you had lots of friends at school but what about boyfriends? Was there anyone special?'

Elinor didn't reply straight away, instead she shrugged and made a face. 'There was someone, Michael, but I'll tell you about him another time.' She looked at all the records propped up on the shelf above the table housing the record player. 'That's some record collection you've got. How often do you buy one?'

'I buy a record each month from my wages, usually from The Music House in Hamilton Road. They have a great stock of records in there. This one I'm going to play is my latest, think you'll like it.' Joanne turned the knob and the disc fell down on to the turntable. Once the arm holding the needle came across and made contact with the disc, the music started and Fats Domino's voice resonated around the room.

The two girls sang along with Fats and when it was finished Elinor picked up another disc. 'Can you play this one?' she asked, as Joanne put the Fats Domino disc back into its cover.

'*See you later, alligator*' by Bill Haley and the comets started to play and the two girls danced and swayed around the room, in time to the music. They sang along with that number and other top hits until Mrs Scott called up to them that supper was ready.

Chapter Five

Tuesday, 7th February, 1956

'A letter for you, Elinor,' Aunt Muriel said, coming into the kitchen with the mail on a cold and drab morning. She laid the airmail letter down at Elinor's place on the breakfast table.

'Thanks.' Elinor picked up the letter, eagerly anticipating news from Michael at last. She experienced a moment's piercing disappointment when she saw the letter wasn't from Michael but from her friend, Dorothy Eastcroft. But, as she'd last heard from Dot at Christmas, she was keen to hear what her friend had been up to since then.

She excused herself from the table and went upstairs to her room to read Dot's news. She sat down on the dressing table stool and ripped open the airletter.

31st January 1956
Dear Elinor
It seems so long since Christmas when I last wrote to you. Thanks for the Christmas card and the enclosed letter. I was glad to hear that your journey from Melbourne back to Scotland was smooth. It's lovely that you can stay with your aunt and uncle meantime but I'm sure you'll all be keen to get a place of your own soon. Don't forget to send me your new address when you do.

I notice you mention someone called Joanne in your letter. Is she someone you've met since you got back to Scotland or had you known her previously? She sounds a fun person.

Last week I flew up to Brisbane for the Australian

Tennis Championships. The temps soared and it got to 108 by early afternoon. I attended the games with Robyn Cherry and Marilyn Paxton from Scots' youth group. They both say hi Elinor and we missed having you with us. We saw some exciting matches. Your British player, Angela Mortimer, is a superb athlete and a real fighter, although she didn't make it to the Final. Our great Aussie player, Lew Hoad, gave a fantastic performance in the Men's Singles and he also won the Doubles with his fellow Aussie, Ken Rosewall. It was a wonderful experience to get to the Milton Courts to watch the tennis and we all felt sad when the Championships came to an end and we had to return to Melbourne.

Three weeks ago I went camping to Hall's Gap in the Grampians with Scots' youth group. You'll remember the fun times we've had with the group. We had a great weekend, with rambles in the bush during the day and songs round the campfire at night. The koalas are really tame around these parts and quite a few ambled through the campsite while we were sitting there. The ground is parched with the recent drought conditions and we had to watch out for snakes when we were on firewood searches. Surprisingly enough, there weren't any notices banning fires but we were extremely careful about putting out the fire completely before we retired at night.

I wonder if you've found yourself a job in Rutherglen? I didn't do as well in my exams as I'd have liked so decided to give up ideas of University. I got myself a job in nursing. I'm working at the Royal Melbourne Hospital, training on the job, in a general medical ward. In addition to my practical training on the ward, I also attend tutorials. Liking it so far. I have a great group of girls in my intake and we also have two male nurses training with us.

Mum and Dad and I attended an excellent choir concert at Scots Church recently. Quite a number of choirs from various churches around Melbourne joined together and the massed voices were fantastic. Mum was saying after the concert how much you folks would have loved it. Life at Scots goes on much as before and many of your friends there ask us how you are getting on back in Scotland. So although you might be on the other side of the world, Elinor, you are not forgotten here in Oz.

We have a great crop of peaches in the garden at the moment, both yellow and white fleshed ones. We have to hurry out each morning at dawn to pick them before the birds get to them. Our oranges and lemons are doing well too. There're so many plums we could never eat them all so Mum is going to use some of them to make jam.

Well, I can see the end of the paper looming up so I'll close for now and look forward to hearing from you soon again, Elinor. I must try to write smaller next time so that I can get more on the letter.

Look after yourself and give my love to your mum and dad. My folks say hi to all of you over there.

> *Love from Dot*
> *xxx*

'I had a letter from my friend, Dorothy Eastcroft, today,' Elinor told Joanne later, when she went round to

Johnstone Drive to play records. 'It's the first time I've heard from her since Christmas so it was great to get her news.'

'I haven't heard you mention anyone called Dorothy. Was she one of your school friends?'

'No, she and I were in the same church group. Mum and Dad and I attended the services at Scots' Church in Melbourne, a Presbyterian Cathedral that was built by the first Scots' settlers in the city. We sat in the same pew as the Eastcrofts and Mum and Dad became friends with Tom and Frances from the word go. Dot invited me to go along to the church youth group and she and I became friends too.'

'Did they live near you in Brighton?'

'No, Brighton is on the coast. The Eastcrofts live in Blackburn, one of the eastern suburbs, more countryside. Australia is such a huge country that people travel much greater distances than we do here. Dot's parents have a Holden saloon car so they often used to drive down to Brighton to visit us at weekends and we would spend all day on the beach.'

Joanne placed one of Dean Martin's hits, 'Memories Are Made of This' on to the turntable, then sat down beside Elinor on the bed. 'So does Dot know your boyfriend, Michael?'

'No, they've never met. I haven't heard from Michael since I was on the ship, as he doesn't like writing letters. I thought at first Dot's letter might have been from him.'

'You must miss Michael,' Joanne said, her head moving in time to Dean's voice.

Elinor nodded and tears slid down her cheeks. 'I miss him terribly,' she sobbed and, seeing her distress, Joanne lifted the needle off the record. She sat back down and took Elinor's hand. 'Do you want to talk about it?'

Elinor didn't reply immediately and sat staring down at her feet. Then she slowly lifted her head and nodded. She began haltingly to tell Joanne about her romance with Michael and then it all came tumbling out about what had happened on the ship and how sad she was that she hadn't heard from him for so long. Her friend listened without interrupting and by the time she had stopped speaking both she and Joanne had tears streaming down their faces.

'You're the only person I've told about what happened on the ship. Mum and Dad don't know anything about it.'

'Well, I'm glad you told me,' Joanne said, stroking the back of Elinor's hand in an attempt to comfort her friend. 'It's always better to tell someone about such things. And I can assure you that I will not tell another living soul; your secret is safe with me.'

Elinor wiped away her tears when Mrs Scott called them down for supper.

***

'Would you like to have this, Elinor?' Aunt Muriel said the following evening, handing her niece a thick book with dark blue covers. 'The book belonged to my father, your Grandpa Weir, who died before you were born. As the elder daughter, it was given to me on his death.'

Looking at the book, Elinor saw that the title was 'Rutherglen Lore' by W. Ross Shearer. The Rutherglen Coat of Arms appeared on the bottom right hand corner of the front cover with the motto of the Burgh, EX FUMO FAMA, printed on it. The book's spine was slightly damaged and she noticed that some tears on the pages inside had been repaired by the use of sellotape.

'What does the motto mean?'

Her aunt smiled. 'If I've remembered any Latin from my days at Rutherglen Academy, I think it means out of smoke comes fame. Probably refers to the many factories there were in the Burgh at one time.'

Seated in her armchair at the side of the fire, Susan looked up from the novel she was reading. 'The only Latin I remember is what was on our school badge. Sapientiae Timor Domini Initium, which I recall means the fear of the Lord is the beginning of wisdom. But Muriel, by right that book should go to Rita or Brian.'

'No Sis, my two have no interest in Rutherglen or its history. Rita has settled in London and says she will never come back up here to live and once Brian gets his Degree, he's determined to go and work in America. You're interested in our history, Elinor, and I'd like you to have the book. You were never interested in it were you, Sis?' she said as an afterthought to Susan.

Susan's face wrinkled. 'Not really. I'm happy for Elinor to have it so long as Rita and Brian have no objection.'

Elinor opened the book at the first page. 'According to what it says here the book was first printed in 1922. It was written to coincide with the Eight Hundredth Anniversary of Rutherglen receiving its Royal Charter,' she said, turning back to Aunt Muriel.

Her aunt smiled. 'Rutherglen was Scotland's very first Royal Burgh and the book is valuable nowadays as there aren't many copies in general circulation.'

'Thanks, Aunt Muriel. I'll treasure it,' Elinor said, planting a kiss on her aunt's cheek. Both Aunt Muriel and Mum were proud of their Ruglonian heritage, especially Aunt Muriel, and her aunt's pride had rubbed off on Elinor.

Susan buried her head in the novel once more while Muriel, seated on the other side of the fireplace, carried on turning the heel on the socks she was knitting for George.

Elinor sat at the kitchen table, browsing through the Evening Times and, after she finished reading the news, she moved on to job vacancies, circling the ones that sounded promising. Being an experienced painter, Dad had been snapped up by the local Council soon after he came back from Australia. Joanne had returned to her work in the Chamberlain's office following the Christmas and New Year break and by now boredom was gripping Elinor. That, and the lack of money she had to spend, made her redouble her efforts to find a job.

'What about this job?' Elinor announced and, for a moment, Aunt Muriel's pins stopped clicking and Mum looked up, her finger at her place in the book.

Office junior required for Colvilles Steelworks, Eastfield, Cambuslang. Applicant would be expected to have shorthand and typing skills. Anyone interested should apply via the box number below.

'That would be a good job, love,' Susan said to her daughter. 'Colvilles has always been known as a fair employer.'

Muriel smiled at her niece. 'You'll get stationery in the bureau drawer in my bedroom. If you write your application, you can post it tomorrow. Strike while the iron's hot, I always say.'

'Thanks, Aunt Muriel.' Elinor went off to the bedroom, recalling that her aunt's conversation had always been sprinkled with proverbs.

Shortly afterwards, silence reigned, apart from the scratching sound of Elinor's fountain pen nib on the paper and the clicking of Aunt Muriel's needles. When she finished writing her letter of application, Elinor sealed it in its envelope and stamped it, then started to write to Michael. It was a very long time since she'd heard from him, in fact he'd only sent her two letters, but she reminded herself constantly that writing was a real chore for Michael. Her eyes were moist as she wrote the letter. She still missed him dearly but as the weeks went by she was gradually settling back into life here, a life that Michael had never been a part of.

Chapter Six

Thursday, 16th February, 1956

Elinor received a reply from Colvilles within a few days of sending her application, inviting her to attend for interview today, 16th February. She arrived at the front door of their offices earlier than her appointed time of three o'clock.

The Commissionaire at the door ushered her in and the girl on duty at the reception desk took Elinor's name and gave her an encouraging smile. 'If you take a seat in the waiting room, Mr Harvey, the office manager, will see you soon.' Choosing a seat in the far corner of the room, out of view of the receptionist, Elinor played with her fingers, unable to keep her nerves at bay.

Shortly afterwards a white-haired woman approached and showed Elinor to Mr Harvey's office upstairs on the first floor. After introducing Elinor to the manager, the woman slipped out of the room again. Mr Harvey got to his feet and shook hands with Elinor, directing her to a chair on the far side of his desk, facing him.

'Thank you for attending, Miss Bonnington.'

Elinor sat with her hands clasped, resting on her lap.

'So are you in employment at the moment?'

'No, my parents and I returned to Scotland just before Christmas. We lived in Australia for two years but Mum was homesick so we came back.'

'And what did you work at in Australia?'

'I didn't. I was at school and left to come back to Rutherglen. I would have been ready to start work or go to college when the school finished at Christmas for the summer break.'

Mr Harvey smiled. 'And how did you like having a hot Christmas?'

'Christmas day at the beach was lovely but I still feel there should be snow at Christmas.'

'And have you brought any certificates or references with you?'

She slid her school certificates, plus the character reference that Mr Wilkes, the minister, had given her, across the desk to him. Although Mr Wilkes had only known Elinor a short time, he knew her family background and had been happy to recommend her for employment.

Mr Harvey studied the paperwork carefully before speaking again. 'We were thinking of employing someone with work experience but I see you have shorthand and typing certificates.' He held up the reference from the minister. 'Malcolm Wilkes is a friend of mine and if he vouches for you, you're alright. If we take you on, you won't go and disappear off to Australia again, will you?'

She shook her head. 'No, we're back for good.'

'If we employed you, we'd train you up,' he explained. 'The experienced typists work on the invoices and correspondence and you, as the new start, would type out the envelopes for their work. You'd move on to typing invoices and letters once you had gained more experience.'

He looked to see how she had received this and when he saw her nod, he continued. 'As well as typing, you'd need to relieve the telephonist on the switchboard at lunchtime. Don't worry,' he said, noticing the look of alarm on her face, 'we would train you on the switchboard. Do you think you could handle all that?'

'Yes,' she replied, hoping she sounded more confident than she felt.

'I'll give you a note of the salary we're offering

before we take things any further,' Mr Harvey went on. He told her what the rates of pay were and that she would be required to work from 9-5 Monday to Friday and until midday one Saturday in each month. 'The steelworks close down fully only twice a year, that is during the Glasgow Fair Holiday Fortnight each July and for a few days at New Year. This means that some of our office staff are on duty on Public Holidays.'

'Are staff paid extra for working Public Holidays?' She hoped her question didn't sound too cheeky.

But he didn't seem to mind at all. 'The policy isn't to pay staff for those days but you get a day off in lieu. And you normally stop early on any Public Holiday you do work. Are you happy with all that?'

'Yes,' she said, aware that she didn't really have anything to compare as this would be her first job. But to her, never having earned before, the wages sounded like a fortune. She could check with Dad when she got home.

'If there's nothing else you want to ask me, we'll get you to type a letter or an invoice for us.' Assured that Elinor had no further questions, Mr Harvey lifted the phone sitting on his desk. 'Could you ask Mrs Marshall to come up to my office, Edna?' he said to the person on the other end of the line. A few minutes later the lady who'd brought Elinor to his office came back in. 'Peggy, could you find a typewriter for Miss Bonnington and give her something to type?' Peggy nodded and once again Mr Harvey shook hands with Elinor.

'I'm Peggy Marshall, the supervisor in charge of the typing pool so, if we employ you, I would be your immediate boss,' Peggy told Elinor on the way downstairs. When they walked into the typing pool, Peggy collared one of the girls. 'Isabel, can you let Miss Bonnington use your typewriter, please?'

Isabel nodded. 'Yes, I've got some photocopying I can do.'

Elinor, who'd heard of a photocopier but had never seen one, watched Isabel go over to a machine in the corner of the room and pull two sheets of paper out of separate black plastic bags.

'Not too many offices have a photocopier,' Mrs Marshall said, noticing Elinor's interest in what Isabel was doing. 'We use negative and positive paper which are fed through a tray of chemical solution to produce a copy. Right,' she went on, returning to the job in hand, 'you can use Isabel's typewriter while she's busy.'

The typewriter was an Adler, a German machine, and much more modern than the ancient relic Elinor had used at Symonds High. She typed a letter and an invoice, then gave them to Peggy before being ushered out of the pool.

'Bye,' the same receptionist on the desk called to Elinor as she left the office.

'I hope to see you again,' the Commissionaire said and winked at her.

Dad was at work when she arrived home but Mum and Aunt Muriel were in the front room. Both looked up expectantly as she walked in, keen to hear how she got on at the interview.

***

Friday, 17ᵗʰ February, 1956
Dear Dot

It was great to receive your airmail a couple of weeks ago and hear all that you had been up to. I was so jealous about not getting to the tennis in Brisbane or going to the camp at Hall's Gap with you. Our weather isn't good enough to go camping – you'd freeze to death if you tried!!

My main news is that I have a job. I had an interview yesterday for a post in the offices of Colvilles steelworks near here and they contacted me this morning to offer me the job. I'm really excited about starting next Monday, 27th February, and earning some money at last. My friend, Joanne, is already working in a local office so now that we will both be earning we will be able to go out more often to the cinema or the theatre. I hope you are still enjoying the nursing, Dot. I'm sure you will be a very caring nurse for your patients.

You were asking me how I knew Joanne. She and I were in the same class at school before I left to go overseas. Since coming back here, Mum and Dad and I have been attending Wardlawhill Church on a Sunday with Aunt Muriel and I met Joanne there as her family worships in the same church. We've resumed our friendship as though we'd never been apart which is lovely. I was telling her about you and how we met at Scots' Church.

Joanne lives quite near Aunt Muriel's house and I go round often in the evening so that we can play records. Joanne has an enormous record collection, says she buys a disc each month from her wages. She has been to visit us at Aunt Muriel's house but I'm looking forward to inviting her to our house once we buy one. Mum and Dad are keeping an eye on house sales in the paper and if we pass a house with a 'For Sale' notice they always make enquiries about it.

I'm sorry this letter is so short, Dot, but I've promised Mum that I'll help her with the shopping. I will definitely write more next time. Mum has asked me to tell you that she will write to your mum soon too.

Love from Elinor
xx

Chapter Seven

Saturday, 26th May, 1956

With this being one of Elinor's Saturdays off, she was able to join her mum and dad in viewing the house they'd seen advertised in Melrose Avenue, not far from Aunt Muriel's house. Thanks to the money Dad had earned in Melbourne, they were in a position to put in an offer for the house.

Elinor had been employed in Colvilles for almost three months now. Under her colleague, Edna's, guidance she was shaping up to be a proficient telephonist. The switchboard had five outside lines and fifty internal extensions so she was kept extremely busy when working on the board. When she was in the typing pool, Elinor enjoyed working her way through the envelopes she had to type for the older girls' work. But she'd been delighted yesterday to be called into Peggy's office and told that she could now type some invoices and letters herself.

She got on well with the other girls in the typing pool, and had formed a friendship with Freda Conroy, who lived in Hamilton. Elinor had never been to Hamilton but Freda told her that it took about half an hour to get there by bus.

Arriving at the house in Melrose Avenue that they'd come to view, Susan and Elinor stood at the front gate. Arms linked, mother and daughter looked up the path to the front door. Unlike the other houses in Melrose Avenue, which were all semi-detached built in red brick, this detached house was in a lighter colour of stone with a tower shape design on its frontage. The garden was badly overgrown with bushes, some of which almost obscured the front door.

Elinor was first to speak. 'The garden's like a jungle, makes me think of Prince Charming hacking his way in to rescue Sleeping Beauty. Or have I got my pantomimes mixed up?'

'Come on, girls,' her dad said, standing behind them and pushing them gently inside the gate. 'Let's go and have a gander. The estate agent should be waiting inside for us.'

They rang the bell and the estate agent let them in. He introduced himself as Mr Allan. 'Sorry the place is so cold but it has been unoccupied and unheated for almost a year.'

'Why is that?' Susan queried.

'The previous owner had a long stay in hospital. She recently moved into a nursing home, where she died after only a few weeks. I understand she was an elderly lady, who didn't attend to necessary house repairs as she should have done. Because of this, the nephew who is selling the property is willing to let it go for below the market value.' Mr Allan handed Andrew a prospectus with information about the house. 'I'll leave you all to have a look round at your leisure. Give me a call if you need any further information.'

They looked round the downstairs part first, beginning with the front sitting room.

'It's so cold in here.' Elinor shivered despite the warm day.

The interior of the house proved to be as run down as the garden. The carpets were worn, some even with holes in them. The furniture was ancient and covered in layers of dust. Garish patterned paper covered the walls. There had been burst pipes and the house had been flooded, leaving some rotting floorboards behind it. There were cobwebs hanging from the ceilings and light fittings. Overall the house wore an air of long neglect and shouted out for care.

'Well it's certainly seen better days,' was Susan's verdict after they'd looked round the ground floor. 'I like the layout of the house though and I'm sure you could make a lot of improvements, Andrew.'

They went upstairs to explore further. 'How do you like the house, Elinor?' Andrew asked, when his daughter came into the bedroom he and Susan were standing in.

'Despite the dreadful state it's in, I really like it. Could I have this bedroom looking over the back garden?'

Susan laughed. 'I think this one might be earmarked for your dad and me.'

'Will we put in an offer?' Andrew asked, when they came out of the house after parting company with the estate agent.

Susan took her husband's arm, smiling up at him. 'Yes, let's try for it. It's certainly handy for the shops and transport into town.'

'I wonder what happened to all my school chums?' Elinor mused aloud as they passed Rutherglen Academy at the end of the road. 'Sheila Cosgrove, Yvonne Mathews and the others. Must ask Joanne if she knows where they are now.'

Her mum chuckled. 'I spent many happy years at the academy before you, Elinor, but I've lost track of people years ago. I suppose everyone goes their separate ways once they leave school.'

Back at Parkhill Drive, Aunt Muriel opened the door at once. 'Come away in and tell me all about the house you saw. Did it live up to your expectations?'

Chapter Eight

Wednesday, 12th September, 1956

'Do you want to come with me to the Troc on Saturday night?' Freda asked, when she and Elinor were having lunch in the staff canteen. The two girls had become close friends during the months Elinor had worked in Colvilles and usually spent their lunch hour together.

Elinor's face screwed up into a question mark. 'The what?'

Freda laughed at her expression. 'The Troc. It's one of our local dance halls. The correct name is the Trocadero but all of us Hamilton people call it the Troc.'

'I've never been to public dancing before, Freda. I don't know how to dance.'

'I'm not very good myself but we can learn. And the band there is fantastic, makes you want to dance. My parents said you're welcome to stay overnight at our house instead of travelling home alone on the bus late at night.'

'I'd like to come with you, Freda, but I'll have to check with my mum and dad,' Elinor told her friend.

'Sure. That's fine by me. You can let me know before Saturday.'

For the first time Elinor became aware of a sandy-haired chap sitting on his own at the table to her left. She could just see his face behind the newspaper he was reading. She didn't think she'd seen him in the canteen before as she felt sure she wouldn't have forgotten such a handsome guy. She quickly banished her feeling of disloyalty to Michael; after all it was a very long time since she'd heard from him. Surely if Michael had wanted to keep their relationship alive, he'd have written to her, despite his problems with spelling.

Freda sighed and pushed her seat back from the table. 'I guess we'd better return to our desks. No rest for the wicked, eh?'

Freda had started working in Colvilles the year before Elinor and she'd kept the younger girl right about the way things were done in the typing pool. After work, the two girls usually walked together up the long avenue that led from the steelworks to the main road where they got their buses home. Freda waited at the one side of the road for the bus to Hamilton, with Elinor's stop on the opposite side where she got on the Rutherglen bus.

The girls returned their used crockery to the serving hatch where Sarah, the canteen supervisor, took it from them. 'Thanks, girls, maybe see you tomorrow. We're going to have steak and kidney pie on the menu.'

Freda beamed. 'Oh, yummy, can't wait.'

Elinor gave a sideways glance as she followed Freda out of the canteen and the good-looking chap was still seated at his table.

Chapter Nine

Saturday, 15th September, 1956

With all the work that had needed doing to the house in Melrose Avenue, the Bonningtons had only moved in a little over a month ago. Although grateful for Muriel and George's hospitality over the previous nine months, they were enjoying living in a home of their own once more.

Susan came out of the kitchen when Elinor was coming downstairs that evening, wearing her new green dress which complimented her hazel eyes. 'Elinor, are you sure this place you're going to is quite safe? And that this Freda Conroy's parents are happy for you to stay overnight?'

Elinor sighed. 'Yes, Mum.'

'After all, there are plenty of dances here in Rutherglen without you having to go all the way to Hamilton.'

'Oh Mum,' Elinor said, 'Hamilton is only about half an hour's bus journey away. It isn't like it was far out in the country. Freda said she'll meet me when I get off the bus and take me to her house in Low Waters Road so that I can leave my overnight bag before we go to the dance. And I'll be able to meet her mum and dad at that time.'

'I don't like you going so far away to dances. You are only eighteen after all.'

Andrew joined them in the hallway and gave his daughter a wolf whistle when he saw her dressed for the dance. 'Give her a break, Susan,' he said to his wife. 'What harm is she doing by going to a dance? You'll have to let go of the apron strings soon, you know.'

Susan squeezed her daughter's hand. 'I know you find me an old fuss pot, Elinor, but you'll understand when you have your own children. You hear of bad things happening to young girls at these dance halls.'

Elinor hugged her mum, laughing as she did so. 'Don't worry, we'll be quite safe. Freda's been to the Troc before and she said the people who go there are all respectable.'

'Well at least let Dad walk you to the bus stop.'

'But there's no need. It's only a five minute walk.'

'Of course it is, love,' Andrew said, looking at his daughter with raised eyebrows. 'Anyway, I'd only cramp your style.'

Susan laughed and threw her hands up in the air. 'Okay, I know when I'm outnumbered. Go and enjoy yourself, Elinor, but be careful.'

'Will do,' Elinor promised, pulling on her coat. She picked up her overnight bag and glanced at her reflection in the hall mirror on the way out.

**

'You're right about the fantastic band,' Elinor whispered to Freda as the two girls returned to the seating area after coming off the dance floor. 'The music really makes your feet tap, doesn't it?'

'Knew you'd enjoy yourself,' Freda said, smiling at her friend as they sat down.

Seconds later the music started up again for a foxtrot. 'Can I have this dance?' a chap came over and stood in front of Freda, holding out his hand.

Freda excused herself to Elinor and walked off with him. A moment later a lad approached Elinor for a dance. She recognised him as the chap who'd asked her to dance about half an hour earlier. As he whirled her around the dance floor, she found herself wishing she was in Michael's arms but dismissed the thought immediately because she was having such a good time. When she got back to the seating area, she spotted Freda still on the dance floor with the same lad who'd asked her up for the foxtrot. By now they were dancing a quickstep and it was obvious Freda was thoroughly enjoying herself.

Freda danced the remainder of the evening with the same chap and, although Elinor herself didn't want for a partner, she didn't get a chance to speak to Freda again until they were in the cloakroom at the end of the evening.

'Jack has offered to walk us back to my place,' Freda told her while they were waiting in the queue to collect their coats. 'He lives quite near me.'

'You seem to have got on well with him. Are you going to see him again?'

'Yes, he's asked me out on Wednesday. He's a lovely guy, Elinor. Works with Colvilles too, he's an electrician in Dalzell steelworks in Motherwell.'

It was clear to Elinor that Freda had fallen head over heels in love with Jack, and on their way back to Low Waters Road, she was sure that Jack felt the same way about Freda. When they reached Freda's front gate, Elinor tactfully turned away, leaving Freda and Jack a chance to say goodnight.

'Night, Elinor,' Jack called quietly as he walked away from the gate.

'Night,' she replied, raising her hand in a wave while Freda turned the key in the lock.

By the time they got into the house, Mr and Mrs Conroy had gone to bed and as the girls crept upstairs, they heard heavy snoring coming from the bedroom. 'It's my father,' Freda whispered, 'my mother sometimes has to move into the spare room when it gets too bad.'

Too excited to sleep, the girls lay in bed chatting quietly. They discussed the dance and the people they'd met there.

'That red-haired chap you danced with was quite handsome,' Freda said to Elinor. 'You know the one who came from Motherwell. I wondered if he'd made a date with you.'

'No, he didn't ask me out. There were a couple of boys I didn't enjoy dancing with, especially the one who was about 5' tall, but on the whole I was lucky with the partners I had. You're keen on Jack, aren't you?'

'He's gorgeous and I just can't wait to go out with him next week.'

Sleep gradually overcame the girls. Elinor's thought as she drifted off was one of thankfulness that they didn't have to get up early for work next morning.

Chapter Ten

Christmas Day, 1956

Elinor's hands shook slightly as she held the two letters. It had been a shock when, just before Christmas, two of the airmails she'd sent to Michael were returned to her, bearing a red and white 'Gone Away' label across the front. In the year that had passed since she'd last heard from him she'd been forced to accept that he must have met someone else in Melbourne. She'd no idea where these two letters had been in the intervening months; they'd been written not long after her arrival in Scotland when hope of a future with him was still a possibility.

She made the mistake of reading through the letters and before she'd reached the end of the first one her tears were flowing freely. As sure as she'd been of having come to terms with the fact that she'd never see Michael Lynch again, she admitted to herself now that her love for him burnt as brightly as ever.

Australia was such a vast country that he could be anywhere. She thought the likeliest solution was that his family had moved north to Queensland to be near his sister and her family. But, with no address for his sister, there was no way she could check out her suspicion.

'Elinor, are you nearly ready?' Susan's voice floated up to her from the hallway. 'Aunt Muriel and Uncle George will be here any minute now.' The Bonningtons were looking forward to welcoming Muriel and George for the first Christmas dinner in their new home. Last Christmas they'd all enjoyed dinner at Parkhill Drive so Susan was delighted to be returning the hospitality this year. Rita and Brian were both spending Christmas with friends so, without the Bonningtons,

Muriel and George would have been on their own.

'Coming, Mum.' Elinor wiped the tears from her face and checked in the mirror that her underskirt wasn't hanging down under her dress. Then she joined her parents downstairs to await their visitors.

***

'What a happy time we've had. Thank you, Sis.' Muriel embraced Susan.

'Thank you for coming, it wouldn't have been the same without you.' Susan turned to receive a hug from her brother-in-law. The two men shook hands and Elinor kissed her aunt and uncle goodbye.

They stood at the front door and waved their guests off. 'I'm glad they came. It would have been lonely without them,' Susan said. 'Muriel says the dinner will be at hers next year.'

Andrew chuckled. 'What are you two like? Let's get this Christmas over before we start thinking about next year.'

Elinor had been disappointed not to spend Christmas day with Joanne but she, like Elinor, also had relatives visit for Christmas dinner. The two girls had gone to the Christmas Eve midnight service at Wardlawhill and were planning to meet tomorrow, Boxing Day.

Despite not seeing her best friend, Elinor felt contented as she slipped in between her sheets that Christmas night. The meal had come up trumps and Mum's Christmas pudding had been superb. Elinor had found a little silver sixpence wrapped in greaseproof paper in her piece of pudding. Mum always put sixpences in the pudding and it was fun to see who found them. Uncle George had even eaten his way through a second portion but had remained unlucky.

After their meal, they'd left the washing-up to listen to the Queen's Speech. They all sat around the radio and heard the clear tones of the Monarch wish them and all her subjects around the globe a very happy Christmas.

Once the dishes had been done, they'd played some games. Chinese checkers and Ludo both had an airing, after which they'd played charades and a Christmas quiz that Uncle George had compiled. Lots of cheating went on but a great time was had by all.

Chapter Eleven

Saturday, 14th September, 1957

Susan walked into the kitchen, where Elinor was wrapping up the crystal vase, an engagement gift for Freda and Jack. They'd decided to become engaged on the first anniversary of their meeting at the Troc and, since Elinor didn't have a regular boyfriend, Freda had suggested she bring Joanne with her to the party in the Castle Rooms at Uddingston.

'We won't be getting married for a couple of years yet,' Freda had told Elinor, 'we'll need to save a lot more money before the wedding.'

Elinor signed the gift card from her and Joanne and sellotaped it on to the box. 'There,' she said, standing back to admire her handiwork.

'That looks good, love. I take it Joanne has seen the gift.'

'Yes, Mum, of course she has. Don't you remember, Joanne and I went together to choose it?'

Susan tapped her fingers against her brow. 'Of course you did, love. Think I must be going senile in my old age.'

'You're far from senile,' Elinor said, and returned the scissors and the roll of sellotape to the kitchen drawer. 'I'm going upstairs to dress before Joanne gets here.'

Susan sat down at the kitchen table and picked up the Rutherglen Reformer, their local paper which came out once a week. She hadn't had a chance to read it in the last couple of days. With Andrew playing in a tie at the bowling green, followed by a dinner afterwards, she planned to sit with her feet up and enjoy having the house to herself this evening.

Upstairs, Elinor slipped her white lacy blouse over her

head and stepped into her red and black flared drindl skirt. She drew her red belt around her waist and fastened it with the butterfly clasp at the front. She fixed her jewellery before pushing her feet into a pair of red high-heeled shoes that she'd bought last week. Elinor didn't like wearing new shoes to a special event, preferring to 'break them in' beforehand, but this pair were as comfortable as slippers. A squirt of her favourite Yardley perfume and she smiled at her reflection in the mirror. She was putting on her coat when she heard a ring at the doorbell.

'Hello, Joanne,' she heard her mum say, 'come in for a minute. Elinor's just about ready.' By the time she got downstairs, her mum and Joanne were standing together in the hallway.

'Dad waited outside in the car,' Joanne told her.

'It's really good of your dad to run you both over to Uddingston to the party and even kinder that he is going to collect you at the end of the evening,' Susan said. 'Don't forget to collect the gift from the kitchen table,' she reminded Elinor, who scurried away to get it.

***

'What a great party it's been,' Elinor said to Freda a few hours later, when she and Joanne were getting ready to collect their coats from the cloakroom. 'The band was super and so was the buffet. And your ring's gorgeous,' she added, taking her friend's hand to admire once more her beautiful two-stone diamond engagement ring.

'Yes, it's magnificent,' Joanne agreed. 'Thank you very much for inviting me to your party.'

'You're welcome, thank you both for coming. And also for the gift. We'll open our gifts when we get home and then I can thank you properly.' Jack, who'd been chatting to some folk nearby, joined them. 'Elinor and Joanne are getting ready to leave,' Freda told him.

He threw his arm around Freda's waist and smiled at her two friends. 'Thanks for coming and helping to make our party such a success.'

'We wouldn't have missed it,' Elinor told him. 'But we need to get our coats now, as Joanne's dad has poked his head in the door to tell us he's parked outside.'

Their farewells said, they donned their coats and got into Mr Scott's car, glad to have transport home and not to have to wait for a late night bus.

Chapter Twelve

Saturday, 5th October, 1957

Elinor came out of the bathroom draped in a towel. In her bedroom she quickly dressed in her tartan skirt and warm jumper. Mum thought the skirt was too short and showed off too much of her legs but Elinor herself rather liked it. I'm always told I have shapely legs, she thought, so why not show them off.

She frowned when it occurred to her that Michael would have liked her in this skirt. She always felt sad when Michael and the baby she'd lost came into her mind. But it was futile to look back. She'd told Joanne about what happened on the ship, knowing she could trust her friend to keep it to herself. She sighed and went off to brush her teeth. On her return to the bedroom, she opened the blind to the feast that awaited her in the garden; the trees a kaleidoscope of colour, ranging from the palest yellow, through the various shades of green to burnt orange and crimson.

With this being her Saturday off, she'd enjoyed a long lie and a leisurely breakfast. She'd promised to do the shopping for Mum before she went with Joanne to the cinema at three o'clock. Joanne's parents had invited her for tea after the film and later the two of them would listen to some of their favourite records up in Joanne's room.

'What do you want me to bring from the shops, Mum?' she asked, walking into the kitchen where Susan was busy cleaning out the cupboards. 'I need to go to the shops now as I'm meeting Joanne this afternoon for the cinema.'

Susan looked up and smiled at her daughter, delighted that Elinor had formed such a firm friendship with Joanne, a girl Susan approved of. Coming from such a respectable family, Joanne was unlikely to lead Elinor astray. 'I've made out a list,' she said, handing it over, too busy with her chores to notice Elinor's short skirt. 'Thanks for doing the shopping, Elinor, I want to stay here and clean up after Dad.' Today Andrew had begun decorating the living room and hallway.

'No problem.' Elinor took Mum's wicker shopping basket out of the kitchen cupboard and pushed two string bags inside. With the shopping list tucked safely inside her coat pocket, she stepped into her outdoor shoes and left the house.

She kept up a brisk pace down Stonelaw Road towards Rutherglen Cross. As an academy pupil, she'd done this walk each day to get her bus home from the Cross. There were piles of fallen leaves lying on the pavement and Elinor couldn't resist her childhood urge of scrunching her way through the leaves, kicking them aside as she walked.

On reaching the Cross, she looked along Main Street. She loved living here. On both sides of the street flower beds, bursting with colour, alternated with beech and sycamore trees along the wide pavement. Rutherglen was a thriving business community and, although there were some company-owned stores, most of the shops that lined Main Street were run by local families, with the business being passed down from father to son. Some of the shops had been run by the same family for generations.

Mum and Aunt Muriel had impressed on Elinor from a young age that for centuries Rutherglen had been a busy industrial and commercial town while Glasgow was still only a village. 'Not even a dot on the map,' had been Mum's way of describing Glasgow.

'In the early days Rutherglen had busy shipyards,' Aunt Muriel boasted. 'These shipyards traded with countries all over the world. When a ship arrived at Rutherglen Quay, a bell would ring to alert the townspeople, who'd make their way down to the quay to buy or sell goods.'

'Why did the shipyards close down?' Elinor asked her aunt.

'The demise of the shipbuilding here in Rutherglen stemmed from the bridges that were built over the River Clyde, at Dalmarnock and beyond. This curtailed the passage of large ships into Rutherglen, halting the shipbuilding and allowing instead the industry to flourish nearer the centre of Glasgow.'

Elinor stood outside Boot's the Chemist on this autumn morning, and looked towards the Town Hall halfway along Main Street. The building towered high above the others that surrounded it, the Union Jack waving from its flagpole. Just then the clock struck twelve times, reminding her that she needed to get a move on.

Crossing to the other side of the street, Elinor went into Hamilton's dairy, a family-run concern. There was a long queue in the dairy and while she waited her turn her thoughts once more centred on Michael and how much she'd loved him. Despite having her letters returned to her, a little flame of hope still flickered in her heart that one day she'd get a letter from Michael. She'd made no mention of the miscarriage in her letters to him, wanting to spare him the pain she'd suffered.

'Can I help you?' The assistant's voice broke into her reverie. He stood behind the counter, wearing a light brown button-through overall. His specs were sitting on the top of his bald head, giving him the look of an air ace. The name Biggles came into Elinor's mind.

'Two pints of milk please.'

The man placed the bottles into her wicker basket sitting on the wooden counter.

'And I want half a pound of butter and a piece of

cheese,' she told him, and watched him pat the butter into shape. He put the two wooden spatulas into a bowl when he was finished and moved on to the cheese.

'About that size?' he asked and placed the wire cutter across the cheese.

'A bit more please,' she said and nodded when he moved the wire to the correct place.

Dairy shopping done, Elinor continued on her way along Main Street. She nodded and smiled at passers-by, feeling blanketed in the warmth of the local people.

Dad often joked about being brought up in Cambuslang and how he was looked on as an 'incomer'. 'Rutherglen's such a parochial wee town, Elinor,' he would tell his daughter at such times, with a twinkle in his eye.

Susan bristled even though she knew he was joking. 'Not parochial, just friendly.'

Elinor stopped on the pavement outside the library to look at the Mercat Cross. Rows of steps led up from ground level to the obelisk in the centre. In the back of her mind she recalled Aunt Muriel telling her that there was a time capsule buried inside the monument; she decided to check 'Rutherglen Lore' to see what was mentioned about the Mercat Cross.

Further along Main Street Elinor peered through the railings at the crumbling moss-encrusted gravestones in the Old Parish Church grounds. While waiting for the traffic on Queen Street to clear and allow her to cross the road, she stared up at the statue of Dr James Gorman near the entrance to the church. During the mid to late 1800s he'd been a surgeon in the Burgh and had often given his services free of charge to the poor. Once she'd crossed over Queen Street, Elinor looked back at the statue, erected in the doctor's memory by the townspeople a couple of years after his death. Even cast in metal, Dr Gorman had a kind face.

Elinor stopped beside the cenotaph and waited until the traffic eased sufficiently to allow her to cross the road to Gall's wool shop. Gall and Co. owned multiple shops in the Glasgow area. Elinor had promised to get Aunt Muriel two hanks of wool from Gall's. Her aunt knitted constantly; Elinor remembered on many occasions being asked to hold a hank of wool between her outstretched hands while Aunt Muriel wound the wool into a ball. When no-one was available, her aunt would place the hank over the back of two dining chairs and wind the wool by this method.

'Do you have two hanks of blue wool with that dye number please?' she asked the red-haired assistant in Gall's, handing over the label that had been round the original hanks.

The assistant, dressed in a deep blue button-through overall, with the name Gall's printed in yellow lettering on the pocket, smiled at Elinor. 'I'll check for you,' she said, and fetched a set of stepladders from the back shop to reach the hanks of wool piled up on top of the glass-fronted cases, which displayed jumpers and underwear. 'You're in luck,' the girl said, and brought down the two hanks.

At the end of that row of shops was a gushet, with Main Street on one side and Cathcart Road on the other. According to the Lore, Mary, Queen of Scots, was thought to have ridden her horse down Cathcart Road in 1568 on her way to the Battle of Langside. Elinor didn't know how much truth there was in the story but she liked to think that the Queen had indeed passed through Rutherglen that day. When the traffic lights permitted, Elinor crossed over Cathcart Road to the other side of Main Street and joined the queue in the City Bakeries, a well known Glasgow company.

'A square sliced loaf, please,' she said to the middle-aged assistant.

'Anything else?' the woman asked when she'd put the

loaf down on the counter.

'Two chocolate pear tarts and two French cakes. And could you put them in a box please?' She watched how quickly the woman made up the box and tied it with string. 'I wonder how many of these boxes you've made up,' she joked with the assistant.

The woman smiled at Elinor as she cut the string. 'Oh hen, if I had a penny for every one I've done I'd be worth a fortune by now.'

Emerging from the bakers, Elinor continued along Main Street, passing St Columbkille's chapel, positioned directly across the road from the Town Hall.

The last shop she needed to go to was Warnock's the butcher, another long established family business and one favoured by both Mum and Aunt Muriel. 'One and a half pounds of stewing steak and will you mince it for me please?' she said when her turn came to be served.

'Are you Susan Weir's daughter?' the assistant asked Elinor when she brought the minced beef to the counter.

'Yes, I am.' Elinor smiled when she heard Mum's maiden name being used.

'I was at school with your mother. Tell her Barbara Donaldson was asking for her.'

When Elinor got home her dad was busy measuring the walls on the stairway, with the radio on at a low volume as he worked. 'That you back, love?' he greeted her, 'Mum would have taken a couple of hours longer if she'd gone.'

Susan came into the hallway and tutted, but there was merriment in her eyes as she answered. 'Andrew Bonnington, you're just jealous that I'm more popular than you. Thanks Elinor,' she said, taking the basket from her daughter and carrying it through to the kitchen.

While her mum unpacked the shopping, Elinor slung

her coat over the back of a kitchen chair and glanced down at the most recent Reformer. The paper was lying on the table open at a page with a headline of **ANOTHER LANARKSHIRE MURDER – Woman Found on Kirk o' Shotts Moor**.

'That's yet another murder,' Susan said, noticing Elinor reading the piece. 'A farmer's wife found near a reservoir. Poor woman only went out to gather firewood but didn't return.'

Elinor looked up from the newspaper. 'From what it says here, the police seem to be linking it to that murder of the young girl found on an East Kilbride golf course a year or so back and also to the murder of the three people in the bungalow in High Burnside.'

'Looks like it,' Susan agreed. 'Let's hope they catch the murderer soon before any more innocent people are killed. That's why I worry so much about you coming home from dances late at night, Elinor.'

'Mum, you worry too much,' Elinor said and closed over the paper.

Then she remembered the lady in the butcher's shop. 'By the way, Mum, Barbara Donaldson served me in Warnock's and said she was asking for you.'

'Oh yes, Barbara and I used to sit together in the academy.'

'Is that someone else you went to school with?' Andrew called through from the hallway. 'I think half the population of Rutherglen were in your class, Susan.'

Susan made a face to Elinor and ignored the jibe. 'I've made you a ham sandwich before you go to the cinema. What film are you and Joanne going to see?'

'The Bridge on the River Kwai. It's showing in the Odeon on Main Street this afternoon. And Mrs Scott has asked me round to their house for my tea afterwards.'

'That's nice of her. And I think it should be an interesting film even if there's a lot of killing in it. Still, the war did happen so people should know about it in the hope that no such barbarity will occur again.'

'Barbarity,' Andrew called from the hallway, where he was pasting a strip of wallpaper. 'Is that you describing your treatment of me?' he said, grinning, and then ducked as Susan made to throw an imaginary object at him.

Chapter Thirteen

Wednesday, 15th January, 1958

'What are your plans for your day off?' Susan asked Elinor at breakfast time.

'I thought I'd take the tram into town and have a look at the clothes in the January sales.' Elinor had taken a day in lieu of Christmas day, which she'd worked.

After breakfast, Elinor walked down to the tram stop on Stonelaw Road near to the Cross. By her reckoning the next tram was due to leave the terminus at Burnside in about five minutes' time. Elinor had heard a rumour that the tramcars were to be withdrawn from service over the next few years, most likely to be replaced by buses or trolley buses. She was sad about this as she always enjoyed her journey into the city centre on the tram.

A couple of minutes afterwards a girl about her own age, her red hair pulled back into a pony tail, came round the corner at Boot's the chemist and joined her at the tram stop. By the time the No 18 tram arrived there were four people in total waiting to board it.

The downstairs section was full so Elinor climbed the stairs to the upper deck, where she chose the double seat above the driver. The red-haired girl sat down beside her. They didn't speak until the conductor came upstairs calling 'fares please'. Both girls held out the money for their ticket. Elinor's weekly bus ticket only covered two journeys a day to and from her work at Eastfield and couldn't be used on the trams. The conductor moved on further up the tram to collect fares and Elinor's neighbour turned to her. 'I feel as though I've seen you before but I can't think where. Do you work in

Rutherglen?'

'No, I work at Eastfield.' Elinor looked closer at the girl. 'Do you work locally?'

'I work in Gall's, the wool shop at the far end of Main Street.'

Elinor raised her hand, her forefinger pointing upwards. 'That's it,' she said. 'I come into the shop often for wool. My aunt's a keen knitter and always has something on the pins.'

The girl smiled. 'Great, we've solved the mystery. I'm Rose Peters by the way.'

'Elinor Bonnington. Are you not working today?'

'I'm on a week's holiday from work. What about you?'

'I've got the day off. Do you live in Rutherglen, Rose?'

'Yes, in a tenement flat in Mitchell Street. It's through the pend beside Woolworth's,' Rose explained when Elinor looked at her blankly. 'And you?'

'I live in Melrose Avenue.'

'In the posh houses.'

Elinor laughed. 'I wouldn't call myself posh. I used to live in a tenement flat in Rosebank Street in Cambuslang, but later we lived in Australia for two years. Dad earned good money over there and it allowed us to put a deposit on our new house when we returned to Scotland.'

'Did you go to school in Cambuslang?'

'No I was a pupil at Rutherglen Academy. I had to come to Rutherglen because Cambuslang only has a junior secondary school. What school did you attend, Rose?'

'St Columbkille's. I left school at 15 and worked first in Woolworth's but after six months I got the job in Gall's. I like it there.'

They chatted on during the journey and by the time they got off the tram in Argyle Street they'd almost exchanged their life histories.

'See you again,' Rose said, when they parted company outside Lewis' Polytechnic, where she wanted to shop.

'Yes, I'll no doubt be in Gall's again soon.' Elinor walked on towards Arnott Simpson's store, certain that she'd just forged a new friendship.

***

'Looks like you've had a successful day's shopping,' Susan said, when Elinor arrived home in the late afternoon.

'There were some fantastic bargains.' Elinor dropped her shopping bags on to the settee in the living room. 'I'll need to go easy on my spending until the next pay day. By the way, a man's been arrested for some of the recent murders that have taken place in Lanarkshire.'

'Who told you that?'

'I saw it on the board outside a newsagent's shop I passed on West Nile Street.'

Susan's response was to switch on the radio and set the volume at low. 'The news should be on shortly, so we'll hear about it then. Now what about letting me see the new clothes you've been treating yourself to?'

Elinor spread her new clothes out over the back of the settee, accompanied by many 'oohs' and 'aahs' from her mother.

'Why don't you try them on for me?'

'Okay.' Elinor was happy to oblige and, once she'd donned the garments and received her mother's approval of her choices, she carried them upstairs to her room.

'On the tram into town today I was sitting beside a girl who sometimes serves me in Gall's,' she told her mother, on her return downstairs. 'Her name's Rose Peters and she's very friendly. We had a good old chin-wag on the way into town.'

Susan smiled at her daughter. 'That's nice, love. Here's the news starting now,' she said, and turned up the volume.

'Yesterday a man was arrested and charged with the spate of Lanarkshire murders committed over the past few years,' the newsreader said. Once the newsflash was over, Susan switched the radio off once more. 'Thank goodness they've arrested him. Now we'll all be able to sleep peacefully at night.'

Elinor nodded. 'Where did they say he came from?'

'From Birkenshaw. Mind you, I can't help feeling sorry for his mother. Imagine having a son who's committed such offences. That'll be your dad now,' Susan said to her daughter, as they heard the front door opening.

Chapter Fourteen

Saturday, 12th July, 1958

'What train are you going for?' Susan asked Elinor, when they were clearing away the breakfast dishes.

'Joanne has a timetable and says we can get a ferry from Ardrossan at eleven o'clock. That gets us over to Arran just before midday. We can come back on the last ferry, about half past seven. We thought we might do the bus trip round the island as neither of us has been any further than Brodick and Lamlash before.'

'So you'll need to allow about an hour for the journey from Glasgow,' Susan said, adding a squirt of Fairy liquid to the boiling water in the basin. She put on a pair of rubber gloves to protect her hands, the skin of which had been very dry recently.

'We're aiming to get a train from the Central just before ten, so we'll try to get into town by about quarter to ten at the latest.' Elinor took the tea towel from its hook beside the sink. 'I'll help you with the dishes before I get ready.'

'No, love, I'll manage. You need all your time so you aren't running late.'

'Are you sure?' Elinor was pleased when her mum nodded as she had still to get dressed and put on her make-up, before meeting Joanne at the Cross.

'I see the serial killer was hanged in Barlinnie yesterday,' Andrew said to them both, lifting his eyes from the newspaper. 'They seem to think that he murdered either eight or nine people. I don't expect we'll ever know exactly how many victims there were.'

Elinor was still standing in the doorway. 'I read in the

paper that the police arrested him because he'd spent some new banknotes which he'd stolen from the house in Uddingston where he murdered three people. They were able to trace him from the numbers on the notes.'

'At least now I can go to bed and sleep when you go out at nights, Elinor,' Susan said to her daughter. 'I was worried sick while he was on the loose.'

Elinor shrugged. 'I suppose most people felt uneasy knowing what was happening but it's great that they caught him eventually. Too late for the poor people he murdered but it's a relief that the police have solved the crimes.' She closed the door behind her and went upstairs to her bedroom.

Elinor decided to wear trousers today as the forecast was for changeable weather. She put on a lightweight pair, in case the sun came out and her heavier slacks would be too hot. She folded up her plastic raincoat with the hood and squeezed it into her shoulder bag.

'Right, I'm off,' she said to her mum and dad, who were both still in the kitchen. 'What are you two going to do today.'

'Your mum and I thought we'd go down to Largs for the day and get a walk along the prom.' Her dad folded up his newspaper and put it into the rack beside the fireplace.

'Well have a good time. See you tonight.'

'Okay, love. Have a great day.' Susan walked Elinor to the front door.

She kissed her mum on the cheek. 'We will. Bye.'

'Bye.' Susan stood at the door and waved her off.

Chapter Fifteen

Friday, 28th November, 1958

Susan stopped for a moment as she passed the kitchen table where Elinor was tying the final lavender bag with a piece of tartan ribbon. 'These are lovely, Elinor. They should sell like hotcakes.'

'Do you want me to take any of your home baking with me, Mum?' Joanne's dad was picking Elinor up shortly so that she and Joanne could leave their contributions in the church hall for tomorrow's Christmas Fayre. It was better to take things on Friday night and save a mad rush on Saturday before the Fayre opened.

'No, I'll take the fruit bread and cakes with me tomorrow but you could take my shortbread and tablet with you tonight. I'll put them into tins which will be easier for you to transport,' Susan said, fetching a couple of empty biscuit tins from her stock in the kitchen cupboard.

'And what about the aprons you've sewn? Will I take those?'

'Good idea.'

By the time Joanne arrived, Elinor and Susan had everything ready to be put into the boot of Mr Scott's car.

'We won't be late home Dad, so don't bother coming back for us,' Joanne told him, when she got out of the car at the hall. 'We can walk home together.'

'Okay, if you're sure.'

'Thanks, Mr Scott,' Elinor said, clutching the two biscuit tins tightly. 'It'll be no bother coming home as we won't have anything to carry.'

He put on his indicator and gave them a toot as he

drove away.

Once in the hall, the girls left everything on a window sill as the tables were just being put up. Some of the B.B. Officers and Elders were busy carrying folding tables from the downstairs hall and setting them up where the Committee ladies instructed.

One chap caught Elinor's eye. She didn't recognise him from church but felt sure she'd seen him somewhere before. She racked her brains but couldn't think where. 'Who's that dishy chap over there?' she asked Joanne quietly. 'The tall sandy-haired one, wearing a blue sweater.'

'That's Colin Dawson, he's the B.B. Captain. Yes he is very handsome, isn't he?' Joanne raised her eyebrows at her friend. 'And I think he's single.'

'Oh.' Elinor smiled, looking interested.

'Are you two girls planning to stand there all night gossiping or are you going to give us a hand to put the covers on the tables and lay out some of the goods?' Mrs Bruce, one of the Committee members, called over to them.

'Sorry, Mrs Bruce,' Joanne replied, 'of course we'll help, we were just trying not to get in the way. Do you know my friend Elinor?'

'Yes, you're Susan's daughter, aren't you?' Seeing Elinor nod, Mrs Bruce went on. 'I know your mum from the church guild. Now, will you two start laying out things on the fancy goods stall so that Mrs Duncan and I can sort out the grocery items?'

The two girls set to and did as they were requested. By the time they had organised the fancy goods stall to Mrs Bruce's satisfaction the men, including Colin Dawson, had disappeared.

In bed that night a tall chap wearing a blue sweater featured in Elinor's dreams.

Chapter Sixteen

Saturday, 16th May, 1959

Elinor sat at the dressing table in her bedroom at Melrose Avenue. She'd grown to love the house in the three years they'd lived here and her life in Melbourne now seemed such a long time ago.

After much negotiation and wheedling on Elinor's part, her parents had allowed her to occupy this room overlooking the back garden. She'd chosen her teak bedroom furniture and Dad had decorated the room in her choice of colours. Mum had sewn some mock velvet pale pink curtains which matched the carpet. The candlewick bedspread on her single divan was white with a pink floral design in the centre. As she looked around the room, she was happy with the choices she'd made.

After a good brushing, she fixed her long hair into a French roll, using almost a packet of kirbie grips to hold it in place. She was seriously thinking of having some of her hair chopped off as it would be easier kept short. Next came her eye make-up, a soft green eye shadow and mascara on her lashes. Finally, she applied her lipstick, a pinky/beige shade which was an exact match for the nail polish she'd applied last night.

She went into her parents' bedroom and looked at her image in the long mirror. Her yellow and white floral patterned dress had a lowered waist which she felt made her look slimmer. She turned sideways to admire her beige coloured court shoes. The small heel looked good with her dress, and wasn't too high for dancing.

'Elinor, Joanne's arrived,' Susan called up the stairs to

her daughter. She smiled when Elinor made her way down. 'You look lovely, darling, don't think either of you girls will be short of dance partners tonight.' Susan was very relaxed about Elinor going out tonight; the dance, run by the 195th Boys' Brigade Company attached to Wardlawhill, was to be held in the church hall. 'I bet this dance won't cost as much as the public dancing you've been to,' she said as she helped Elinor on with her new brown suede jacket.

Elinor laughed. 'Probably about half the price.'

At the sound of their voices, Andrew came out of the living room into the hallway. 'Susan, you can't compare the cost of public dancing with a wee knees-up in the church hall. Have a great time, girls.'

Elinor climbed into the back seat of Mr Scott's car behind Joanne. Mr Scott and Uncle George were the only people Elinor knew who had a car. Joanne looked lovely in a navy and white polka dot dress with a large white collar. A navy blue Alice band on Joanne's blonde hair completed the ensemble.

'Who's organising the dance?' Mr Scott asked when he drew up outside the church hall.

'It's the B.B. Company,' Joanne told him. 'They're having the dance to raise funds for some new equipment they need.'

Mr Scott wound down his car window once the two girls were standing on the pavement. 'When do you want me to come back and collect you?'

Joanne shrugged. 'Not sure. Think it'll be finishing between 11.30 and midnight.'

'Two tickets please,' Joanne said to a tall chap who stood inside the church hall entrance issuing tickets.

Elinor held her breath when she saw it was Colin Dawson. He looked even more handsome than he had on the last occasion she'd seen him.

'Five shillings please, half a crown each.'

After the girls handed over the money, Joanne made the introductions. 'This is Colin Dawson, the B.B. Captain. Colin, this is my friend, Elinor Bonnington.'

'Pleased to meet you, Elinor.' Colin smiled at her and shook her hand firmly. His hand was cool which she liked. She hated touching anyone with sweaty hands.

The band was warming up when the girls walked into the main hall. Some of the B.B. Officers' wives and mothers were bustling around in the kitchen, situated directly off the hall. The women were preparing the supper to be served halfway through the evening.

As Susan had predicted, the girls didn't lack for dancing partners during the entire evening. Colin Dawson asked Elinor to dance near the beginning and continued to partner her all evening. She found him charming.

'Do you live in Rutherglen?' he asked, when he'd first invited her to dance a St Bernard's Waltz with him.

'In Melrose Avenue,' she told him, counting her steps as she spoke. 'Where do you live?'

'I live in Smith Terrace at Farme Cross.' The dance came to an end and he walked her back to her seat, his arm around her waist.

'I think the houses in these terraces at Farme Cross are lovely,' Elinor said, when he sat down beside her. 'One of the girls in my class at the academy lived in Miller Terrace. Nancy Martin, do you know her?'

Colin shook his head. 'Don't think so. You're right about them being good houses but a bit small for my parents, my brother Eric and me. There are only two bedrooms and it means Eric sleeps on the bed settee in the living room.'

While they were chatting, the bandleader announced

the next dance was a quickstep. As the music started, Colin was on his feet once more and held out his hand. 'Would you like to dance this one?'

He led her rapidly around the floor, weaving their way through the other couples. 'Where do you work?'

'I'm in the typing pool in Colvilles at Eastfield,' she replied, trying to keep up with his rapid footwork.

'I work there too, I'm a draughtsman. Come to think of it, I'm sure I've seen you in the canteen at lunchtime,' he said, as they headed back to their seats once the music had stopped.

She nodded, realising for the first time that he was the chap she'd seen in the canteen. 'My friend Freda and I do go to the canteen most days, although sometimes we take a packed lunch and have it in our staff kitchen in the office.' With his sandy hair and blue eyes, Colin was one handsome guy. When she fancied lads these days, she no longer felt disloyal to Michael, having long ago accepted that their relationship was over.

Colin's voice brought her back to the present. 'Looks like the buffet's ready. Let's go and grab a plate before all the food has gone.' They filled their plates and carried them over to where Joanne and another B.B.Officer were sitting. Joanne introduced the chap as Frank.

'Would you like to go to the cinema next weekend?' Colin asked Elinor later, when they were dancing, cheek to cheek, to the last waltz.

'Yes, I'd like that,' she replied, keeping her cheek against his as she answered.

They continued to discuss their date after the singing of 'Auld Lang Syne' was over, but their conversation ended when Joanne tapped Elinor's shoulder. 'Sorry to rush you, Elinor, but that's my dad back for us. He's parked outside the hall.'

Chapter Seventeen

Saturday, 23rd May, 1959

The following Saturday Colin and Elinor met at Boot's the chemist's corner, a popular meeting place for courting couples. Colin was already there, standing outside the shop, when Elinor arrived.

'Have you any film in mind that you'd like to see?' he asked.

'No, I haven't checked what's on.'

'The Rio cinema is showing 'The Diary of Anne Frank'. It's about a young Jewish girl and her family who hid in a loft in Amsterdam from the Nazis for years during the Second World War. I believe the story is based on some diaries Anne wrote while they were in the loft. Do you think you'd like to see the film?'

'Oh yes, I always like true life stories. And I like the weepies.'

'Hope you've got your hankies then,' he said, and they both laughed.

When they got to Glasgow Road, there was a queue outside the Rio cinema but it moved quickly. 'Two seats in the front balcony,' Colin said to the woman in the cashier's box, sliding a ten shilling note through the slot to her. The woman pushed back the two tickets and his seven and sixpence change. Once they got to their seats, Colin handed Elinor a box of Cadbury's Dairy Milk chocolates, which he'd had in his coat pocket.

'Thank you.' She opened the wrapping paper before the film started so that they could enjoy the sweets without disturbing other patrons by rustling.

She quickly became lost in Anne Frank's world. She sniffed back the tears during the film and her hankie became quite damp.

Part way through the film, Colin put his arm round her and pulled her closer. She enjoyed the feel of her cheek resting against his shirt and the smell of his after shave.

Elinor blinked at the brightness when they came out of the darkened cinema. She loved these lighter nights and they strolled, hand in hand, along Main Street and turned up Stonelaw Road. Elinor found Colin easy to be with and their silences were comfortable with no embarrassment causing unnecessary chatter.

They turned into Melrose Avenue. 'I love these long summer days when it's dark only for a few hours,' she said, 'it's something I missed when we lived in Melbourne.'

'Do they not have the long days?'

'No, summer and winter over there, darkness comes early. Even in summer the light fades instantly in the early evening, almost like a blind being pulled down.'

'What about a walk in Overtoun Park after church tomorrow?' Colin asked her when they were standing at her gate. 'The forecast for tomorrow is good so we could take a picnic and listen to the Salvation Army band. They play in the park most Sunday afternoons from spring until autumn.'

'I'd like that.'

'If you wanted to ask Joanne to come along, I could bring my pal, Dougie McGregor, and make it a foursome.'

'Fine, I'll say to Joanne. I'll see if my mum would make us some sandwiches.'

'Great, if you and Joanne could do the sandwiches, Dougie and I could bring some lemonade.' He kissed her full on the lips and she found herself responding.

'I better go in.' She drew apart when she noticed her

mum at the upstairs window.

Colin's eyes followed hers and he laughed when he saw the face at the window. 'Okay, mustn't get you into trouble. Till tomorrow then.' He kissed her again briefly and walked along Melrose Avenue, whistling as he went.

It occurred to Elinor as she turned her key in the lock that, for the first time since she'd left Melbourne, Michael Lynch hadn't once entered her thoughts during the entire evening.

Thank goodness Dad had arranged for the phone to be installed last month, Elinor thought, as she lifted the receiver off its cradle. They'd had to take a party line and share with a neighbour further down Melrose Avenue. Fortunately he was an elderly man and very rarely used his phone so it left the line mainly free for the Bonningtons.

'Rutherglen 4360', Mrs Scott answered after a few rings. It was only then that Elinor became aware that it was almost eleven o'clock.

'I'm sorry to phone so late,' she apologised, 'but I was hoping to speak to Joanne.'

'That's alright, Elinor,' Mrs Scott said, when she heard the familiar voice. 'She's upstairs playing her records. Hang on a minute while I call up to her.'

Joanne was all for the picnic. 'I know Dougie McGregor. I've seen him at B.B. dances in the past and I've always fancied him. He was in the year above us at the academy.'

'That's great. Colin seemed quite keen to make up a foursome.'

'Dougie's also a B.B. officer but he's a member of the 248th Glasgow Company. They meet in either the West Parish Church or Munro Church.'

Elinor began to yawn. 'Right, see you tomorrow,' she

said and hung up.

***

'Hi girls,' Colin greeted Elinor and Joanne the next day at the end of the church service. 'Dougie's going to meet us in the park and bring the lemonade with him.'

The trio set off to Elinor's house to collect the sandwiches, Elinor taking Colin's arm while Joanne walked at his other side. Susan had made the sandwiches up before going to church and had left them on the kitchen table.

'I never came to the park when I was at school,' Elinor said to Joanne, as they entered via the gate in Overtoun Drive. 'I've only been in here once years ago when we were visiting Aunt Muriel from Cambuslang.'

'So you probably don't know that the park was gifted to the people of Rutherglen by John White, Lord Overtoun.' When Elinor shook her head, Joanne explained further. 'He owned White's chemical works and was one of the major employers in the Burgh. He died a year before the official opening.'

'What a pity he didn't live long enough to see folk enjoying his gift,' Elinor said, as they took the path to their right.

'It was certainly a generous gift,' Colin told her, 'but the down side is that many of his employees in White's have since suffered ill health as a result of all the fumes from the chemicals that they constantly breathed in. Our next-door neighbour is one of these people and he can't work now.'

Dougie was waiting for them beside the ornate Victoria fountain. Once hellos were exchanged, the four of them went into the main part of the park, with trees around the perimeter, many of them bedecked in spring blossoms. Elinor and Colin strolled, arms entwined, ahead of the other two.

They spread out a rug on the grass close to the bandstand and quickly devoured the sandwiches. Dougie sat two bottles of lemonade in front of him, securing them between his feet while he undid the tops. 'We don't have anything to drink out of so we'll need to drink from the bottle.' He gave one bottle to Colin and Elinor, leaving the other for Joanne and him to share.

'Just as well my mother can't see me drinking out of a lemonade bottle.' Joanne giggled as she took the bottle from Dougie. 'She's always such a stickler for decorum at all times.'

After drinking, she passed the bottle back to Dougie.

'Ta.' He took a large gulp, then burped loudly.

Joanne drew him a look but didn't comment. 'I was looking at Cliff's latest album in the Music House in Hamilton Road on Friday night. It's just out this month and there's a gorgeous picture of Cliff on the front.'

'Is that the album featuring his new song, 'Move It?' Elinor asked.

'Yes, it does. He's dreamy, I could listen to him all day.'

'Och, Elvis' new one 'A Fool Such As I' is much better.' Dougie proceeded to give his Presley impersonation, then he and Colin got to their feet and serenaded the girls.

'It's like a cats' chorus,' Joanne said when she and Elinor had managed to stop laughing.

Looking suitably offended, the boys sat down again.

The sun was hot and soon only Elinor remained awake, soaking up the pungent smells around her, while she munched on an apple. Then she lay back, her head close to Colin's. The silence was broken by the hum of a lawnmower somewhere in the distance. Her thoughts went back to the picnics she'd enjoyed with Michael in Melbourne; sitting in the Botanic Gardens surrounded by the fabulous Australian flora and fauna or seated on the grassy bank lining the River Yarra that flowed through the city of Melbourne. But the memories of her time with Michael were fast receding and she was happy to be here with her new friends. The soporific effect of the birdsong soon caused her eyelids to become heavy.

They awoke to the sound of voices and laughter. By now the park was packed, people sitting head to toe, with hardly a blade of grass visible between them. Behind them to their left was another group of teenagers. Elinor gasped when her glance fell on one of the boys in the group. He was the image of Michael and, although she knew it was impossible, she let herself imagine for a moment that it was him. When she looked round at Colin, she realised that he had seen her eyes on the Michael look-alike. Colin was now staring at Elinor with a frown on his face, although he said nothing.

The band members, each one wearing a Salvation Army uniform, arrived and set up their music stands in a semi-circle on the bandstand. At three o'clock the band started to play, their instruments glinting in the sunlight. The audience applauded, many singing along to the familiar hymns. When the band members packed up their instruments, people began to leave and, when Elinor turned round, the Michael look-alike and his friends had gone.

'Let's go out this exit.' Colin pointed to the ornate gates near the bandstand. From there, they walked along Rodger Drive back to Stonelaw Road.

'Will we meet one night next week?' Colin asked Elinor, when he kissed her goodbye outside her gate. 'That is if you want to see me again?'

'Of course I do.' Sure that Colin was still annoyed about the Michael look-alike, Elinor wanted to tell him he needn't worry but she decided it was best to say no more about it.

***

Humming quietly to herself, Jean Dawson finished weeding in the back garden. Jean often told her family and friends that she didn't have to attend church as the garden was her spiritual home. She moved to the front garden and pulled on her gloves to weed the rose bushes; it never ceased to amaze Jean that these magnificent flowers could give you such a brutal scratch.

Noticing that the paper-boy had left the gate open when he delivered 'The Sunday Post' this morning, Jean closed it. It creaked in protest and she made a mental note to oil the hinges. It was also badly needing painted so she'd either do it herself or ask Colin to do it for her. Past experience had taught her that if she waited for Tom, who spend most of his time on the golf course, or for that matter Eric, the gate would creak on forever. Jean loved both her sons in equal measure, but could never get over how different they were. Colin had achieved so much, both in his work and in the Boys' Brigade. Eric was much quieter than his older sibling and spent more time on his own. A bit like me, I suppose, Jean thought.

Colin had met a girl, Elinor, at the B.B. dance last week and he'd taken her out to the pictures last night. Today he was going with her to the park; they were having a foursome with Elinor's friend and Colin's pal, Dougie. Colin had taken longer with his appearance today, so Jean guessed Elinor was special.

'Hi Mum.' Jean looked up from weeding between the narsturtiums as Colin creaked open the gate.

'Hello, son,' she smiled at him. 'Did you have a good time at the park?'

'Yes, we had a great time. The place was packed, probably because it was such a sunny day.'

Jean stood up straight and rubbed her lower back, stiff from crouching down for such a long time. 'I was thinking that the gate could do with oiling, and perhaps a lick of paint. Do you think you could do it for me sometime, Colin?'

'Sure, I'll try and get time next weekend,' he promised, holding the back of his hand over his mouth as he yawned. 'Think I'll have a soak in the bath before dinner.'

***

When Elinor and Colin met on the following Wednesday evening after work, she was pleased that Colin seemed to have forgotten about the Michael look-alike she'd stared at in the park.

'What do you want to do?' Colin asked, as they made their way along Main Street. 'I'm not sure what's on in the cinema.'

Elinor shook her head. 'It's too nice a night to be indoors. We could either go to the park again or maybe walk along to Bankhead Pond. I used to go there a lot when I was younger.'

'I haven't been to the pond before so let's go there.'

They walked up Mill Street and turned into Bankhead Road. The road was busy, as was the pond, because the sunny evening had brought folk out. Elinor and Colin found themselves a place on the grassy slope above the pond, with the hedges of the houses behind them in Milrig Road sheltering them from any breeze.

Colin screwed up his eyes against the strong evening sun. 'Are these cows I can see in that field beyond the trees?'

'Yes, the cattle belong to Mitchell's farm. The farmhouse is up at the top of the hill. A couple of the farmer's sons went to school with me and they used to deliver the milk before they came to school.'

'My mother was asking about you last night,' Colin told her. 'Nothing bad,' he added, seeing the look of alarm on her face, 'just interested in where we'd met and if we were going steady. I think she'd like me to invite you to our house for tea sometime. Would you like that?'

'Yes,' she stammered. 'I would.'

'Well I'll try to arrange it. Maybe at the weekend, although I've promised to paint the front gate for her, so I might do that on Saturday morning. Perhaps you'd like to come for tea that evening?'

Elinor nodded and laid her head on his shoulder, as before enjoying the smell of his after-shave.

Chapter Eighteen

Friday, 29th May, 1959

'Elinor, if you don't get a move on you'll be late for work,' Susan said to her daughter a week later. Elinor was reading something which she'd propped up against the teapot sitting on the middle of the breakfast table.

'Gosh, where's that last half hour gone?' Elinor polished off her last piece of toast spread thickly with Marmite. 'This stuff isn't half as nice as Vegemite,' she said, closing the lid tightly on the jar. Elinor had acquired a taste for Vegemite while living in Melbourne and she felt that Marmite was a poor substitute.

'Well it's the best we can do as you can't buy Vegemite in this country,' her mother reminded her.

'I'll finish reading this on the bus.' Elinor grabbed the sheets of paper and stuffed them into her handbag sitting on the sideboard. She hurried into the bathroom to brush her teeth. When she returned she went over to the mirror above the sideboard and applied her lipstick, then stood back and pursed her lips, to help spread it evenly across them.

'What is it you were reading?' Susan asked, while Elinor was putting on her coat.

'It's the information about the B.B. camp at Nairn in July.'

'So you're definitely going to that, even though you've only known Colin a few weeks.'

Elinor buttoned her coat. 'Mum, it isn't only the two of us who are going. There will be a whole Boys' Brigade Company, plus some other females. Joanne's coming too.'

'And what about sleeping arrangements?'

'Oh Mum, stop worrying, there won't be any hanky panky as you call it. The boys and the officers will sleep in the local church hall; they'll use sleeping bags and camp beds and Phil, an old Army mate of Colin's dad, will be the cook for the fortnight we're in Nairn. We girls will stay in a bed and breakfast place nearby. We'll have our breakfast in the guest house but our other meals will be taken with the Company.'

As Elinor picked up her handbag, she glanced at the clock. 'I'll need to dash or I'll miss the bus,' she said, and raced out of the house. She caught the bus each morning in East Main Street, a five minute walk from the house, less if she put a sprint on.

It was a thoughtful Susan who cleared away the breakfast things. As a mother she still had reservations about Elinor and Colin going on holiday together when they scarcely knew one another. And yet, Elinor was right; they wouldn't be alone in Nairn. She ran some hot water into the basin and squeezed in some washing-up liquid. Then she dropped the plates into the soapy water. It was some comfort to know that the Minister and his wife would be there for part of the time to keep an eye on things.

Elinor got to the bus stop in East Main Street just as the No 76 drew up. She stood back to allow a passenger to get off and was still breathless as she climbed aboard. She smiled at Hannah, the regular conductress, and found herself a seat on the lower deck. She'd scarcely sat down when Hannah arrived, ticket machine and money bag around her waist.

'Fares please,' the conductress said to the gentleman on the opposite side of the passageway from Elinor. 'A single to Hamilton, please,' he said and held up a ten shilling note.

'Have you anything smaller?' she asked but the man shook his head. 'Sorry, I haven't.' Hannah sighed and rummaged in her money bag until she got sufficient change, which she gave to the passenger along with his ticket.

'How are you today?' Hannah turned and smiled at Elinor.

'Fine thanks. Just made the bus by the skin of my teeth.' Elinor handed up her weekly bus ticket which she bought each week from Penman's shop in Farmeloan Road.

Hannah grinned. 'Yes, I saw you haring along the road. But don't worry I wouldn't have rung the bell for the driver until you were aboard.' Hannah punched a hole in the appropriate day on the ticket and gave it back to Elinor. 'Be good and don't do anything I wouldn't do,' she said, as she moved down the bus again.

Elinor smiled at this familiar statement from Hannah; she enjoyed the rapport she'd formed with the conductress who was always bright and cheery whatever the weather. Elinor heard Hannah climb the stairway at the back of the bus and next minute her call of 'fares please' could be heard coming from the upstairs deck. Before Hannah descended the stairs once more, the bus had long since reached Eastfield, where Elinor got off.

Chapter Nineteen

Saturday, 13th June, 1959

'Are you nearly ready to go?' Susan called upstairs to her daughter, a week before Elinor's 21st birthday. 'We can go into Glasgow by train, it's much quicker than the bus.'

'Be down in a mo,' Elinor replied. It was only last week that Freda had suggested to her that she go to Watt Brothers department store in Hope Street to buy a dress for her 21st party. 'My sister got her wedding dress there a few years ago,' Freda told her. 'They have a fantastic range to choose from. Not just wedding dresses, but dance and party dresses too.'

'Will you go there for your wedding dress?' Freda and Jack had set their wedding date for the middle of November.

'I probably will if I don't get anything suitable in the local Hamilton shops.'

Aware her mother was becoming impatient, Elinor pulled on a cardigan over her summer dress and hurried downstairs. 'Right, let's go,' she said to her mother, who was waiting in the hallway.

They walked down Stonelaw Road and crossed over to the far side of Main Street. 'Is it in there that Aunt Muriel buys her budgie seed?' Elinor asked, when they were passing the grain store, run by the Gilchrist family, on the corner of Main and Castle Streets.

Susan nodded and steered Elinor into Castle Street. 'If we move ourselves, we'll get the half past eleven train.' They put on a spurt and hurried into the station entrance in Victoria Street, keeping up a good pace along the wooden walkway and down the stairway to the booking office. They'd barely purchased their tickets when the Glasgow train drew into Platform 1.

Once in Watt Brothers, the assistant directed Susan to a comfortable armchair while Elinor was trying on some dresses. The first few garments Elinor tried on didn't suit her, some were the wrong style and others the wrong colour. She sighed as she tried on the sixth dress, sure that it would be as unsuitable as the previous ones. Instead, she drew in breath when she saw herself in the mirror of the fitting room cubicle.

'Oh Elinor, you look a picture,' Susan enthused, when her daughter came out of the changing room, wearing a classic style white dress. It had a straight skirt with the hemline just under the knee. There was a low neckline but Susan was pleased to see a large white flower positioned at the cleavage. The dress had thin shoulder straps with a tiny bow on each strap. Elinor had done her hair in the usual French roll style and the assistant had given her a white satin Alice band to place on her head. 'You'll look fantastic at your party, darling.'

Elinor was glad that she'd taken Freda's advice to come to Watt Brothers. 'I feel great in it.' She gave her mum a twirl, showing off the white sling-back shoes with the 3" heels to perfection.

'Will you be able to walk and dance in such high heels?' Susan queried.

'Yes, no bother. The shoes are really comfortable.'

'How are we doing?' The assistant, who had also been attending to another customer, now returned and gave Elinor an admiring glance. 'You look superb in that dress. It's a perfect fit.' She indicated for Elinor to turn around and show the dress from all angles.

Elinor obliged and the woman beamed at her. 'It's a really classic design and in a beautiful fabric.'

'I take it the dress would need to be dry-cleaned,' Susan said to the assistant.

'Yes, I wouldn't try to wash it. Safer to take it to the dry cleaners. Is it for a special occasion?' she asked Elinor.

'My 21st birthday party.'

'How lovely. And the dress is just right for that event. When is your birthday?'

'Next Saturday.'

The assistant wrapped the dress carefully in tissue paper and placed it in one of the store's large carrier bags. She put the shoes and the Alice band into a smaller bag. When they left the store, they had a look around other shops in Sauchiehall Street. Then, feeling in need of some refreshment, they made their way down West Nile Street.

'Let's go for a cup of tea before we get the train home,' Susan suggested. 'We can go to Miss Cranston's tearoom in Buchanan Street.'

'But isn't it a bit expensive in there?'

'Yes, but it isn't every day my daughter reaches 21, so let's push the boat out this once.'

The restaurant was on two levels and Susan asked for a table upstairs. The waitress showed them to a window table, where they could look down over Buchanan Street. Shoppers, mainly women, hurried along, each swinging one or two large carrier bags at her side.

'Can we have afternoon tea, please?' Susan asked the waitress.

'Certainly,' the woman said and moved away towards the kitchen.

'I love these chairs.' Elinor looked admiringly at the high backed chair she was sitting on.

'Yes, Charles Rennie Macintosh was a wonderful designer and I always think his rose design is so distinctive, isn't it?' Susan turned to look at the rose panel on the wall beside them. 'You do know that it was Macintosh who designed the Glasgow School of Art?'

Elinor shook her head. 'No, I didn't know that. He must have been a very clever man.'

'Yes, it's such a pity that his work wasn't truly recognised during his lifetime. His wife, Margaret, was also an artist.' They chatted on about Mackintosh and other famous Glasgow people until the waitress returned, carrying a cakestand which she placed on the white starched tablecloth. There were daintily-cut sandwiches on the bottom plate, scones and pancakes on the middle one and the top plate was filled with delicious cream cakes.

They made short work of the sandwiches and sampled a scone, before going on to the cakes. They discussed the forthcoming 21st party while they ate. 'I'll phone the City Bakeries on Monday to confirm that everything is still fine for next Saturday,' Susan said, as she cut a cream horn in half. 'With your birthday cake being made in their bakery, it will just need to be left downstairs when the shop closes.'

The City Bakeries shop in Rutherglen had a well-frequented tearoom in the basement, which was popular for functions, such as weddings and parties. When Susan and Elinor had gone to see the place a couple of months ago, they decided it was an ideal size for the number of guests Elinor planned to invite to celebrate her 21st.

'Do you think there will definitely be 20 at the party?'

Elinor nodded, popping the last piece of meringue into her mouth. She began to count the number on her fingers. 'There'll be Colin and Eric, Joanne and Dougie and of course Freda and Jack. That's six. I've invited Rose Peters and, as she doesn't have a boyfriend, I was hoping she'd get on well with Eric.'

'So that makes seven,' Susan noted.

'Yes, and I've asked Edna, Isabel and Maureen from Colvilles plus their partners, and Phyllis and Diane from church and their partners.'

'That brings the number up to seventeen,' Susan said, as she poured them both another cup of tea. 'And of course Aunt Muriel thinks Rita and Brian will manage up for the party.'

'Well if they do, and bring a partner, that'll be another four.'

'Which totals twenty one and don't forget yourself.'

Elinor smiled. 'Of course. I forgot to count myself. So it looks like it could be twenty two and you and Dad will be there for a wee while so we should cater for twenty four.'

'Why don't we cater for twenty six in case Aunt Muriel and Uncle George decide to come along as company for your dad and me?'

'Yes, that's a good idea.'

'Whether it's twenty six or less you'll have lots of room for dancing. Are you sure Joanne's record player will be good enough for the music?' Susan asked, stirring sugar and milk into her tea. 'We could hire a band for the evening if you preferred.' She and Andrew had decided to stay until the tea and the cutting of their daughter's cake was over and then go home and leave the young ones to dance the next few hours away.

'Of course,' Elinor told her, stretching out for a French cake. 'Joanne's dad is going to drive her down to the tearoom with the record player and some suitable records. Joanne has a huge collection and lots of them are good to dance to. I know that because we often dance to them in her bedroom.'

'That was nice,' Susan said, once they'd had their fill,

and she signalled to the waitress for the check. She looked at her watch as they made their way to the cash desk. 'We should be in time to catch the four o'clock train home.'

Chapter Twenty

Saturday, 20th June, 1959

Andrew pressed down the button, capturing the picture of Elinor posing in front of her cake, which was decorated with pink roses and the words HAPPY 21ST BIRTHDAY ELINOR. He was a keen photographer, if an amateur, and his pictures usually turned out well. 'Right, will we sing to the birthday girl before she cuts her cake?'

The guests joined in with 'Happy Birthday To You' and then someone began to sing '21 Today'. When the singing finally died away, Andrew gave his daughter the nod and Elinor plunged the silver knife into the centre of the cake.

Afterwards they all took their places at the table. Susan, Andrew, Muriel and George sat at the one end of the table to let the young folk sit together. The plates of food were quickly emptied. The staff then served tea and coffee and pieces of birthday cake were handed round.

Elinor was pleased to see that Eric was getting on well with Rose Peters. 'Your brother seems quite smitten with my friend, Rose,' she whispered to Colin.

'I've noticed,' he replied, 'and I'm pleased about it as Eric is usually very shy when he's with girls. I like Rose, she's bright and bubbly and will be good for Eric if they decide to go out together.'

'They would make a lovely couple, wouldn't they?' Then she laughed. 'We're becoming matchmakers.'

'I know, we're like an old married couple instead of teenagers in the first flush of love ourselves,' he said, then stopped speaking when Susan and the Manageress of the shop came up to ask Elinor something.

Elinor was disappointed about the interruption, but she was left with a warm feeling, remembering his words about them being in the first flush of love. It proved he did love her as she'd hoped.

Once the staff had cleared away the crockery and cutlery, the table was pushed back against the wall to leave room for dancing. The four adults said their farewells to the young folk and left the tearoom as the first record was put on the turntable.

George put his hands in his ears. 'What a racket.'

'Yes, it's good to get away from the noise,' Susan said, smiling at her husband when the four of them climbed the stairs to the shop floor, where a member of staff let them out.

'You're showing your age, Mrs B,' Andrew joked.

'I agree with Susan,' Muriel said, once they were outside. 'We can go home and sit with our feet up. What a joy.'

Andrew threw one arm around his wife's shoulders and the other around Muriel. 'Oh to be young again, eh?'

But Susan shook her head, taking Andrew's arm. 'No, love, once is enough for me. No going back.'

***

'You seemed to be getting on well with Eric at my party,' Elinor said to Rose, when they were walking along Main Street on their way to the Odeon the following Wednesday evening. The film 'Ben-Hur' was showing this week and both girls were keen to see it.

'Yes, I really like him, Elinor. He walked me home from your party and he kissed me in the close. He's asked me out this coming Saturday.'

Elinor poked her friend in the ribs. 'Great, and I hope you said yes.'

Rose nodded, blushing furiously. 'I did. We're going to meet at Woolworth's at half past seven.'

'I'm so pleased. He's a really nice boy, even though it's like pulling teeth trying to get a conversation out of him.'

'But you see, I didn't find him like that at all. We chatted away quite happily together. I think both of us are shy, so we're like kindred spirits.'

'Well that's great, Rose, and I'm very happy for you both. We must arrange a foursome sometime with Colin and me. How did your mum and dad take it?'

'They were listening to a play on the radio when I got in so I was able to go to bed without telling them too much. Just said I'd enjoyed the party and the brother of your boyfriend walked me home. Mum asked me more about Eric the following day but I didn't tell her that I'd fallen for a Protestant boy. You know what parents are like about folk of a different religion.'

'I know. It seems so stupid to me as we all worship the one God, whether we're Catholic or Protestant.'

'Same here,' Rose said, linking arms with Elinor. 'Anyway, I don't think it'll make any difference to how Eric and I feel about each other. Not that we said as much, but I sensed he was feeling the same as I did.'

'That's fantastic, Rose.' They turned into the foyer of the cinema. 'Hope the film's as good as everyone says.' The two girls got out the money for their tickets and the problem of the different religion was forgotten for the moment.

Chapter Twenty One

Saturday, 18th July, 1959

'Look, there's a coffee shop over there,' Joanne said, pointing to the café on the opposite side of Nairn Main Street from where she and Elinor were standing.

'It says on the board outside that they serve home baking. Let's go in.'

The other three were lagging a bit behind but Joanne signalled to them that she and Elinor were crossing the road. The girls had arrived in Nairn a little over an hour ago and once they'd unpacked had decided to explore the town.

Elinor chose an empire biscuit with her tea and Joanne plumped for a pineapple tart. They took their place at a window table which would easily accommodate all five of them.

'I had a quick chat with Colin when we got here,' Elinor told her friend. 'He said that when those of them in the advance party got off the overnight train in Inverness early this morning they had only about ten minutes to board the Nairn train.'

'What about all the extra stuff they brought with them?' Joanne knew that the advance party brought some extra luggage needed for the fortnight's holiday. While she was speaking the other girls came into the café and went over to the counter to check on the home baking.

'Colin said it was a nightmare getting the luggage piled on to a porter's trolley and loading it into the train.' Elinor giggled. 'He said, as it was the B.B. officers themselves who did all the lifting and pushing of the trolley, they didn't give the porter a tip and he was none too pleased about that.'

'But they obviously managed to do it before the Nairn train left.'

'Yes but with just seconds to spare. Colin said it was too close for comfort.'

'Did the advance party check out our bed and breakfast accommodation when they arrived?' The girls had travelled on the same daytime train as the main party.

'I think so. Isn't it fabulous, two whole weeks in Nairn?' Elinor moved her chair closer to Joanne's to make room at the table for the others.

'What beautiful baking,' Hilda said, when she sat down next to Elinor. 'There's too much to choose from.'

Mary laughed as she put her tray down on the table. 'There's nothing else for it girls, we'll have to come in every day until we've sampled all the cakes.'

'Eating is a much more enjoyable exercise than going for long walks,' Cathy piped up.

Cathy was Lieutenant Dave Farthing's girlfriend and Elinor and Colin were known to be sweet on one another. Joanne, Hilda and Mary didn't have a particular beau in the B.B. Company but there was plenty of 'talent' for them to choose from.

'Mr and Mrs Wilkes will be arriving on Monday,' Joanne told the others. 'Mr Wilkes can't come over the weekend as he needs to conduct the Sunday services at Wardlawhill.'

Elinor nodded. 'Colin said the entire Company will be attending the service on Sunday morning at Nairn Parish Church, followed by a B.B. parade. I think we're expected to go too.'

Mary laughed. 'Oh yes, no show without Punch.'

'I could do with a sharper knife,' Hilda complained, as she tried to cut her empire biscuit in half. Peals of laughter ensued when the cherry on the top flew off and hit Joanne on the nose.

'At least we don't have to do any cooking,' Elinor said, once the hilarity had died down, 'wouldn't be much of a holiday if we had to do that. Colin said that Phil is an excellent cook. He used to be an Army cook.'

'Thanks,' Joanne said to the waitress as they were leaving the café. 'We're here for a fortnight so with all that delicious baking I think you'll be seeing us quite often.'

The waitress beamed at them. 'That's great girls. We'll be pleased to have you in any time,' she replied, and began clearing the dishes from the table they had vacated.

***

It was on the middle Saturday of the holiday that Colin first broached the subject of their relationship, when he and Elinor were walking, hand in hand, on the beach at Nairn. With the warm sun shining down on them, they were both wearing sunglasses to shade their eyes from the glare. Tonight the entire company would meet up for a party in the church hall, with Phil as usual doing the catering. Some members of Nairn church had been invited to join them, mainly female, as they were a bit short of girls for dancing.

Colin squeezed Elinor's hand tighter. 'It's great to spend some time on our own, isn't it?'

'Sure is. I've enjoyed my time with the other girls but I've missed us being together.' Elinor's foot caught in some stones on the beach and she would have fallen over had it not been for Colin's steadying arm catching her. She grabbed on to his arm and he supported her until she regained her balance.

'Thanks,' she said, feeling breathless and not just from the fall. 'I'm surprised there aren't more people here this afternoon.' She looked at the vast stretch of deserted beach ahead of them. 'Strange isn't it that we haven't met anyone from the camp since we came down here?'

'Some folk probably hit the town and the shops and a lot of the boys were staying around the church hall to have a game of football.'

A short distance on Elinor stopped again and leaned on Colin once more, while she removed her sandals. 'I might as well take these off. With all the wee stones getting in between my toes I'm as well walking barefoot.' She swung the straps of her sandals over her wrist and they moved on.

'Let's have a seat,' Colin suggested when they came to a sheltered spot below some dunes. They perched on a couple of large boulders and relaxed in the sunshine. Happy to be together, with no need for words, the only sound was the gigantic waves crashing in over the rocks. Elinor watched, fascinated, at the wall of water that cascaded in, to end finally in a feeble ripple on the sand.

It was Colin who spoke first. With his arm around her shoulder and her hand held in his, he looked into her eyes. 'I love you, Elinor Bonnington, and I hope you love me.'

'I do.' She smiled up at him and snuggled against him, her reaction to his words showing as little pink spots on her cheeks.

'I know we haven't been dating for long,' he continued, 'and I hope I'm not speaking out of turn. But I really love you, Elinor, and I want to marry you if you'll have me. I hoped you might agree to us becoming engaged at Christmas.'

Elinor made no reply at first and he turned to her, a frown puckering his brow. 'What's wrong, Elinor? Should I have waited a bit longer before telling you of my feelings?'

She shook her head but he could see she was perplexed. 'It's just … I want … I need … I need to tell you something,' the words came out in a rush, 'and afterwards you might hate me. I didn't really want to tell you but I don't want to keep secrets from you. If we are going to be married, then we need to be truthful with one another.'

'I agree about the need for truthfulness but Elinor there surely can't be anything so bad that I would hate you. I love you, my darling, and nothing is going to change that.'

Elinor raised her head and gripped his arm tightly. 'I really hope so, Colin, as I love you so much it hurts and I want more than anything else in the world to be Mrs Dawson. But I need to tell you something first.'

She took a minute or two to begin speaking, while Colin kept his anxious eyes on her face, and when she began to talk the words poured out of her. She gave him all the history of her time with Michael, the night of passion while his parents were in Queensland, her discovery that she was pregnant and the spontaneous abortion she'd suffered.

'You're the only person, apart from Joanne, who knows what happened on the ship that night. Mum and Dad don't know about it,' she said while Colin was absorbing everything she'd just told him.

He tightened his arm around her and leaned forward to kiss her, a kiss as passionate as previously. When they'd drawn apart, he cupped his hands around her face and stared into her eyes. 'Elinor, I love you as much as I did ten minutes ago and I love you all the more because of your honesty. What happened is very sad and my heart goes out to you for what you've suffered but you are still the girl I fell in love with at the dance that night. And, if you'll have me, I still want to be your husband.'

'Oh, Colin,' she whispered, tears glinting in her eyes as she looked at him. 'I love you like mad and of course I want to marry you.' This time last year her feelings for Michael would have got in the way but by now she knew that there was to be no future for them. Suddenly she was aware that she had spoken the truth and that Colin had taken Michael's place in her heart.

'What do you say if we make an unofficial commitment to one another now and I can ask your parents officially at Christmas? That gives me time to save for a special ring for you.'

Elinor's reply was a squeal of delight and she threw herself into his open arms. They kissed again, more intense this time, and Elinor felt herself drowning in passion. Once they'd drawn apart and Elinor's breathing had returned to normal, she whispered, 'I think we'll have to keep our feelings in check until we're married.'

'I agree, although it won't be easy to control ourselves.'

'Well, you know what they say about good things being worth waiting for.' She glanced at her watch. 'Do you think we should make our way back to the town?'

'Yes, let's go and find a café. I could murder a cool drink. Why don't we go down to the harbour café?' When Elinor nodded, he jumped to his feet and pulled her up gently from the boulder she was sitting on.

The hill down to the harbour was steep and Colin's arm tightened around her waist. As they reached the harbour, before they got the length of the café, they heard some yelling. A few of the B.B. boys raced towards them from further along the harbour. They were all shouting at once and gesturing madly towards a large expanse of water between two fishing boats. Seeing a boy's head bobbing up and down in the water, and the name Graham McDougall registering with him, Colin threw off his sports jacket and dived from the harbour wall into the oily water.

Elinor held her breath and covered her face with her

hands, terrified to watch. She knew Colin had life-saving certificates but she was angry at him for putting himself in danger. She took her hands away from her face when she heard the boys cheering and next thing she knew Colin's head and shoulders appeared at the top of the harbour wall, dragging Graham along with him. The other boys crowded round and assisted the officer and boy up over the wall to safety. Colin looked remarkably calm after his experience but Graham's lips were blue and he was visibly shivering from cold. Colin slapped the younger boy's back. 'You okay, Graham?'

Graham coughed and spluttered out some bits of gunge that had got into his mouth while he was in the water. 'I'm fine, Captain. Thanks for rescuing me. I can't swim.'

'Well, let's get ourselves back to the camp and change into dry clothes. Then we'll get you to the local hospital to have you checked over. And I promise I will personally give you swimming lessons.'

Elinor's feelings changed from anger to pride and she ran over, uncaring of his soaking wet clothes, and hugged Colin like she'd never let him go. 'I was so worried,' she whispered into his sodden shirt, 'but I'm so proud of you.'

'I'm fine,' he said gently, taking her hand. 'But I'll be happier once we get Graham seen by a doctor to be certain there will be no lasting effects.'

Chapter Twenty Two

Saturday, 1ˢᵗ August, 1959

'Did you have a good time, love?' Susan opened her arms to her daughter when she came into the house in Melrose Avenue on her return from Nairn.

Elinor dropped her case at her feet. She wanted desperately to tell her mum and dad that she and Colin had discussed marriage but they'd made a pact to say nothing yet to either set of parents. 'We had a super time. And we were lucky with the weather too.'

Susan smiled. 'I can see that from your lovely tan?'

'I've been keeping an eye on the forecast, and I noticed that it seemed to be dry in the Nairn area during the fortnight you were away.' Andrew picked up Elinor's case and carried it upstairs to her bedroom.

'And was the food palatable?' Susan asked as the three of them sat down in the kitchen to enjoy a cup of tea with some of her delicious home baked scones.

'Yes, Phil, the cook Colin had employed, produced some lovely meals for us. He'd been a cook in the Army so he was very experienced. We were also lucky with our bed and breakfast place. The couple who owned it were ever so friendly and they rustled us up a super breakfast every morning.'

'And did Mr and Mrs Wilkes join you all at any stage?' Susan asked.

'Yes, they came up to Nairn for a few days during our first week. They were very relaxed and both of them joined in all the activities with us. And, guess what, Mr Wilkes gave all five of us girls who were there a lovely box of chocolates.

Cadbury's Milk Tray no less.'

Susan smiled. 'How kind of him. And so like Mr Wilkes to do such a generous act.' Mr Wilkes was a man who practiced what he preached. He was known and respected in the Burgh as someone who helped others in the community, irrespective of whether or not they were churchgoers. If you were hurting or in trouble then Mr Wilkes would never turn you away.

'It was indeed kind,' Andrew agreed, and then he laughed. 'Mind you, just as well there were only five of you; otherwise our poor Minister would have been bankrupt.'

Elinor cut open her scone and spread it with butter, before adding some of Mum's home-made raspberry jam. Uncle George occasionally took them up to one of the Clyde Valley fruit farms, where Aunt Muriel and Mum would pick their own strawberries and raspberries for jam making. 'Yummy,' she said, through a mouthful of scone.

Susan took the jam dish from Elinor and spread some on her own scone. 'Uncle George took us up to the Clyde Valley while you were in Nairn so we could pick some more soft fruits.'

'So, did you and the other girls amuse yourselves during the day while the boys were busy with their camp activities?' Andrew wanted to know.

Elinor nodded and swallowed her last piece of scone. 'There weren't really any definite activities, the boys mainly amused themselves, going to the swimming pool and playing football in the fields around the church. I sometimes went round the shops with the other girls. Nairn has some lovely shops, especially coffee shops. Now and again Colin and I went down to the beach on our own or went to the cinema. And we had a party in the church hall on the middle Saturday night and some members of Nairn church came along.'

'And how about the younger boys in the Company?' Susan asked, stirring more milk into her tea. 'Were they well behaved?'

'They were absolutely no bother and none of them seemed to be homesick. There was one scary moment though when a group of boys were fooling around down at the harbour and Graham McDougall fell into the water.'

'Is he Bob McDougall's lad?' Andrew asked.

'I think so. Colin and I were on our way to the Harbour café and heard the other boys yelling to us. Colin dived in to rescue him. He has a life-saving certificate, just as well as Graham can't swim.'

Susan's hand flew up to her mouth. 'Oh dear, that could have been a real disaster if Colin hadn't been there. I bet you were proud of your boyfriend being a hero.' Susan squeezed Elinor's hand. 'It's great to have you home, love. The house was really quiet with just your dad and me here. We really missed you.'

Chapter Twenty Three

Saturday, 15th August, 1959

Elinor's thoughts were on their visit to the Edinburgh Military Tattoo when she joined the queue outside Shearer's fruit shop in the Main Street that morning. The shop was run by Jeannie and Peggy Shearer, another family concern. While Elinor waited, she counted the hours until the bus would pick them all up at the church hall for their journey to the Capital.

Her excitement had been mounting since the day, just over a week ago, that Colin had invited her and Joanne to go to the Tattoo with the B.B. Company. 'A few of the boys have pulled out at the last moment,' he explained. 'The tickets were paid months ago when we booked, so none of the boys are expecting their money back.'

'I'd love to come and I'm sure Joanne will too. The Tattoo is something I've always wanted to see. But I don't think it's fair that we take the tickets for nothing, couldn't we pay even part of the cost?'

'Well that would be a nice gesture. I'll ask the boys concerned and let you know.'

Before she realised it, Elinor was at the head of the queue. 'How's your mother, Elinor?' the assistant asked, as she weighed out some apples and dropped them from the metal dish into a brown paper bag.

'She's fine thanks.' Elinor didn't address the assistant by name, as she wasn't sure if she was Jeannie or Peggy. One sister was tall and slim, while the other was shorter in height and more rotund, but Elinor could never remember who was who. When the quarter stone of potatoes she'd asked for were put into her shopping basket beside the apples, the basket became heavy to carry and she wished she'd left the fruit and veggies to the last.

On her way along Main Street, she popped into the library to return two books for her mum. Being a keen reader herself, Elinor loved browsing along the rows of books lining the shelves. She also liked the peaceful atmosphere in the building, where people spoke in hushed tones so as not to disturb others who were reading at the various tables situated around the main section. As she waited at the desk to be attended, Elinor's eyes were drawn, as ever, to the coloured glass dome in the ceiling at the rear of the main library. The daylight penetrating the dome made the place light and airy. The reading room, situated to the right of the main desk and entered by a separate door, was well used by elderly retired gentlemen who read the papers there each day, at the same time enjoying the social contact with their peers.

Coming out of the library, Elinor continued along Main Street to Wason's the baker. The shop, its frontage painted in blue, had a large window to the right of the doorway where all the goods on offer were displayed. The Bonningtons loved Wason's plain cookies and Susan had asked Elinor to get half a dozen. The shop usually sold out quickly as the cookies were so popular and Elinor hoped this wouldn't be the case today. Fortunately, there were still some left by the time she was served.

The last shop Elinor went into was the Woolworth's store, known to locals as Woolie's. Dad had asked her to get a special type of screwdriver and Mum wanted a box of drawing pins.

Shopping completed, she made her way home again, her thoughts once more on the visit to the Tattoo. She glanced up at the clouds scudding across the sky but they didn't look too ominous and she hoped for fair weather this evening at the Castle.

***

Elinor almost floated down the Royal Mile after the Tattoo performance, the skirl of the pipes and the bright colours of tartan still circling around in her mind. Colin and she walked hand in hand as it would be easy to become separated from your friends in the mêlée that had spilled out of the esplanade area and was now streaming down towards Princes Street. Elinor glanced back and Joanne was a short distance behind them in the company of other members of their group.

'Well, did it come up to your expectations?' Colin asked the question but was certain that he knew the answer.

'I loved it,' she said, her beaming smile confirming her words. 'It was fantastic to see so many acts from all over the world but the pipers and drummers were the best.'

He squeezed her hand. 'Yes, the music really gets your Scottish blood up, doesn't it?'

Just before they reached Princes Street, they took a left turn and headed along the side road underneath the castle where their bus was parked. It was after midnight by the time they got back to Rutherglen, a tired but extremely happy band of young people.

Elinor crept into the house, trying not to waken her parents. 'That you, Elinor? Did you have a good time?' Susan's voice came from her parents' bedroom, when Elinor had climbed the stairs.

She poked her head round the door, her dad's snores continuing undisturbed. 'Yes, Mum, it was fantastic,' she whispered, stifling a yawn. 'I'll tell you about it in the morning.'

'Okay, goodnight love. Sleep tight.'

Chapter Twenty Four

Saturday, 21ˢᵗ November, 1959

'Wow,' Colin said, when Elinor opened the door to him that Saturday afternoon. He took both her hands in his. 'You look fabulous, my darling. I can see you'll turn plenty of heads today.'

'And you don't look too bad yourself.' Her heart raced when she saw how handsome Colin looked in his best suit and sporting a new tie. She loved to see a man wearing a collar and tie, it was something she'd missed in Melbourne. In view of the hot weather over there, very few men wore ties, instead leaving their shirts open at the neck. Colin's black shoes were polished so that you could almost see your reflection in them.

Elinor had chosen a peach coloured dress and jacket for Freda and Jack's wedding and she wore a small pillbox style hat in a matching shade. Best of all was that she hadn't even needed to go into Glasgow to buy her outfit. She'd purchased it in Grieve's dress shop in Stonelaw Road. Mum had lent her a ring with a topaz stone which she wore on her right hand. She hoped very soon now to have another ring on her left hand once Colin had spoken to her parents about their engagement.

'Elinor,' Susan called to her daughter from the back of the house, 'don't keep Colin at the door. Bring him in until Uncle George gets here.' Uncle George had offered to run the young couple to the church and would pick them up at the hotel after the reception. Freda's parents had laid on a bus to transport the guests from the church to the hotel.

Colin followed Elinor along the hall and into the

living room, where the three of them settled down to wait for the car. 'Which church is it Freda and Jack are being married in?' Susan asked her daughter. 'I know you told me but I forget.'

'It's in the Congregational Church in Hamilton, near Hamilton Central railway station. The reception afterwards is to be held in the Commercial Hotel, which Freda said is down on Cadzow Street.'

Susan glanced at the clock on the mantelpiece. 'Uncle George should be here any minute now. He's a good timekeeper so I'm sure he won't be late.'

Spot on cue, they heard a toot and went out to find Uncle George standing outside his vehicle. 'Your carriage awaits you both,' he joked, raising the chauffeur's cap that he'd got from somewhere for the occasion. With much laughter Elinor and Colin climbed into the back seat of the car and with a couple more toots Uncle George drove off.

'Here we are,' Uncle George said, as he drew up outside the Congregational Church in Hamilton. 'At least you've arrived in good time.'

'Yes, the service isn't due to start for another fifteen minutes.' Colin got out on his side of the car and went round the back of the vehicle to hold Elinor's door open for her. She stood on the pavement beside him for a moment, before a sudden gust of wind blew her hat off. Colin hared after the hat, rescuing it just before it was bowled across the road. Elinor put the hat on again and held it down with her hand.

'Don't hang around,' Uncle George advised them from the driver's seat. 'Best to get inside where it will be warm and you can take your seat. Will I come back for you just before midnight?'

Colin shook hands with him. 'That would be great thanks. Do you know whereabouts in Cadzow Street the

Commercial Hotel is?'

'No, but I'll find it. I can always ask a passer-by if I'm stuck.'

'Thanks for bringing us, Uncle George.' Elinor leaned into the vehicle and kissed her uncle on the cheek, his moustache as ever tickling her face.

'Enjoy yourselves,' he called, and waved as he drove off.

'Bride or groom?' the usher at the church door asked them as they entered.

'Bride,' Elinor told the young man, who handed her an Order of Service before ushering them into a pew.

'Aren't the flower arrangements magnificent? Freda's aunt is a florist and she did the flowers as a wedding gift. And I like the hymns they've chosen.' Speaking quietly, Elinor held out the Order of Service for Colin to read.

A few minutes later Jack and his cousin, who was best man, entered the church from the vestry and stood in front of the communion table to await the bride. Soon afterwards the organ music changed from 'Jesu Joy of Man's Desiring' to the traditional piece announcing the arrival of the bride. Elinor turned and smiled at Freda when she swept past their pew on the arm of her father, to take her place beside Jack.

'She looks like a princess,' Elinor whispered to Colin, as the last strains of the music died away and the minister began to speak.

***

'Well, how was the wedding?' Uncle George asked once they had driven away from the Commercial Hotel and headed for the main road to Rutherglen. This late at night the road was almost empty, so they were unlikely to encounter any hold-ups.

'It was wonderful,' Elinor told him. 'Freda looked so

beautiful and Jack's speech was good too. She gave her bouquet to her aunt and all the ladies at the wedding were given a favour.' She opened her bag and felt the little piece of orange blossom tied with tartan ribbon, which she would put in the display cabinet in the front room when she got home. 'The band played all our favourite tunes to dance to, didn't they, Colin?'

'Yes, and they fed us well. The meal was delicious and there was more food later in the evening too.'

Uncle George chuckled. 'A man after my own heart, Colin. The ladies love all the finery but we blokes are more interested in the grub.'

Elinor tutted, in mock disapproval. 'Honestly, what are you two like?' she said, laughing.

Uncle George drove home via Farme Cross, where he dropped Colin off at his front door, before making sure Elinor was delivered home safely.

Chapter Twenty Five

Sunday, 20th December, 1959

'There's something I wanted to ask you.' Colin's glance took in both Susan and Andrew as he spoke to them across the dining table. It was the Sunday before Christmas and he'd been delighted to accept an invitation to lunch at Melrose Avenue after church.

About to take a drink of her coffee, Susan now replaced the cup on its saucer. She stared at him with a puzzled look on her face. In the seven or eight months that Colin had been dating Elinor, she'd come to like him and she hoped his next words weren't going to spoil that impression. She sensed Andrew, who was sitting next to her, straightening up in his chair.

On her side of the table, Elinor edged nearer to Colin, holding his hand under the table as he continued to speak. 'Elinor and I love one another,' he told her parents, turning to smile at Elinor, who was gripping his hand as if her life depended on it. 'We would like to become engaged on Christmas day and hope you will give us your blessing.' He sighed, relieved that he had finally said it.

The stunned silence that followed was broken by Andrew. 'In my opinion lad, you're from a respectable family and a hard worker from all accounts. But more importantly to me, you have been kind to my daughter and treated her well. I know Elinor loves you so I have no objection to the engagement.'

'Thank you, Dad,' Eleanor said, laying her head on Colin's shoulder.

Susan at last found her voice. 'I'm so pleased, I hoped you two would get together as you seem right for one another. Have you bought the ring yet?'

Colin smiled at her. 'No, we didn't want to buy it until we got your blessing.'

'Colin and I are taking a day's leave from work on Tuesday to go into town.'

Susan beamed at the young couple. 'I have an idea. Why don't we all, the two families, have Christmas dinner together so we can all see your rings at the one time? Your parents will be welcome here, Colin. There will just be the three of us and Muriel and George are joining us.'

'That would be lovely, Mrs Bonnington, if you're sure that won't be too many people. Don't forget, my young brother Eric would be with us too.'

'That's fine,' Susan said, unable to stop smiling at the good news. She looked at Andrew who nodded his agreement. 'There would be nine of us but this table has two leaves that can be inserted so it should accommodate us all.'

'And I know, if you'll allow them, that my parents will want to supply some of the food for the dinner,' Colin told her.

'That's very kind. I've probably got sufficient food in but if your parents want to bring an extra dessert I'm sure it won't go amiss.'

'Have you got the length of deciding on a date for the wedding?' Andrew asked. 'After all, Elinor, your mum and I need time to save up our pennies for the big event,' he went on, his eyes behind his glasses glinting with merriment.

The young couple looked at each other. 'I would love to be married in June at midsummer,' Elinor told her parents. 'It's an awfully long time until June 1961 so I wondered if we could make it June 1960.'

Susan's eyes widened. 'Gosh that's only a few months away. It doesn't give a lot of time to get everything arranged. Still,' she continued, seeing disappointment smear Elinor's shining eyes, 'I'm sure if we started immediately after Christmas we could manage it.'

'Thank you, thank you.' Elinor jumped up and ran round the table to embrace both of her parents at the one time.

***

'How did it go?' Susan asked two days later, opening the door as Elinor and Colin came in the front gate. Unable to concentrate on housework or cooking, she'd been constantly going to the front room window to watch out for them. A few minutes ago she'd seen them coming along Melrose Avenue from Stonelaw Road.

They kicked off their footwear in the front porch. Their coats were speckled with snow from the flakes that had started about ten minutes ago. 'It was dry when we got off the train but on the way from the station the snow started,' Elinor told her as she hung up her coat. 'Maybe we'll get a white Christmas after all.'

'Perhaps, although they aren't forecasting snow for Christmas day. Let's go into the front room where the fire's lit,' Susan suggested. The 6' tall Christmas tree Elinor had helped to decorate stood in the corner near the bay window, the star on the top twinkling in the firelight.

They'd scarcely parked themselves on seats when Elinor proceeded to tell her mum about their purchase. 'I've got a gorgeous ring, Mum. There were so many to choose from but I fell in love with this one the minute I saw it. We got it in a jeweller's shop in the Argyll Arcade. Colin is going to keep it until Christmas day,' she said, 'it's so exciting.' She took hold of Colin's hand. 'Can we let Mum see it?'

'Okay, but don't tell the others what it's like as we

want to surprise everyone on Christmas day.' He pulled a little red box out of the inside pocket of his jacket and carefully opened it. He handed the box to Susan; a magnificent solitaire diamond sparkled up at her from the ring's position nestling in the groove inside the box.

'What a beautiful ring,' Susan said softly. 'You've done Elinor proud, Colin, that ring must have cost a pretty penny.'

'I've been saving hard since we were at Nairn in the summer.'

She handed the ring back. 'Well, thank you for letting me see it and I look forward to it being placed on Elinor's finger on Christmas day. I promise I won't tell anyone what's it's like, not even Andrew when he comes home from work. It will be much nicer for the others to have the surprise on Christmas day.'

Elinor's face was radiant. 'It won't be long until I can wear it, only another three days.'

Susan grinned at her future son-in-law. 'Be careful you don't lose it, Colin.'

'Don't you worry,' he laughed, 'I'll guard it every minute of the day until Elinor is wearing it.'

Chapter Twenty Six

Christmas Day, 1959

It proved to be a very merry Christmas indeed.

The Bonningtons warmed to Jean and Tom Dawson on first sight and Muriel and George also enjoyed the extra company for the festive occasion. Eric was fairly quiet but Elinor had warned her parents that he was shy. Jean brought a big bowl of trifle and a box of chocolate mints to accompany the after-dinner coffee.

When the meal was over and they were at the coffee stage, Colin got to his feet. He drummed his spoon on his saucer as he'd seen people do in films. Once he'd got everyone's attention, he began. 'Ladies and gentlemen, I have an announcement to make.' His audience laughed, most of them guessing what he was about to tell them.

But Colin was determined to make it formal. He pushed his chair back, got down on one knee and held the engagement ring up to Elinor. 'Elinor Bonnington, will you do me the honour of being my lawful wedded wife?' he asked.

Blushing happily Elinor's 'yes' could be clearly heard and a cheer went up around the table when Colin placed the ring on the third finger of Elinor's left hand. After the excitement of the announcement was over and congratulations had been given, a toast was drunk to the young couple. Then the table was cleared and the men settled down in the front room, where they began to put the world to rights, while the ladies went into the kitchen to wash up after the meal. 'I'll to the washing Elinor,' her mum said, 'and you can help with drying. We don't want you to put your hands into detergent when you've only worn your ring for half an hour.'

'It was so kind of you to invite us to share your Christmas dinner, Susan,' Jean Dawson said when she was drying the cutlery. Over dinner, the two women found that they had a lot in common and both were delighted about the engagement of their offspring.

'You're welcome, Jean. It was great for us all to be together and to get acquainted before the wedding next year. Elinor tells me that she and Colin want to make it June of next year so we don't have long to get everything organised.'

Elinor came into the kitchen, carrying a trayload of used dishes. 'Is that someone taking my name in vain?'

Susan looked round from the sink and smiled at her daughter. 'I was telling Jean that you and Colin would like to have the wedding in June.'

'Yes we would. Midsummer's day if possible.'

'You'd have a chance of fair weather at that time of year but I think we'll need to set to early in the new year as a wedding needs a lot of planning.' Jean carried the cups and saucers she'd previously dried over to the kitchen worktop, then turned to her future daughter-in-law, who was standing beside her. 'Have you got any ideas about the sort of dress you'd like, Elinor?'

'It's all happened so quickly I haven't really decided yet. But I thought I'd take a look in Watt Brothers. I got a dress for my 21st party there, and they've got a huge selection to choose from. Can we go there sometime in January, Mum?'

'Good idea,' Susan said. 'Why don't you join us, Jean, and maybe you and I could have a look at dresses for the mothers of the bride and bridegroom.'

Jean's face lit up. 'I'd love that. With having two sons, I might not have another chance to go with a bride to choose her wedding dress. Who will you have as your bridesmaid, Elinor?'

'I'm going to ask my friend Joanne when I see her tomorrow. She and I have known one another since we were at the academy. Joanne might come with us on the dress hunting.'

Putting the washed pots on to the dish rack, Susan ripped off her rubber gloves and rinsed out the basin. 'That makes sense, love, Joanne would want to help you decide on your dress and she could look at bridesmaid's dresses at the same time. It's going to be an exciting day out,' she said, smiling at Jean.

The talk continued on the theme of next year's wedding until the women were ready to join the men in the front room for a game of cards.

Chapter Twenty Seven

Saturday, 9th January, 1960

The day of the dress hunting proved a success. The four of them were able to sit together on the train journey into Glasgow; Elinor and Joanne facing Susan and Jean. 'Will we go straight to Watt Brothers?' Susan suggested, 'and if we don't get what we're looking for there, then we can move on to other stores.'

'Good idea,' her companions nodded their agreement.

The chat on the train was all about wedding wear. Alighting at Central Station, they made their way up Hope Street to the store. Inside, they took the lift up to the wedding department on the fifth floor, where they were greeted by a smiling assistant. 'Good morning, ladies, how can I help you?'

There was a thick pile carpet beneath their feet and the wood-panelled walls smelt of lavender furniture polish. In this luxurious atmosphere, rows of wedding dresses hung on racks beneath the large windows, which looked down on Sauchiehall Street.

Elinor explained what they were looking for.

'I'm sure we'll be able to find something to suit you all,' the assistant told her, and offered Susan and Jean a seat on a comfortable-looking sofa facing the dress rack, while the girls perched on two separate upright chairs.

'I think your dress should be first, Elinor,' Susan said and the assistant invited Elinor to browse along the row of dresses.

'What do you think of this one, Joanne?' Elinor held up one of the dresses and Joanne went over to look at it and some others that had taken Elinor's eye. The girls chose a few

121

and the assistant led Elinor into a cubicle to try them on. She modelled the dresses one by one but none of them matched the style of dress she had set her heart on.

'Never mind,' she said, once she'd changed into her outdoor clothes again, 'what about the rest of you trying something before we leave the store?'

But Joanne shook her head. 'I think my dress should be left until we get yours, Elinor. We want my style of dress to tone in with yours.'

This idea was agreed and the two mothers then had a look. They were both able to find an outfit; Susan's in a beautiful shade of apple green, while the colour of Jean's was described as mulberry.

Once the two outfits were placed in the store's large carrier bags, the four of them made their way up Sauchiehall Street to another shop called 'The Wedding Belle'.

It was when Elinor emerged from the changing room wearing the fourth dress she'd tried on that the others gave a gasp and nodded excitedly, all speaking at once.

'You're beautiful,' Joanne said.

'Oh darling, that's perfect,' said Susan.

'I love it,' was Jean's comment.

'This is it, just as I imagined it.' Elinor walked across the floor, wearing the heavy brocade straight dress with a large matching bow at the waistline. A long veil slid along the carpet behind her; the veil was attached to a sprig of orange blossom which the assistant had pinned on to Elinor's hair. When she got to the far end of the room, she turned round to walk back and Joanne raced over to gather up the veil and guide it over the carpet behind Elinor.

When the assistant was certain that Elinor was satisfied with the dress, she turned her attention to a bridesmaid's dress for Joanne. With Joanne's blonde curly hair she suited most colours but eventually they plumped for a deep pink shade in a similar style to Elinor's dress. The assistant produced a large artificial flower in the exact shade of the dress which she affixed to the side of Joanne's head.

'Magnificent' was the overall consensus.

When they came out of 'The Wedding Belle' Susan said to the others, 'Let's go up to Bradford's for lunch to celebrate the success of our dress hunting.'

They walked along to the tearoom, which was situated near Charing Cross. 'Andrew is treating us to lunch because it's a special day,' Susan told them.

'How kind of him,' Jean said, 'it's a real treat to eat in a posh restaurant.'

They started with home-made broth and chose the main course of steak pie. Their dessert was ice cream and fruit.

'Gosh, I'm so full I can hardly move,' Jean said, pushing her chair back from the table a little. 'Don't think I'll eat another thing today.'

'Oh no, don't say that,' Susan said. 'I was about to suggest we finish with a pot of tea and some of the delicious strawberry tarts they serve in here.'

Jean raised her eyebrows. 'Oh well, if you twist my arm…'

When they left the teashop, they made their way down to Central Station to get the train back to Rutherglen.

***

'I hear that you've all got your dresses for the wedding,' Mrs Scott said to Elinor, when she was round at Joanne's house a few evenings later.

'Yes, we were so lucky to get them all on the one day. Joanne really suits the shade of pink. Why don't you both come along to our house soon, so that you can see Joanne wearing it?'

'That would be lovely, Elinor. We'll do that.'

'And of course you and Mr Scott will be invited to the wedding,' Elinor said, 'so you'll be getting an outfit yourself.'

'How kind of you to invite us. We'd love to come.'

Elinor smiled. 'I can't have a wedding and not have my bridesmaid's parents with us to admire their daughter in her new dress. You could have brought your dress here, Joanne, but I hoped on the wedding day we could get dressed together in my house.'

Joanne and her mother both nodded. 'Yes, that's the best idea,' Mrs Scott said.

Joanne got to her feet. 'Mum, Elinor and I are going upstairs to play my new record.'

'Is it the Neil Sedaka one?' Elinor asked, as they got into Joanne's bedroom.

'Yes, it's his latest one, 'Oh Carol'. It was released last year.'

Elinor settled herself down on Joanne's bed, while her friend placed the disc on to the turntable and put the volume up high. Next minute the delightful tones of Neil Sedaka serenaded them with his new song and the girls joined in with him. They played the disc over and over until Mrs Scott came into the bedroom to ask them to turn down the volume. 'I'm sure people walking by on the street must be able to hear it,' she said.

Chapter Twenty Eight

Tuesday, 22nd March, 1960

Today at half past ten Elinor and five other girls from the typing pool met Mr King, the Works' Safety Officer, in the foyer, ready for their tour of the steelworks. The last time Mr King had conducted one of these staff tours, Elinor had been on holiday. Thelma Green, who was a recent start in the typing pool, was among the group of six.

Thelma was a replacement for Freda who, because of the company rule, had to leave their employ on marriage. This rule would apply to Elinor herself after her wedding in June. She wasn't too concerned about that as she and Colin both wanted to start a family soon after their marriage.

Elinor sensed Thelma's antagonism towards her right from the word go and decided to steer clear of the new girl. She didn't enjoy this situation but it helped to know that it was a two-way thing. Initially Elinor was hurt by Thelma's sarcastic comments but by now an uneasy truce had grown up between the two. They'd never be friends but at least Thelma had stopped trying to wound her by words and they more or less ignored one another.

Before the tour started, Mr King issued them with safety helmets. 'These must be worn at all times while you're in the works. I suggest you put them on right now.'

Elinor took the blue helmet he gave her and turned it over, to reveal a metal frame inside. 'What's this for?' she asked, holding up the helmet to show the frame. She'd barely uttered the words before Thelma cast a withering look in her direction. Without needing to speak, Thelma's look said 'what a stupid question.'

She was very relieved at Mr King's next words. 'That's a very good question and one I'm often asked. The steelworks can be a dangerous place because of the machinery and loose pieces of masonry and metal that can fall down from time to time. If any object were to hit you,' he said, looking around the group, 'your helmet would likely cave in but that frame would protect your skull and save your life.'

Mr King led the girls, crocodile style, across the concourse from the office block to the entrance to the works. The first thing to hit Elinor was the noise and the oily smell coming from some of the machines. You could hardly hear yourself think never mind speak and Mr King had to shout above the racket of the machinery to tell them about anything they were viewing.

'Let's go up to the melting shop,' Mr King said, once they'd seen around the ground floor level. He shepherded the girls to a narrow metal stairway. 'Be careful and hold on to the handrails,' he advised.

The heat in this bay was overpowering and Elinor wondered how the men working there could survive it. One man opened the chamber and the girls were glad of the dark glasses they'd been issued with. The intense colours of the molten material inside were blinding. Elinor watched in fascination as another workman pushed a long metal object, the end of it shaped like a bowl, into the furnace. He used this tool to mix the material around inside the chamber.

They were all pleased to move away from the heat to the cooling bay and from there to the loading bay. There was a ringing sound each time a large sheet of steel was conveyed from a machine and rolled on to the long lorry that would transport it to wherever it was bound.

Although the tour had been interesting, the girls

agreed that they were happy to return to the relative quiet of the typing pool.

***

On her way home from work Elinor got off the bus in Rutherglen Main Street and hurried through the Pend into Mitchell Street, passing Rose's tenement home on her way. She was so glad that Rose and Eric were going steady now and great that they weren't letting a difference in religion spoil the love they shared. At the top of Mitchell Street, Elinor went along Greenhill Road and turned left into Macdonald Street, where she and Colin had been allocated a house by a local factor. It was a short street built on a hill, with three tenements on either side. Their flat was in No 5 at the top of the hill on the left hand side.

There was a shop on one corner of Macdonald Street and Greenhill Road, with a church on the opposite corner. The shop sold everything from a packet of kirbie grips to folding garden chairs, and was locally known as a jenny a' thing.

She raced up the tenement stairs two at a time to the top floor, where she arrived breathless at their front door. Colin, who'd taken a day's leave from work to be in the flat for the carpet fitter, led Elinor into the front room, holding his hands over her eyes. 'Well, what's the verdict?' he asked, releasing his hands.

A sea of soft green met her gaze. 'It's gorgeous,' she breathed, and walked across the floor, her feet leaving patterns in the thick pile. She knelt down on the carpet and drew her hand across the pile, enjoying the feel of the strands between her fingers. Colin knelt down beside her and kissed her. She responded immediately and they lay down together on the soft pile, happy to be in one another's arms. Their passion intensified until Elinor pushed her hands firmly on Colin's chest and drew herself back. 'No, darling, we have to wait until after the wedding. It's only another seven weeks.' She sighed. 'I love this flat and I wish we could move in right now.'

Colin laughed and pulled her to her feet. 'I doubt if your mum would think much of that suggestion. Apart from which, we would have neither furniture nor a cooker.' The cooker in the kitchen had been so old and dirty that they'd had it taken away by the cleansing department and a new cooker was on order for them.

'I hope all our new things will be delivered before the wedding,' she said, as the two of them went into the kitchen where an old carpet of Colin's parents' had been laid. Although there were a couple of worn patches, the grey carpet with the yellow and orange flowered design still had a lot of wear in it.

'Looks alright, doesn't it?' Colin threw his arm around her and nibbled her ear.

Elinor put her head on his shoulder and snuggled up against him. 'Yes, it was very kind of your mum and dad to give it to us and we should get a few years out of it.' They moved into the bedroom which was adjacent to the kitchen and looked around. 'I think this linoleum is fine, if we just put a carpet runner on top,' Colin said. 'Probably best to wait until the bed is delivered before we decide on that.'

'You're right, that's what we'll do.' Elinor stood in the middle of the room and pointed over to the corner behind the door. 'The bed will fit in there and we've got space for a wardrobe or a chest of drawers here,' she said, pointing to the wall at her side. Then she wandered over to the window and stared out at the view over Denholm's hill behind the tenement. 'At least we're looking out on a grassy area rather than into another tenement building.'

Colin looked at his watch. 'There isn't anything else

we can do here tonight, darling, so why don't we go home?'

'Yes, it's been a long day for you,' she said, picking up her shoulder bag and putting on her gloves.

'And you've been out all day too. How did your tour of the works go?'

'Very interesting. Mr King is such a pleasant man.'

'Yes, he's a good sort, the old school. Was the new girl in the party, Thelma whatever her name is?'

Elinor nodded. 'Yes but there were four others so I didn't need to have any conversation with her. I can't wait to move in, it'll be wonderful to have our own home,' she said as Colin locked the door and dropped the key into his jacket pocket.

'Your dad says he'll come at the weekend and do some more painting in the bedroom and lobby. I'll come too and be his labourer for the day.' He put his arm around her waist and they made their way downstairs and out into the evening spring sunshine. From Macdonald Street they walked, arm in arm, to Melrose Avenue where he left her at the front gate and proceeded to continue down to Farme Cross and home.

Chapter Twenty Nine

Saturday, 23rd April, 1960

Elinor nudged Colin. 'I think ours is the next stop. Freda said to get off at the stop after Equi's.' She pointed through the bus window to the shop that combined a fish and chip restaurant with an ice cream counter.

They stood up and went downstairs, gripping the handrail tightly as the bus lurched round the corner into Almada Street. Once off the vehicle, they walked across the road. Following Freda's directions, they turned into Guthrie Street, where Freda and Jack lived in the first tenement on the ground floor.

Freda's face lit up when she opened the door. 'Come in,' she welcomed them and led the way into the kitchen, where Jack sat in an armchair, reading the Daily Record. He got to his feet at once. 'Welcome to our humble abode,' he said, smiling at them both.

Elinor gave Freda the tulips she and Colin had bought in Galt's flower shop in Rutherglen before getting on the bus. 'I chose yellow ones, as they looked so springlike.'

'Oh, thank you, they're gorgeous. The flowers I had were just thrown out yesterday.' As she was speaking, Freda picked up the empty crystal vase sitting on the table.

Elinor recognised the vase as the one that she and Joanne had bought Freda and Jack for their engagement. It crossed her mind that she hadn't known Colin at the time of the engagement party. It didn't seem believable somehow, she felt she'd known Colin forever. She pulled herself back to the present. 'What a lovely bright room this is.'

By this time Freda was filling the vase with water.

'Yes, we like it. Let me put the tulips in water and then I'll show you our bedroom.'

'Jack and I wondered if you'd like us to take you a walk along the River Avon,' Freda said, once she'd let them see the bedroom. 'We could go from there into the Palace grounds.'

'I didn't know Hamilton had a palace,' Elinor said.

'We don't have one any longer. The palace belonged to the Duke of Hamilton but it was demolished in the 1920s. Some people say it was demolished because of subsidence but others maintain that it was to cut down on the amount of taxes the Duke had to pay.'

'Was it the Duke of Hamilton who built the mausoleum?' Colin asked.

'Yes, but only some of the Dukes lie there. The others are in a grave in the Bent cemetery. There's a large monument in a secluded part of the cemetery, listing the names of the Dukes who are buried there and telling you something about each of them. If you're interested, we can show you the monument sometime.'

Jack laughed. 'Right, enough about graveyards. Let's get off while it's sunny.'

'How are you getting on with my replacement now, Elinor? You know, Thelma what's 'er name?' Freda asked the question as she and Elinor walked along the banks of the Avon, behind Jack and Colin, who were deep in conversation about football.

'Green, that's her name, Thelma Green. Things are better between us. I don't think we'll ever be best buddies but she's stopped criticising me so much.'

'Who does she think she is? A new start trying to tell you how to do things and you in the office for years.' Elinor could hear the indignation in Freda's voice as she spoke.

'She doesn't actually tell me what to do. She just has this annoying habit of treating anything I do with derision; how I work, what I wear, and so on.'

'Cheek,' Freda said, and shook her head.

Elinor shrugged. 'Maybe I'm being too sensitive. Anyway, what about your new job, Freda? How are you enjoying it?' After her marriage, Freda had secured employment locally in a lawyer's office in Quarry Street, Hamilton.

'Oh, it's great. The girls I work with are lovely and my boss is also very pleasant. Best of all is that I can walk to work and can get a longer lie in bed in the morning.' By this time they had entered the green area that was known locally as the palace grounds, even though there was no palace any longer. The two girls now overtook the men, who were watching some young boys playing football. 'Would you and Colin like to come to Equi's before you go home?' Freda asked, as they came off the green and back on to the pavement once more. 'We'd be happy to have you back to ours for tea but the flat is a bit cramped for four of us so we thought it would be nice to eat out for once. What do you say?'

'That would be lovely.' They turned to find that the men had almost caught up with them. 'Freda has suggested we all go to Equi's for something to eat,' Elinor said to Colin. 'You happy with that?'

'Sure thing,' he replied. 'Sounds good to me.'

'Do you think we'll get a table without booking?' Jack asked his wife. 'You know how popular Equi's is.'

Freda glanced at her watch. 'I think we're early enough to get a table before it gets busy.' She took Elinor's arm as they continued to walk. 'Equi's are famous for their fish teas and their ice cream is delicious. People come from all over Lanarkshire to buy it.'

'Sounds yummy, let's go.'

'The smell of cooking makes me realise how hungry I am,' Colin said, as they settled down into a booth table at the restaurant.

The food was as wonderful as Freda had promised. They all tucked into their fish, chips and mushy peas, served with bread and butter and pots of tea, and still had room to squeeze in a delicious ice cream sundae afterwards.

'I don't think I'll eat again for a week,' Elinor said, as they were leaving the restaurant.

Colin laughed. 'Well, I won't eat until at least supper time.'

'Thanks for a lovely day.' Elinor hugged Freda, as she and Colin were about to board the bus to return to Rutherglen. She blew a kiss to Jack and the two men shook hands.

'We've enjoyed it too. Come again soon,' Freda called, waving as the bus drew away from the stop.

Chapter Thirty

Tuesday, 21st June, 1960

Because of having to arrange the wedding in a short space of time, Elinor and Colin couldn't get a booking for their reception on a Saturday and, as Elinor had set her heart on being married on Midsummer's day, their wedding took place on a Tuesday.

Elinor's bouquet of yellow tea roses and freesia shook as she gripped her dad's arm and they walked together down the aisle in Wardlawhill Church, with the organist playing the wedding march. Magnificent vases and sprays of flowers decorated the sanctuary and the church vestibule. Joanne, her taffeta gown rustling, followed a couple of steps behind Elinor's long train as it rippled its way over the royal blue carpet.

Colin was standing in front of the communion table with Dougie, his best man, and he turned round and smiled at Elinor as she neared the bottom of the aisle. Elinor moved over to stand beside him and smiled at him through the veil covering her face. Colin took her hand, his fingers caressing her soft skin.

Giving the young couple an encouraging smile, Mr Wilkes started the wedding service. 'We are gathered here today, in the presence of God, to join together this man and this woman in holy matrimony,' he began and soon afterwards the congregation sang the first hymn 'Love Devine'. After a prayer and a bible reading, the vows were taken and Joanne lifted Elinor's veil away from her face so that, in traditional form, Colin could kiss his bride.

While the wedding party were in the Vestry to sign

the marriage register, two of Susan's friends sang 'I'll Walk Beside You'. Then the wedding party left the church where a group from the Boys' Brigade Company had formed a Guard of Honour on the steps outside the church.

***

At the reception in the Co-operative Hall on Main Street, the meal and the speeches were over. Most of the ladies adjourned to the powder rooms and the men stood chatting in the ante room and hallway until the staff had cleared away the tables for the dancing to begin.

At the request of Elinor and Colin, the first dance was to Pat Boone's popular number, 'I'll Be Home'. They'd danced to it at the B.B. dance the night they'd met. The newlyweds led the way, dancing cheek to cheek to the silky tones of Mr Boone.

Soon afterwards they were joined on the dance floor by Joanne and Dougie and the two sets of parents.

During the evening the band played lots of recent hits, such as 'Cathy's Clown' and 'Three Steps to Heaven'. Elinor and Colin stayed at the dance until almost the end, determined to get the most out of their wedding reception.

'I think I better go and change out of my dress,' Elinor said around eleven o'clock. They were booked into the Central Hotel overnight, to be handy for their train to Morecambe tomorrow where they would spend a two week honeymoon.

Colin nodded. 'Right, while you're doing that, I'll go and check on the taxi to take us to the hotel.'

Elinor slipped past the guests on the dance floor and went into the room they'd been allocated. She took off her wedding dress and laid it over a chair for her mum to take home at the end of the reception. Dressing in her turquoise going away suit, she fixed her hair and re-applied her lipstick.

When Colin appeared to tell her the taxi was waiting

in front of the hall, they collected their luggage and left the room. They hoped to slip away unnoticed but Dougie had seen to it that this wasn't going to happen. He rounded up the assembled guests, who all spilled outside on to the pavement as the honeymooners were leaving. Dougie had somehow managed to tie tin cans and Just Married notices on to the back bumper of the taxi. The taxi driver tooted his horn as he drove off and the newlyweds were sent off to the rattle of the cans and loud cheering from their guests.

Chapter Thirty One

Tuesday, 28th June, 1960

'Happy, Mrs Dawson?' Colin asked a week later, when he and Elinor were sitting in their swimwear on a quiet stretch of the beach at Morecambe. They'd found this spot, close to the guest house, on their first day in the resort. By now they'd become possessive of it and felt annoyed if anyone dared to invade their privacy.

Elinor laid her head on his shoulder. 'Extremely happy, Mr Dawson.' She entwined her fingers in his and ran her other hand down his arm. 'I wish we could stay here forever, Colin.'

'You'd miss Rutherglen and everyone we know there if you did.' He played with her fringe as he was speaking.

'Yes, I would. I'd miss Mum and Dad and Joanne and all my other friends. But I'm glad we've still got another week's holiday here.'

'Do you want to take the bus into Blackpool tomorrow?'

'That sounds lovely. I haven't been to Blackpool before.'

'It's much busier than Morecambe. My mother always says it's like Argyle Street with a beach.'

She lifted her head off his shoulder and squinted round at him. 'Will we rouse ourselves and go back to the guest house? Give ourselves time to get changed before dinner.'

'Yes, good idea.' He got to his feet, holding out his hands to help Elinor up off the sand.

***

The following day they set off after breakfast and enjoyed the train journey from Morecambe to Blackpool. During the journey Elinor spotted a tall tower that she recognised from picture postcards. 'There's Blackpool Tower.'

'Yes, you can see it from miles away,' Colin told her.

When they drew into Blackpool station, they made their way towards the compartment door. When the train came to a standstill, Colin opened the door and jumped down on to the platform before helping Elinor down beside him.

Hand in hand, they strolled out of the station exit into a crowd of people, the like of which Elinor had never witnessed before. The pavements were clogged by cheery groups of holidaymakers, some of them wearing hats with the words 'Kiss Me Quick' on them and many of the shops they passed were selling holiday rock.

'I can see why your mother made the comment about Argyle Street,' she said, holding on tightly to Colin's arm as they wended their way through the masses thronging the promenade.

Colin brushed his hand over hers that lay on his arm. 'Don't worry darling, if we walk further up to the north shore it will be much quieter there. Let's cross over to the promenade side and get away from some of the crowd,' he said, steering her across the road when the traffic allowed.

Finding a secluded spot on the north shore beach, they hired a couple of deck chairs. Removing their top layer of clothes, they lay in their swimwear to soak up some summer sunshine. 'This is the life,' Colin said, rubbing his hand gently up and down her arm.

'Yes, I'd like to stop the world and stay here like this for ever. I know we will have the usual ups and downs that all married couples find but I can only see happiness ahead for us.'

He squeezed her hand. 'I'm sure there will be problems ahead, we can't expect to go along unscathed, but our love will help us to overcome any troubles that come our way.' Then he turned to her and grinned. 'What are we like? Spending our honeymoon discussing problems ahead. Race you for a paddle,' he said, diving to his feet.

Elinor took on the challenge and almost got to the water as quickly as he did. Fifteen minutes or so later they came back up the beach, their wet, salty arms entwined, and dropped down on their deck chairs again. The hot sun made them drowsy and they were soon asleep.

It was almost four o'clock when Colin wakened and got up from his deck chair. 'What about making our way back into the centre of Blackpool now and get something to eat?'

Elinor looked up sleepily, shading her eyes with her hand to see his face better. She yawned. 'When does the show start?' The guesthouse owners had booked them seats for a variety show at the Tower theatre this evening.

'It begins at seven o'clock but it'll take us some time to walk back to the Tower and we could eat before the restaurants get too busy.'

'Good idea.' She stood up, letting the warm sand dribble through her toes. On the prom, she spread out the towel on the wall between them. 'Can you remember who the stars are in tonight's show?' she asked, as she used an edge of the towel to wipe away the sand from between her toes.

Colin used the other end for his feet. 'Tommy Steele and Alma Cogan are the main stars, and I think the landlady said Eddie Calvert was in the show but I can't remember the other acts.'

Elinor was singing 'Bell Bottom Blues' when they

came out of the show that night. 'Wish I could stop singing that song,' she said, 'I can't seem to get it out of my head.'

'Yes, it's a catchy tune.' Colin took her arm in his and they strolled down the long pier in the warm, starry evening.

They stopped at the side of the pier for a few moments, listening to all the sounds around them. There was a splash down below as a holidaymaker went for a late night dip.

'When's the train back to Morecambe?'

'The last one is just after midnight but I think there will be a couple more before then.' Colin bent over in the darkness and kissed her. 'Ready to head for the station?'

'Yes. I'm really sad at the thought that tomorrow is our last day in Morecambe.'

'Well we must make the most of it,' Colin said, as they merged into the crowd of holidaymakers around them.

***

Two days later, after breakfast in the guesthouse, they were on the train home from Morecambe. When they walked into the flat in Rutherglen, Colin dropped their cases in the hallway and picked up the mail lying behind the front door.

'Good old Mum,' Elinor called from the kitchen. 'She's left us in bread and milk.'

'She's a good sort. We're lucky to have such good support from our parents.'

'Yes, from both sets.' Elinor was aware of how kind Mr and Mrs Dawson Senior had been to them. 'It's great we've still got the rest of the week on holiday. It'll give us time to get unpacked and everything washed and dried before going back to work.'

'Are you nervous about starting your new job?' Elinor had left Colvilles before she was married as was the custom in the firm and a couple of days before the wedding had obtained a job in the offices of the House of Fraser store in Buchanan Street.

'I am a bit but right now all I need is a cup of tea,' she replied, going over to the sink to christen the modern style whistling kettle, one of their wedding gifts.

Chapter Thirty Two

Monday, 11th July, 1960

Elinor's first day in her new job went well. When she first
arrived, she had an introductory tour from the department
head, Miss Cochrane. As one of the members on the interview
panel a few weeks previously, Elinor had met Miss Cochrane
before. The well-spoken lady was dressed in a tailored navy
suit, with the collar of her white satin blouse visible
underneath her jacket. Her silvery white hair was swept back
into a bun at the nape of her neck and she wore sturdy navy
court shoes with a wedge heel.

It was obvious from the outset that Miss Cochrane ran
a tight ship and demanded high standards from her staff. But
from what Elinor gleaned during their conversation and what
was confirmed by her later chats with other members of staff,
Miss Cochrane was very fair in her dealings with staff.

'I think I'm going to be happy in the store,' Elinor
told Colin, when they were having dinner that evening. Elinor
had peeled the potatoes in the morning before going to work
and when Colin came home a short time before Elinor, he
switched on the gas ring under the potato pot and laid the table
for their meal.

'What are the bosses like?' Colin asked, as he took his
last mouthful of mince.

'Miss Cochrane, the department head, is very
pleasant, quite old-fashioned and strict but fair. She is honest
and you know exactly where you stand in your dealings with
her. I much prefer that to those people who are sweet to your
face and tell another story behind your back.'

Colin smiled. 'We've all met them. What about the

142

rest of the staff?'

'They made me very welcome but the one I warmed to most was Wendy Butler. She showed me how things were done in the office and came with me to the canteen at lunch time.'

'That's good. Is Wendy about your own age?'

Elinor's brow wrinkled. 'It's hard to say. She seems around my age but when she told me she's worked in the store for over ten years, it made me think she might be older. She's married with a young son. Very cheery and got a good sense of humour, so I think we'll be good friends.'

Their meal over, Elinor gathered up the used crockery and carried it over to the sink. 'And how were things in Colvilles today?' she asked Colin, while they were washing the dishes together.

'I had quite a pile of stuff to get through on my return, so there wasn't much time for a catch up. John White sends you his best wishes and was sorry he didn't make the wedding as his wife was in hospital. He was pleased to hear we'd enjoyed our stay in Morecambe.'

'And is Mrs White home now from hospital?'

'Yes, and she seems to be recovering well from her operation.' Colin glanced out of the window as he was hanging up the tea towel. 'Do you fancy a walk through the park since it's a nice night?'

Elinor dried up the draining board and the bottom of the basin. 'Yes, that would be lovely. We should go now while there's still a lot of daylight left.'

She took Colin's arm as they walked down Macdonald Street on to Greenhill Road. Once on the main road in Mill Street, they turned left and walked uphill towards Overtoun Park. The ornate park gates at the top of the hill sparkled under the blood red sky. 'Red sky at night, a shepherd's delight,' Elinor recited, as they walked through the gate into the park.

Chapter Thirty Three

Monday, 15th August, 1960

Elinor raced out of the store and crossed over Buchanan Street to get to Argyle Street. She ran in between the traffic, with car horns blaring at her. By some miracle she arrived unscathed on the opposite side of the road, and got to the bus stop just in time to jump on to the bus for Rutherglen. She climbed the stairs to the upper deck and, panting for breath, sat down near the front. She'd been working in the House of Fraser store for five weeks now and enjoyed her job very much.

Once her breathing became normal again, she took Dot's airmail letter out of her bag. She'd only skimmed over it on her way into town this morning and she and Wendy had lunch together, so this was her first chance to digest Dot's news properly.

5th August, 1960

My Dear Elinor

Thanks so much for the beautiful wedding pictures you sent me. The dresses are superb and the men have scrubbed up well too! As I said previously, Mum and Dad and I would love to have accepted your invitation to the wedding but neither Dad nor I could have got a long enough holiday from work. But we toasted you all on the big day just as the service would have been about to start; it was nearly bedtime over here.

Your honeymoon in Morecambe sounds fantastic and

the wonderful weather you had would have been the icing on the cake.

I was pleased to hear you liked the tablecover I sent you and the tea towels from Mum and Dad. I chose that tablecover as I know the wattle was your favourite bush when you lived here. Our wattle bushes in the garden have started flowering as spring has come early this year. The gum trees at the bottom of the garden are bare right now but they should flower soon.

I'm still enjoying my time with the Glen Waverley singers and we are booked for a concert in October when we will be performing in Melbourne Town Hall. We will be singing some works by Handel and Bach and we're also performing one of my favourites, March of the Hebrew Slaves, from Verdi's Nabucco. We will also include some popular pieces from the musicals.

I've arranged a holiday with two of my colleagues. We leave Melbourne in early September and travel on the overnight train to South Australia. We are joining a coach tour through the Red Centre and hopefully the temperatures won't be too high in September. We will go through the desert country to Coober Pedy, where we'll visit an opal mine. Might try to bring some stones back and have them made into jewellery. From there we'll journey on to Ayres Rock, which we hope to climb. Then it will be on to Alice Springs and, while there, the guide will take us on a visit to the Flying Doctor Service. Our tour finishes in Alice Springs, from where we will fly home. None of us have travelled through the Red Centre before so we are very excited about the trip. I'll let you know how we get on next time I write.

We are extremely busy at work just now so we are desperate for the holiday to come round so we can get a break away from routine.

I hope your new job in the House of Fraser store is going well and you have some pleasant people to work with. It seems strange to me that Colville's have a rule that you have to leave when you marry as nothing like that applies here. Still, as you say, you aren't too bothered as you and Colin hope it won't be long until you start a family.

Well my dear, I'll stop now as I'm running out of news.

Much Love from Dot
xx

Elinor felt really close to Dot as she read the letter, going over it a second time to make sure she didn't miss anything. By the time she returned the letter to her handbag, she noticed that she was only a couple of stops from home.

Chapter Thirty Four

Saturday, 10th September, 1960

Elinor and Colin had teamed up with Joanne and Dougie that Saturday afternoon. They'd decided to spend some time in Overtoun Park and enjoy the fair, or the 'shows' as the locals called it. The fair visited Rutherglen every September, always sited in the park. The children of the fairground people attended one of the local schools during the month they were in the Burgh. Elinor felt that moving from school to school must be disrupting for their education.

Joanne and Dougie had recently announced their engagement and now Elinor was looking forward to their wedding to be held in Wardlawhill Church on Christmas Eve.

'Let's have a go on the Waltzer,' Dougie suggested to the other three as they watched the ride go round, screams of delight coming from the people in the gondolas. The Waltzer came to a halt and the occupants of the gondolas spilled out, laughing and jostling their way off the carousel and down the steps.

Dougie and Colin scrambled aboard an empty gondola and held open the metal safety bar until the girls had joined them. Elinor and Joanne squeezed into the middle and Colin pulled the metal bar towards them again. Once the gondolas were full and the fairground operator had collected the payment for the ride, the music started and the carousel went round, slowly at first before gradually picking up speed. The two girls held on tightly to the bar as the operator came round each gondola in turn, pushing so that it spun even more rapidly. Elinor clung on to Colin's arm as they raced round.

When the Waltzer finally stopped and they came off

the carousel, Joanne's face was devoid of colour and she felt very sick. Elinor also felt somewhat squeamish, but she was sure hers was for a different reason. She'd been sick a few times in the morning lately and hoped she might be pregnant. She hadn't yet said anything to Colin, for fear of raising false hopes.

'Come for a walk away from the fairground,' Dougie said, putting his arm around Joanne, and the two of them moved away to a quieter part of the park, leaving Elinor and Colin on their own. 'Let's try rolling the pennies,' Colin suggested, but they were unsuccessful at winning any coins, simply losing whatever change they had. They moved on to another stall where you paid sixpence and were given three rings. The object was to throw your ring towards any item on display, hoping your ring would fall over it and win you a prize. 'Hard luck,' Colin said when Elinor's three rings had all missed the target completely. Then it was his turn; the first two he threw missed winning a prize but the final ring landed over a small brown teddy bear with a blue ribbon round its neck.

'Your prize,' the stallholder said, smiling as he handed the bear over to Colin who, in turn, gave it to Elinor.

'Thanks,' she said and rubbed the bear's fur against her cheek. 'He's so soft and cute, I think I'll call him Brownie.'

When Joanne and Dougie returned, Joanne looking much better, they both admired the bear. They tried the ring-throwing but fared no better than Elinor. When they tired of the fairground, the four of them had a walk to the other end of the park close to the bandstand, where they sat on the grass for a while.

It became colder when the sun went down, and Dougie was the first to broach the subject of food. 'Don't know about you lot but I've got hunger pangs.'

'Do you want to come back to our flat for something to eat?' As she voiced the words, Elinor was trying to think what they had in the cupboards that they could offer their friends.

'Why don't we go down to Marie's café and buy fish suppers,' Dougie suggested.

'Good idea. Then nobody has to cook,' Joanne said. 'You can all come back to my house afterwards and we can listen to records. Mum and Dad are away on holiday so we could bring the record player down to the front room as we won't be disturbing anybody.'

With agreement all round, they made their way down Stonelaw Road to the café on the corner of Greenhill Road, a favourite place for young courting and married couples. Their order placed at the counter, Colin fed some money into the juke box and soon they were sitting at the table singing along to Lonnie Donegan's hit song, 'My Old Man's a Dustman'.

***

Back at Joanne's house, the four of them listened to records and danced to the music. 'This is my latest disc, I bought it last week,' Joanne said and next minute the plaintiff tones of Brenda Lee rang out.

'Put on this Brian Hyland number,' Dougie said, once the music had died away. 'It's a lot cheerier.' Next minute the four of them were dancing around the room and singing at the tops of their voices.

Chapter Thirty Five

Saturday, 24th December, 1960

Colin, dressed in his best man's attire, was reading this week's Rutherglen Reformer when Elinor came into the kitchen in Macdonald Street. He gave a wolf whistle when he saw her. She had still been in her underwear when he'd left the bedroom a short time ago but now she was wearing her deep crimson velvet bridesmaid's dress. The seams on the dress had been let out in the past couple of weeks now that Elinor's pregnancy had been confirmed and she was beginning to show a little. She and Colin were both thrilled at the prospect of being parents.

Following their engagement, Joanne and Dougie had asked them to be their attendants at today's wedding. With it being winter, Elinor and Joanne had white fur stoles to wear over their dresses.

'Will you fasten my pendant, darling?' Elinor asked and stood still while Colin fastened the catch of the pendant Joanne and Dougie had given her as a gift for being bridesmaid. It was a lovely gold heart-shaped piece of jewellery with a dark red stone in the centre.

The pendant sat prettily above Elinor's cleavage. 'Perfect,' he murmured, his fingertips brushing against her skin as he fingered the little gold heart.

Elinor moved over to the mirror above the fireplace. She smiled when she saw the pendant. 'Yes, I love it and I'll really treasure it.'

'Have you got everything you need?' Colin asked, tucking his wallet into the inside pocket of his jacket.

'Yep,' she said, and a minute later they heard a toot outside. 'That'll be Mr Scott now.'

'Everything running to plan?' Colin asked, as he helped Elinor into the back seat of the car, before sitting in the front beside Mr Scott.

Mr Scott nodded and turned on the engine again. 'So far so good. It's turmoil at the house of course but once I drop you there, Elinor, you can make sure Joanne is properly dressed. After Elinor is at Johnstone Drive, I'll run you to the church, Colin, where Dougie will be waiting for you. Then I'll drive home in time to escort Joanne in the wedding car.'

Colin turned and grinned at him. 'Has it been a fraught morning?'

'You could say that,' Mr Scott replied, once he'd turned off Mill Street into Johnstone Drive. At the front gate, Colin jumped out and assisted Elinor up the path and into the house without allowing her dress to trail on the ground.

Twenty minutes later, Elinor was waiting in the vestibule of the church when Joanne came up the stairs on her dad's arm. At the entrance to the church, she sorted out Joanne's dress and her long train before following father and daughter down the aisle, the same one that she herself had walked down six months ago. Being the 24th December, the beautifully decorated Christmas tree stood at the side of the pulpit and at the end of each pew was a spray of holly, the red berries glistening in the glow coming down from the overhead lights. Sitting on top of the communion table were some red Christmas candles which also added to the Festive atmosphere.

**

When they arrived at the reception, the cake was cut, with many photographs taken, and then the company sat down to an excellent meal. Coffee over, the speeches began, given by Mr Wilkes, the Minister, the best man, the bridegroom, the bride's father and finally the bridegroom's father.

Once the formalities were over, the wedding party

were able to relax and enjoy the rest of the evening. Like Elinor and Colin six months previously, the bride and groom stayed and danced until almost the end before setting off for their honeymoon in London.

When Elinor and Colin finally arrived home, she kicked off her shoes and dropped on to the sofa, putting her stockinged feet up on to the stool that Colin placed in front of her. 'Am I glad to get out of these shoes. My feet are aching after dancing and standing around so long.'

'I'll put the kettle on and make you a cuppa,' Colin offered. 'You probably shouldn't have been on your feet so long in your condition,' he said a short time later, when he brought over her mug of tea. 'Your ankles do look quite swollen, darling.'

'I'll be fine after a sleep.' She took a drink of tea and sighed, feeling revived already.

Chapter Thirty Six

Wednesday, 17th May, 1961

The early morning sun was streaming through the large windows of the ward in Bellshill Maternity Hospital, encircling Elinor and her newborn son in a blaze of light. Colin couldn't help thinking of the Madonna and child. Cradling baby Jeffrey in her arms, the proud new mother's face was aglow when she looked down at him. His well-formed eyebrows arched above clear blue eyes. He had the cutest nose she'd ever seen and his tiny lips were apart as though he was smiling at her. Every tiny feature was assembled in perfect symmetry; a miracle indeed.

'He's beautiful,' Colin whispered, putting his pinkie inside the doll-like hand. 'Thank you, darling.'

Elinor beamed up at her husband, her heart bursting with happiness. 'We did it together, we make a good team, don't we?'

Colin nodded and bent to kiss her. Then he brushed his lips gently against his son's soft cheek. 'I'm glad it's over. I was worried sick when they said it was a difficult labour. I almost wore a hole in the linoleum pacing up and down the corridor.'

'I think the first pregnancy is the worst but it's all been worth it,' Elinor said, and she held her son even closer. For an instant the happenings on the ship almost six years ago came into her mind but she dismissed the thought immediately, refusing to let anything negative take away the joy of this moment. 'Why don't you go home and get some sleep, darling?' she suggested, concern showing on her face, 'you look shattered.' Colin had accompanied her in the ambulance to the hospital yesterday evening and he'd remained here since, until his son was safely delivered two hours ago.

'Think I will go home and later on I'll freshen up and come back to see you both this evening. I'll bring your mum and dad.' Colin had passed his driving test in January and now had a Hillman car, which was a great boon in getting around. 'My mum and dad are hoping to see Jeffrey tomorrow. Look after Jeffrey till I get back,' he whispered. The baby's name came naturally to him as they'd decided on Jeffrey for a boy early on in the pregnancy; or Fiona if the baby was a girl. Colin drew his hand over Jeffrey's downy hair and kissed Elinor again before he left the ward.

After he'd gone, Elinor rocked Jeffrey back and forth in her arms. 'You'll soon be needing a feed, won't you, Jeffrey?' she whispered. She wanted to feed him herself so hoped there would be no problems in doing so.

A few minutes later a nurse bustled into the ward and pulled the curtains round Elinor's bed. The nurse was middle-aged and of a stout build and came across as a motherly sort of woman. 'Okay, Mrs Dawson,' she said in her lovely Irish brogue, 'what about us seeing if this young man of yours is ready for a feed?' Nurse Doyle, as Elinor read it on her identity badge, showed her patient how to get the baby to the breast and shortly afterwards, satisfied that he was sucking well, she slipped out again, leaving mother and son contented and happily bonding.

***

That evening when Susan and Colin came into the ward, Elinor and Jeffrey were both having a snooze, Elinor in her bed and Jeffrey in his cot at the side of the bed.

Susan went straight over to the cot to admire her first born grandchild while Colin drew a chair in to the side of the bed and laid his hand over Elinor's. A few minutes later Elinor wakened and smiled at her husband and her mother. 'I was just having forty winks,' she said.

'Jeffrey is gorgeous, and at 7 pounds, 12 ounces he's a good weight,' Susan congratulated her daughter. 'Colin says you did really well considering it was a difficult labour.'

'I'm fine Mum and I'm glad you could come.'

'Try keeping me away. Dad's here too but with only two visitors allowed in the ward at a time, we'll take it in turns to come in.'

'I'll go out in five minutes and let him come and see his grandson,' Colin promised, then turned back to Elinor. 'Have you had a good rest darling, and how did Jeffrey's first feed go?'

'Great,' she replied, smiling proudly at her son, snug in his cot at her side. 'He took to it straight away. Nurse Doyle said she thought he'd been here before.'

Shortly afterwards, Colin went out and Andrew came in, grinning from ear to ear. 'Well done, love,' he said to his daughter and kissed her forehead. 'And this is my grandson, is it?' he added, standing at the cot and staring down at the sleeping baby. When he looked up again his eyes were moist. 'What a handsome chap. And here he is, not even 24 hours old yet, with his whole life in front of him.'

Susan started chanting the well-known nursery rhyme.

Monday's child is fair of face
Tuesday's child is full of grace
Wednesday's child is full of woe
Thursday's child has far to go
Friday's child is loving and giving
Saturday's child works hard for a living
But the child born on the Sabbath day is bonny, and blithe, and good and gay.

Horror registered on Elinor's face. 'I don't want Jeffrey to be full of woe.'

Susan laughed. 'Of course not, darling, it's only a rhyme, Jeffrey will be full of joy.'

The visiting hour flew by and before she knew it Elinor was saying goodbye to her parents and Colin, who had come back into the ward for the last five minutes. 'Nurse Doyle reckons I should be allowed home within the next few days because Jeffrey is feeding so well,' she said to Colin.

'That's great, darling.'

'Enjoy the rest while you're in here, Elinor, as it will help you to get your strength back before you come home,' Susan cautioned. 'But I'm looking forward to you and Jeffrey getting home soon and I can give you a hand to get into a routine.'

Chapter Thirty Seven

Tuesday, 23rd January, 1962

Afterwards Elinor always remembered that it was on the day Jeffrey got his first tooth that it happened; a bleak January day, barely four weeks after Christmas.

'Ouch,' she cried, at breakfast time when she was feeding her son some solids from a plastic spoon. 'He's got a tooth through, Colin. He bit my finger.'

Colin looked up, his mouth full of toast, and made a face at Jeffrey. Once he'd swallowed his toast he stretched out and touched the infant's sticky hand. 'Did you bite your mum, Jeffrey?'

The baby gurgled and beamed at Colin, a lone tooth just becoming visible on his lower gum, a gum that looked red and sore.

'Poor wee mite. I'll put some gel on your sore gum, darling, and that'll make it all better,' Elinor crooned to Jeffrey, who stared at her as though he understood every word. Leaving him strapped into his high chair, Elinor went to the cupboard for the gel that the chemist had sold her. She pulled Jeffrey's finger out of his mouth and applied the gel to his hot, puffy gum. Then she wiped away the dribbles from his chin with the already sodden bib tied round her son's neck before dropping it into the laundry basket.

Colin meanwhile glanced at his watch. He scooped the toast crumbs on his plate into his empty cup and put his cup and saucer on top of the plate. 'Right, I'll have to love you and leave you,' he said, and went to clean his teeth before going to work. Shortly afterwards he returned, wearing his heavy coat. He picked up his briefcase, kissed Elinor and

Jeffrey and rushed out.

When she heard his footsteps going downstairs, Elinor carried Jeffrey to the front room window and waved the baby's hand to his dad down on the pavement below. It was a ritual by now that Colin looked up at the window when he came out of the tenement close.

**

It was at almost quarter past five, fifteen minutes before Colin was due home from work, that there was a ring at the doorbell. She opened the door to Mrs Anderson, her downstairs neighbour. 'There's a call on my phone for you, Elinor,' she said, unable to keep the panic out of her voice. 'Come quick hen, it's your Aunt Muriel who wants to speak to you.'

Elinor rushed past the middle-aged lady and then remembered Jeffrey was asleep in his cot. 'Could you stay here with Jeffrey, Mrs Anderson? He's in a sound sleep so is unlikely to waken up.'

'Of course, hen,' her neighbour said. 'My door's on the latch so you can let yourself in.'

'Thanks.'

Downstairs, Elinor listened to her aunt's voice explaining everything but part way through she dropped the receiver on to the phone table, unable to take in what she was hearing.

'Hello … Elinor, are you still there? … Hello,' Aunt Muriel's voice came over the air waves.

Elinor sat down on Mrs Anderson's living room floor, her head in her hands. Hearing Aunt Muriel's voice again, she lifted the receiver to her ear. 'Sorry, I'm trying to take it in. Jeffrey's having a nap at the moment but I'll put him into his pram and push him round there.'

'No, don't do that Elinor. I'll stay here and you can

wait until Colin gets home and he can bring you and Jeffrey then.'

'Okay,' Elinor replied, unable to find the words to argue with her aunt, who seemed to be dealing well with everything at Melrose Avenue.

'I'll need to go,' Aunt Muriel told her, 'one of the policemen wants to speak to me.' And with that she hung up.

Jeffrey was still asleep in his cot in the bedroom and Elinor, red-eyed and tear-stained, was sitting on the couch staring at the carpet when Colin got home. 'What's wrong? What's happened?' he asked, kneeling down at Elinor's side, scared by the distressed look on her face. 'Is Jeffrey alright?'

Elinor shook herself out of her despair to answer him. 'Jeffrey's fine, he's napping,' she said, to put his mind at rest on that score. 'It's Dad,' she murmured, her voice no more than a whisper, 'he's dead. Dad's dead,' she repeated, trying to convince herself that she wasn't making it up.

Colin took her hands in his. 'Why ... how ... what happened?'

Elinor looked slightly bemused as she told him. 'Aunt Muriel said two policemen came to the door when she was visiting Mum this afternoon.' She stopped speaking for a moment and swallowed deeply. 'It seems that Dad and his mate were decorating a house in Kirkhill when he slumped down on to the floor. By the time the ambulance crew got there, Dad was dead from a massive heart attack. The policemen came to break the news to Mum.' Elinor felt as though she was describing something she'd read in a novel.

'How did you hear? Did your Aunt Muriel come to tell you?'

Elinor shook her head. 'No, she phoned Mrs Anderson downstairs, who came up to get me to the phone. I only got word about fifteen minutes ago so I didn't try to contact you as

I knew you'd be on your way home.'

'Oh my God. We need to get round to Melrose Avenue now.'

'Yes,' she said, holding on to Colin's hand as she got up from the couch. 'I'll go and lift Jeffrey, he's slept long enough anyway. I can feed him at Mum's,' she added, as she went into the bedroom to rouse her sleeping son.

Chapter Thirty Eight

Monday, 29th January, 1962

The funeral day was grey and drizzly, which added to the pervading low mood and grief. Susan's next door neighbour Mrs Mullin, a grandmother herself and a retired midwife, looked after Jeffrey while the family were at the funeral.

The first service was held in Wardlawhill, conducted by Mr Wilkes. With the Minister knowing Andrew and his family so well, it was a most personal service. Afterwards the close family members and friends got back into the cars arranged by the undertaker and drove to Linn Crematorium for the commital service. The church service had been busy but through the darkened windows of the funeral car Elinor sighted a crowd of extra mourners waiting outside the crematorium. This second service was shorter, during which Colin paid a moving tribute to his father-in-law. Elinor bore up well, her first tears coming as she saw the coffin descend under the red velvet sheet edged with gold braid that covered it. Feeling her mum's shoulders shake, Elinor put her arm around her.

'You're all holding up very well,' Elinor's cousin, Rita, said as they sat together at the light lunch in the Masonic Hall in Melrose Avenue after the funeral.

'We can't do anything else, we have to keep strong for Mum,' Elinor replied, brushing the tears from the sides of her eyes with her fingers. 'I'm glad you and Brian were both able to be here. It means a lot to Mum that her only niece and nephew are with her.'

'We wouldn't have done otherwise.'

Rita had come up from London on a few days' leave

to attend the funeral and, despite his exams coming up soon, Brian had also managed to get away. Rita turned away when an old acquaintance put a hand on her shoulder and spoke to her.

When they finally arrived back at Melrose Avenue, Muriel hugged Susan. 'You sit and put your feet up, Sis, and I'll switch the kettle on. And I think you also need something stronger, so I'll pour you a wee sherry too.'

Susan sighed and obeyed Muriel's instructions. 'Yes, it's been a long day.'

A short time later Mrs Mullin brought Jeffrey back. This helped to cheer them up, with everyone taking it in turns to hold the baby on their knee and admire how big he was becoming.

Chapter Thirty Nine

Friday, 27th February, 1962

Elinor placed Jeffrey's high chair beside her at the table. She tied a waterproof bib around him and ate her own dinner with one hand, her other hand being used to feed the baby. With Jeffrey now nine months old, Elinor had decided to start him on solids. She had tried him a couple of times previously with a small tin of baby food, such as mashed up fruit or blended soup, but this was his first taste of the food she and Colin were eating.

Colin took his last mouthful of roast beef and potato, then pushed his empty plate to one side, while he watched Jeffrey. The baby was staring down at the spoonful of food Elinor was offering him. 'What are you giving him?'

'I've put some mashed potato in the dish and poured a little gravy over it, to see how he likes it.' Elinor had put a small amount on to the plastic spoon, which she now held gently at her son's lips. 'Want to try some potato, darling?' she coaxed, moving the spoon back and forward along his tiny lips.

At first Jeffrey kept his mouth tightly closed and wrinkled his brow as he smelt the food. Then slowly his lips opened and he took some from the spoon, sampling the unusual taste. His perplexed look remained until he finally swallowed the food. Then the sound of 'umm' that he made and his beaming smile showed his approval.

'Think he likes it.' Colin got up and carried his empty plate and Elinor's over to the sink. He put the plates into the basin and squirted in some Fairy Liquid before adding the hot water.

'Yum, yum, yum,' Elinor said to Jeffrey, as he ate the rest of what she had in the dish. She smiled at Colin, when she handed him the empty dish. 'Well that seemed to be a winner. I'll try him with a little fruit and jelly shortly. It'll be so much easier when he's eating more or less what we are.'

'Do you want me to run Jeffrey's bath?' Colin asked, once they'd finished the dishes and the baby had eaten a little mashed banana and a couple of spoonfuls of jelly.

'That would be great, darling. Then once he's in bed and had his story, we can settle down to watch 'The Black and White Minstrel Show'.' Elinor and Colin had recently invested in a small 14" television set and were enjoying watching the programmes, despite the rather poor reception they received.

Chapter Forty

Saturday, 28th February, 1962

'Hi Mum, thought I'd pop round to see how you were doing,' Elinor said, when she arrived at Melrose Avenue that afternoon. 'Thought if you felt up to it, we could perhaps make a start on clearing out Dad's wardrobe.' She knew it was going to be a heartbreaking job for them but felt it was better to do it now than later. 'Unless you'd prefer to do it yourself,' she finished off lamely.

Her mother didn't make an immediate response. 'What about Jeffrey?'

'Colin's going to take Jeffrey out for a wee while. With it being a fairly mild day, Colin thought perhaps he'd take him to Bankhead Pond and let him play on the grass there. He's got a tartan rug to put down on the grass,' she added, before Mum worried about Jeffrey getting cold.

Elinor herself had often played with Rita and Brian at Bankhead Pond as a child when she and her parents were visiting Aunt Muriel from their home in Cambuslang. She used to enjoy taking off her sandals and socks and paddling over the stones in the pond. Through the trees on the opposite side of the pond you could see the cows grazing on the fields belonging to Mitchell's farm.

'It's a bit dangerous to let Jeffrey loose there with the pond,' Susan said.

'Don't worry, Mum, Colin won't let him out of his sight for a second. Jeffrey loves going there and likes to see the 'moo' cows as he calls them. Now, what about Dad's clothes?'

'Would be good to get them sorted out right enough.

Some of his shoes and suits have hardly been worn.'

Elinor followed her mother upstairs. 'What about sorting them out into different piles, Mum? Anything useable could be donated to the Salvation Army. You know how Dad always said they were the most practicing Christians, so he'd like that. Any special items might be accepted by Uncle George or one of Dad's friends. We could keep a separate pile of things you just want to throw out.'

'Would Colin like to wear Dad's watch and maybe his wedding ring?' Susan asked as she opened the jewellery box sitting on the dressing table. She held up the watch and the ring as she was speaking.

'I think he would, Mum,' Elinor said, her tone gentle. 'But why don't we sort out the clothes first before we discuss that?'

Susan nodded and the two women started on their task. They worked in silence, apart from an occasional 'where do you want this to go?' or 'I suppose this will be thrown out?'

Elinor looked up from sorting through a pile of socks when she heard her mum give a choked sob. 'This was your dad's favourite.' Her mum sniffed back the tears as she held up the fairisle v-necked pullover that Dad always wore when he went to the bowling green.

Elinor moved closer and hugged her mum, trying desperately to keep her emotions in check. 'I know, Mum. It's so sad to see these precious things but the sooner we finish the better.'

A short time later it was Elinor who started weeping. She held out a book towards her mother. It was 'War and Peace' by Leo Tolstoy and on the front page she'd written 'To Dad, Happy Christmas, Love from Elinor.' Blinded by tears, she got to her feet. 'Let's go downstairs and have a cuppa.'

Susan nodded, looking exhausted by now. Downstairs

she dropped into an easy chair in the living room, letting Elinor bring her a cup of tea and a piece of fruit bread.

They chatted about Andrew and the happy memories he'd left with them and, afterwards, they returned to their task, refreshed and feeling stronger. Soon they had every item in its appropriate pile.

'I'll ask Colin to collect the stuff for the Salvation Army, Mum, and he'll take them in the car.' How glad Elinor was that her husband had learned to drive. 'Now, let's go to the Rowan Tree for some lunch.' She wanted to get her mother out of the house for a wee while and the Rowan Tree teashop on Stonelaw Road was only a five minute walk away.

'I've been thinking,' Susan said, while they were in the teashop. 'Now you don't need to give me an answer straight away, you'll obviously want to discuss it with Colin, but my house is too big for me on my own. I'd like to stay though, because my memories with your dad are there. I thought you, Colin and Jeffrey might move in with me and we could all stay together.'

When Elinor didn't reply straight away, she went on, 'I know it's a big decision but I wouldn't interfere in your life together. You two would save on rent in Macdonald Street and you know my house will be yours when I go, love. I would enjoy having the company in the house and I could babysit Jeffrey any time you wanted to go out for the evening.'

Elinor spoke for the first time. 'It sounds like an idea worth considering, Mum, but of course I'd need to discuss it with Colin, then we can let you know our decision. I don't like to think of you there on your own and it might be something that we can all benefit from.'

Susan smiled at her daughter. 'Okay love, think about it, that's all I'm asking.'

Chapter Forty One

Wednesday, 19th September, 1962

Elinor patted her five month bump as she stood in front of the full length mirror. She turned round to see herself in profile, then smiled and rubbed her stomach. Yes, she thought, I don't look too massive in my new dress and the autumn shades suit me. Anyway, why should I feel embarrassed about my size? She and Colin were both looking forward to their new arrival at the end of January. Jeffrey was over the moon about 'mummy and daddy buying me a brother or sister' soon. Elinor had explained to him that they didn't know yet if it would be a boy or a girl. He didn't seem to mind as long as he had a playmate.

It was only eight months since Dad's death and it had been a difficult time for them all. It was hardest for poor Mum but her close relationship with Jeffrey had helped her a great deal. Giving up the rental on the Macdonald Street flat and moving in with Mum had worked well too and the house was big enough to allow them all sufficient space. She knew that Mum enjoyed feeling useful; today, for instance, she was taking Jeffrey to the play park and on to visit one of her friends.

Elinor sat at the dressing table and sprayed some of her favourite Chanel No 5 behind her ears and on her wrists. Colin had bought it for her birthday in June and she saved it for special occasions. As she fixed her hair, she thought back to the day a few months ago when Eric and Rose had told Colin and her about their wedding plans. The couple had been at Melrose Avenue for dinner and afterwards, while Susan was upstairs reading a bedtime story to Jeffrey, they'd broken their good news.

'We knew my parents would insist on a wedding in St Columbkille's and Eric's folks would want us to marry in Wardlawhill,' Rose told them, snuggling against Eric as she spoke.

'We're in love and want to marry without any bitterness and arguments,' Eric said, 'and that's why we've arranged to be married in the Registry Office in Rutherglen.'

Colin slapped his brother on the back. 'Good for you both to stick to your guns. How were the parents about your decision?'

Rose made a face. 'Mine were furious at first, although they've calmed down a bit by now. Your mum and dad weren't quite so angry, were they?' she said to Eric.

'No, but I think they were disappointed all the same,' he said, 'I suppose we expected that reaction though, didn't we?'

Rose nodded and clasped his hand tighter.

'Well you know Elinor and I are behind you, aren't we, darling?' Colin turned to his wife for confirmation.

'Definitely,' Elinor agreed. 'Good luck to both of you,' she said, hugging first Rose and then Eric.

'It's strange to think that I'd never have met Eric if I hadn't served you in Gall's that day,' Rose said to Elinor, when the two men had gone out into the garden, Colin keen to let his brother see how well his runner beans were doing.

'And we only became friends when we met that day on the tram going into town. I don't think we stopped gassing during the entire journey.'

'I know,' Rose agreed, laughing at the memory.

It occurred to Elinor now how quickly the time since that day had flown in and here she was dressing for Rose and Eric's big day.

Now that her hair and make-up was done, and her jewellery in place, she put on her low heeled court shoes. Low heels would be better in her condition, especially if she was dancing. She certainly didn't want to have a fall and cause any damage to the baby.

Once she was happy with her appearance, she donned her black jacket. The jacket was wool but by this time in September the weather often turned cool and she'd be glad of it when they were coming home.

When she arrived downstairs, Susan and Jeffrey came out of the living room. Elinor lifted her son into her arms and hugged him. 'Be a good boy for Grandma Susan. Where's Colin?' she asked, as she handed Jeffrey over to her mum once more.

'I'm here,' Colin said, from behind her. 'I was checking the car was ready for us. I'll wash my hands and we can get off,' he added, going into the kitchen.

Susan stood at the front door, Jeffrey in her arms, to wave them off.

***

'Do you want to go home, darling? You look a bit tired.'

Elinor looked up at Colin and smiled. 'I am a bit wearied with all the excitement but I don't want to spoil the evening for you.'

Colin shook his head. 'You won't. With Jeffrey sleeping poorly last night, I'm a bit shattered myself by now. We've had a super time and it's great that everything has gone off so well for Eric and Rose. I don't think it would be rude to excuse ourselves now and head off.'

'Okay,' she agreed, relieved at the thought of having an early night. 'Let's go and say our farewells'.

'Thank you for being with us,' Rose said, hugging

them both in turn, while Eric kissed Elinor and threw his arm round his brother's shoulders. 'Hope you've enjoyed your day.'

'It's been lovely,' Elinor told them. 'We wouldn't have missed it for the world. But Jeffrey has some more teeth coming through and we had practically no sleep last night.'

'You've all that to look forward,' Colin said, grinning first at his brother and then at Rose.

Colin and Elinor turned away when other guests arrived to speak to the happy couple.

Chapter Forty Two

Hogmanay, 1962

It was just after eight o'clock when Colin carried Jeffrey into the living room, wrapped in a fluffy pale blue bath towel. 'There you go, Grandma,' he said, smiling at his mother-in-law, 'this young man wants Grandma Susan to dry him and get him into his pyjamas.'

Susan took Jeffrey on to her lap. He was tall for his age and his speech was much clearer than many twenty month olds. 'What a lovely clean boy you are, Jeffrey,' she murmured, the smell of baby powder wafting up as she opened the towel. Jeffrey gave her an angelic smile, showing off his teeth, six on top and four below. He ran his chubby fingers down Susan's face as she dried him down and put on his nappy. Soon she had him in his pyjamas ready for bed.

'Do you want me to read Jeffrey his bedtime story?' Susan asked Elinor when she came into the living room to fetch some cutlery from the sideboard drawer. 'It would give you more time to prepare the food.'

Elinor kissed her son's soft cheek and ruffled his blond curls. She made a mental note to get his hair cut soon. She'd prefer to leave it as it was with his gorgeous curls but a few people recently had taken him for a girl. 'Would you like Grandma Susan to tuck you in, sweetheart, and read you a story?'

The infant nodded. 'Kwa, Gan, Kwa,' he said, smiling at his grandmother.

'Yes, Quack, Quack,' Elinor agreed. 'It's his favourite story at the moment, Mum. And I warn you, don't try to leave anything out as he knows every word. That's great, Mum, while you read Jeffrey his story, I can get on in the kitchen.'

She set to making some sandwiches and used two full loaves as there would be a lot of folk to feed. Aunt Muriel and Uncle George were coming along later this evening to bring in the New Year with the family and she'd invited Joanne and Dougie, Jean and Tom, and Rose and Eric to pop in after the Bells.

Elinor could hardly believe there were only a few hours to go before 1963 came in. And what an exciting New Year it's going to be, she thought, laying her hands across her eight month bulge. Her heart swelled with joy, a New Year and a new baby. The new arrival was expected on 29th January and Elinor was due to give birth once again in Bellshill Maternity. Mum had been knitting non-stop, all in lemon and white of course until they knew the sex of the baby.

By the time Susan got Jeffrey off to sleep and came downstairs again, Elinor had all the food prepared. She had plates of sausage rolls, cocktail sausages, sandwiches with a few different fillings and a selection of cakes and pastries laid out on the dining table. A big pot of broth sat on the stove just to be heated and there was a large bowl of trifle in the fridge.

'You've got enough there to feed an army,' Susan commented.

'Don't forget the food is to do us into the wee small hours. The men will be having a wee dram at midnight which will give them an appetite.'

Just after nine o'clock there was a ring at the doorbell and Susan went to answer it. 'Come in,' she greeted Muriel and George and the three of them joined Elinor and Colin in the front room, where they had some music playing quietly on the record player.

Elinor got up from her chair immediately, smiling at her aunt and uncle. 'Give me your coats and have a seat,' she said, indicating to the chairs, one on either side of the fireplace, where a fire was blazing brightly. Although each room in the house had electric radiators under the window sill, she and Colin still liked to use smokeless fuel occasionally.

'You can't beat a coal fire on a cold night,' Muriel said, standing in front of the fireplace and rubbing her hands together. 'Even if it does mean cleaning out the ashes next day.'

'What will you have to drink?' Colin asked their guests, once Elinor had hung their coats up on the hallstand.

'I'll have a sweet sherry please, Colin,' Aunt Muriel said, taking her seat at the side of the fireplace.

'And you, George?'

'A whisky for me, lad.'

They all sat down with their drinks and chatted until Elinor told them a short time later that the soup was ready and would they come to the table.

After they'd eaten their fill, they moved back into the front room. 'Will we switch on the telly to watch the Hogmanay show when it comes on?' Susan asked.

'It's just after eleven but we can leave the sound down meantime so that we can still chat,' Elinor suggested.

About twenty minutes later Elinor let out a shriek and jumped up from the settee. There was a damp patch where she'd been sitting and water ran down her legs and dripped on to the carpet.

Susan ran to fetch towels, calling over her shoulder to her son-in-law. 'Colin, go next door to Mrs Mullin and tell her Elinor's waters have broken.'

'At this time of night?'

'It's okay, she'll be up as her son and his wife were coming tonight. Hurry,' she said, as she returned with the towels with which she padded Elinor before helping her

175

upstairs to her bedroom.

'Should I not take Elinor to Bellshill?' Colin called up from the foot of the stairs, forgetting he'd been drinking alcohol.

'There's no time,' Susan replied sharply, 'get Mrs Mullin.'

Colin shot off and returned with Mrs Mullin. 'Phone an ambulance, Colin,' the woman instructed him and disappeared upstairs to attend to Elinor.

After he'd made the phone call, Colin sat with George in dazed silence in the front room, while Muriel went into the kitchen to boil the kettle. She noticed the time on the kitchen clock; leaving twenty to twelve. She carried the water upstairs and Susan took it from her at the bedroom door. 'Shouldn't be long now,' she told Muriel.

Downstairs Muriel passed the message to the two men. She busied herself in the kitchen, while George went to the back door to have a cigarette. For the next fifteen minutes, Colin paced up and down the length of the hall, trying to hear what was going on upstairs. His footsteps kept in time with the tick of the grandfather clock sitting against the wall.

Just before the hour, through the open front room door, he could hear the cheer on the telly as the countdown to midnight began. There were a couple of piercing cries from Elinor and then, as the Town Hall clock chimed midnight, he heard a baby's cry. At the same instant, the strains of 'Auld Lang Syne' came from the television.

Colin raced upstairs and was met by Susan as he opened the door. 'You've got a beautiful daughter,' she told him, 'Mrs Mullin is tying the cord at the moment.'

Mrs Mullin finished what she was doing and called over her shoulder to Colin. 'How did you get on with the ambulance?'

'On its way.'

'Good. It's best to have Elinor and the wee one checked out at the hospital but all seems in order.' She moved aside to let Colin come to the bedside.

'She's beautiful, darling,' he said, 'just like her mum'. He bent over and kissed Elinor gently on her lips. She smiled up at him, too exhausted to speak.

'Welcome, Fiona,' he whispered to the baby and brushed his hand over her mop of black hair.

When they heard the siren, Susan ran down to open the door to the ambulance crew.

PART II

Chapter Forty Three

Monday, 6th May, 1963

'How are you managing with Fiona?' Nurse Middleton asked, as she sat in the living room in Melrose Avenue, facing Elinor, who was cradling her 4-month-old baby daughter. The nurse, who was a Health Visitor or 'Green Lady' as she was known because of the colour of her uniform, had been assigned to the family to ensure that they were coping with the new baby.

'Very well. Fiona's no bother during the day and sleeps soundly at night. I've got her off her two o'clock feed now and she sleeps from about nine o'clock until six in the morning.'

'That's great news.' Nurse Middleton got up and came over to where baby Fiona lay in her mum's arms. 'What a pretty girl you are,' the nurse murmured, putting her finger through the infant's partly open hand. 'She's got a good grip there too.' Taking her seat again Nurse Middleton said, 'I'm sure it must have been a shock to be told of Fiona's condition.'

Elinor nodded slowly and drew her baby closer. 'I suppose we were although, looking back, I think both Colin and I guessed before we were told officially that Fiona had Down's Syndrome. I think it was the shape of her eyes that alerted us although of course we both hoped we were wrong.' She stopped speaking for a moment and brushed her fingers over the baby's soft downy cheek. 'Dr Orchard, our G.P., told us first of his suspicions and this was confirmed when we were referred to a Consultant at the Sick Children's Hospital a couple of months ago. That was when we were told that you would be attending to offer us support.'

'And I will continue to visit you monthly, just to

advise on any wee problems that come up. And of course you can contact me in between should it be necessary.' Nurse Middleton smiled at Elinor. 'I'm so glad you've accepted the way things are. Some parents turn their backs on their handicapped child.'

Elinor shook her head. 'That's so cruel, as if it's the baby's fault that he or she is handicapped.' When Fiona became a bit restless, Elinor lifted her up to her shoulder and stroked her back. The infant immediately began to make contented noises, with her head cradled in the curve of Elinor's neck. 'Colin and I said from the word go that Fiona was ours and we loved her no matter what her condition.'

'That's excellent and I'm sure Fiona will thrive due to your attitude. I can see how well looked after she is. How does your son? – she glanced at her notes – Jeffrey, how does he relate to Fiona?'

'He adores his wee sister and hugs her constantly. We've to watch that he doesn't get too excited and suffocate her. My mother has taken Jeffrey out to the swing park for a wee while.'

'Good. That gives Jeffrey lots of attention from his grandmother and allows you to spend time getting to know Fiona.' Nurse Middleton checked her records again. 'I see Fiona has had her first injection and she'll be due another one when she reaches six months. I'll note it in my diary and I can give it to her in a couple of months' time.' She got to her feet and put on her trenchcoat, green to match her uniform. 'I'll see you next month, Mrs Dawson, but remember you can ring the clinic to speak to me in between if you have any questions or problems.'

'Thanks, it's good to know you are on hand.' Elinor got to her feet, still holding Fiona up at her shoulder, and saw Nurse Middleton out.

About half an hour later, Susan and Jeffrey returned from the swing park, with Jeffrey excitedly telling his mum that he'd been on both the swings and the frying pan. 'How did Nurse Middleton's visit go?' Susan asked, as she helped Jeffrey out of his coat.

'She's very pleasant and it's reassuring to know that I can phone if I need advice about Fiona.'

'What sort of age is she?'

'It's difficult to say, Mum. Maybe in her fifties, but she could be younger. She's really trying to help though and that's the main thing.'

'And was she quite happy with Fiona's progress?'

'She was delighted to see how well she was doing. She's going to give Fiona her next injection in two months time so it's great that I won't need to take her to a clinic or the G.P. surgery.'

'Excellent, I'm so pleased.' Susan rubbed her hands together. 'There's quite a cold wind outside. Think I'll put the kettle on.'

Chapter Forty Four

New Year' Day, 1965

When Elinor opened the front door, Joanne tottered in, with her eighteen month old daughter, Lorna, clinging to her skirt. Joanne grasped a brightly wrapped parcel in one hand, while two baking tins were balanced precariously in the crook of her other arm.

'Here, let me help you.' Elinor relieved her friend of the baking and carried the tins into the kitchen, where she lifted their lids. 'Gingerbread men **and** angel cakes. How lovely.'

'We can't have you preparing everything yourself. What a spread,' Joanne said, when she turned to the table, laden with chocolate krispie cakes, iced cakes covered in smarties, tablet, jelly babies, chocolate buttons and in the centre of the table a birthday cake with two pink candles.

'Mum helped me,' Elinor told her. 'I've also got sausage rolls and some sandwiches although I don't think they'll be as popular with the kids as the sweet things.'

'Yeah, you're right. But not to worry, we adults can scoff the sannies. Where's the birthday girl?'

'She's here,' a voice said behind Joanne and she turned to find Susan standing with Fiona in the kitchen doorway. Fiona wore a cherry red velvet dress with a lace collar.

'Oh what a pretty dress. Happy birthday darling,' Joanne hugged her. 'Fancy you being two already. It seems only yesterday that I came to see you when you were one day old.'

Lorna toddled over to Fiona and the two kids stared at each other for a moment. Then Fiona threw her arms around the younger girl and stroked her blonde hair.

Elinor smiled. 'She treats Lorna like her dolly.'

'Do you want to give Fiona her birthday gift?' Joanne held out the parcel to her daughter and together they gave it to Fiona. In the process the gift fell on to the floor.

'Hope it isn't breakable,' Susan said, sitting on a chair and lifting Fiona and the parcel on to her knee.

'No, it isn't.' Joanne lifted Lorna into her arms and they watched Fiona rip open the parcel to reveal a bedtime story book and a colouring book and pencils.

Elinor smiled at her friend. 'Thanks, Joanne, she loves colouring and insists that Colin or I read her a story every night before she goes to sleep.' The bell rang once more and Elinor opened the door to Rose, Eric and wee David. 'Come in, come in,' she welcomed, standing back to let them enter. 'Let me take your coats and come and join the party.'

By this time everyone had moved into the front room where the party games were going to take place. 'Gosh, you're getting to be a big boy, aren't you?' Elinor said to David and tickled him under his chin. He giggled and when she opened her arms, he came into them. At six months old, he looked tiny beside the girls.

'Where's Colin?' Eric asked Elinor.

'He and Dougie decided they were going to make a New Year's Resolution to get more exercise and walked up to Cathkin today.' Elinor looked at the clock above the mantelpiece. 'They'll be back any minute.'

When two of Elinor's neighbours and their children arrived, she made the introductions. 'This is Maureen from two doors down, and her daughter. Emily,' then, turning to the second woman, she said, 'and Janet is my neighbour from across the road, and her daughter, Mandy.'

Rose and Joanne shook hands with the two women.

'Nice to meet you,' they said, and they all found themselves a seat, either on the settee or in one of the comfortable armchairs.

'Happy New Year,' Eric said suddenly, holding his hands out to include everyone.

Elinor laughed. 'Gosh yes, all the best for 1965. I always think of today as Fiona's birthday rather than New Year's day. I'll get you all something to drink.'

'Before that, Fiona has birthday presents to open.' Rose handed Fiona a parcel as she was speaking, which turned out to be a summer dress. Emily and Mandy also had gifts for her.

Elinor picked up the wrapping paper and scrunched it into a ball. 'I think Fiona's a bit overwhelmed by all the attention. I've just remembered Jeffrey's in his room playing with his train set. Mum could you let him know our guests have arrived?'

'Sure.' Susan was halfway upstairs when Colin and Dougie arrived back, their faces glowing from the fresh air and the climb up to Cathkin Braes.

'I'm glad to see you both,' Eric said. 'Save me from all these females.'

'Is your friend from Hamilton coming today, Elinor?' Joanne asked, when she followed Elinor into the kitchen to get out glasses for their drinks.

'You mean Freda? She and Jack were hoping to come and bring Alistair but they were out at a party last night and she said it would depend on how hung over Jack was. He wouldn't drive if he'd been drinking a lot.'

'Sensible man.'

By the time Colin had dispensed the drinks and handed round the glasses, Freda, Jack and Alistair arrived.

'So glad you could make it,' Elinor said to them,

when they came into the hallway.

Freda took off her coat and handed it to Elinor. 'The party was cancelled at the last minute, so Jack was fine for driving today.'

'Great, because that gives us a full house. Come in and I'll introduce you to everyone.'

Jeffrey arrived downstairs at that moment. 'Do you want to come up and see my train set?' he said, when he saw Alistair. Jeffrey was a couple of months older than Alistair and they played well together.

'Well only for ten minutes,' Elinor instructed them, 'because we're going to start the games soon.'

Chapter Forty Five

Thursday, 24th June, 1965

Elinor was enjoying some rare leisure time at home that morning, with the two children at the park with Grandma Susan. She put down her duster when she heard the mail drop through the letterbox.

There were a few envelopes that looked like bills but she let out a whoop of joy when she saw the airletter from Dot. Forgetting about the housework, she made herself a mug of coffee and sat down to read the letter.

18th June 1965

My Dear Elinor

How lovely it was to receive your last letter, enclosing photos and giving me news of the kids. Fiona looks so cute and I just wanted to lift her up and hug her. I know how shocked you and Colin were to discover that Fiona was suffering from Down's syndrome but, as you say, she has brought a great deal of love to your family and now you couldn't imagine life without her. I can scarcely believe that Fiona is 2½ already. Where does the time go?

I smiled when I read about how protective Jeffrey is of his little sister. He looks such a gentle boy and I can well imagine that would be the case. I was surprised when you wrote that Jeffrey was due to start school next year as I knew he had only turned 4 last month. But then I remembered that kids over there start school at aged 5 unlike here where it is 6.

Fiona will miss him when he goes to school.

I'm still living in Blackburn with Mum. As you know, over the past year I was thinking of trying to find a place of my own; I felt at 27 I was too old to still be staying with my parents. However, after Dad's death at the end of last year, I didn't think it right to leave Mum on her own straight away. She's done very well since then, and I'm proud of how she's coped with her loss, but she is becoming more dependent on me. I've decided to shelve the idea of moving out meantime. Instead Mum and I are going to have some improvements done on the property. The workmen are due to start next week. They will give us a new roof and the next part of the plan is to extend the kitchen and living area, with the dual purpose of giving us more space inside but leaving us a smaller garden to work on.

Mum and I often talk about the old days when you and your mum and dad lived in Melbourne. We'd love to see you all again and you'll be welcome to visit anytime. We've got plenty of room for you all. I do understand, of course, that it's a big undertaking with two small children but I wanted you to know that the invitation is there for you. With both our mums being widows now, I'm sure they'd enjoy spending time together.

Mum and I are going to Surfers' Paradise next Monday for a two week vacation. Our motel, Rosella Bay – isn't it a gorgeous name? – has been recommended by friends who tell us that the facilities on offer are excellent. We are both looking forward to enjoying some Queensland sunshine as it's pretty chilly in Melbourne right now. I'm sure you'll remember how cold June and July are. We had a very dry summer and autumn so the reservoirs are low. Although cold, winter hasn't so far brought much rain.

I was thinking the other day that it was in Surfers' Paradise that your friend Michael's sister used to live. Do you still hear from Michael these days?

Elinor spilled some of her coffee with the shock of seeing Michael's name on the page. She hadn't mentioned him in any of her recent letters to Dot and thought her friend would have forgotten about him. At the sight of his name, a lump formed in her throat.

She fetched a cloth from the kitchen and wiped up the puddle of coffee, before sitting down again to finish reading Dot's letter.

Work is going much as ever. There has been a change in personnel in our ward recently so I'm missing some of my previous colleagues but the new guys seem quite a good bunch. I attended a Seminar on 'Infectious Diseases' in Canberra earlier in the year and enjoyed it very much. There were twenty people on the course, with just three of us from Melbourne. Quite a few people came from hospitals in Western Australia.

It was my first time in Canberra and I found it a lovely city. On one of our free afternoons I went with a colleague to the Australian Parliament Building. We sat in on a debate which we found most interesting. I was fascinated to watch the stenographers who were taking verbatim notes on the debates. They must have colossal speeds in shorthand.

Take care Elinor and love to all the family. I look forward to hearing from you when you can fit letter writing in with your chores as a wife and mother.

> *Your ever loving buddy,*
> *Dot.*
> *xxxxx*

Elinor still had the letter in her hand when Susan arrived back with the children. Jeffrey raced into the living room and jumped up and down at the side of his mother's chair. 'I was on the swings and the see-saw,' he told her, 'and Fiona was on the baby swing, weren't you Fi?' he said to his little sister.

Fiona nodded and toddled over to Elinor to climb up on to her knee. 'Cream,' she said, her eyes glowing.

Elinor kissed her daughter's cheek and cuddled her close. 'Did Grandma Susan buy you ice cream?'

'Es.' Fiona smiled up at her mum and giggled.

Elinor tickled Fiona's tummy and she giggled again. 'Well I don't think you and Jeffrey will be ready for lunch just yet. Will we wait a wee while?'

'Probably best,' Susan agreed. 'Who's the letter from?'

'Dot. And she's asking for you. She and her mum would like us all to go over on holiday some time but I can't imagine us making that journey until the kids are bigger.'

Susan shook her head. 'No, too far and too tiring for them. Still it was kind of Frances and Dot to suggest it. Maybe they could come over here to visit us.'

'Maybe,' Elinor said, going upstairs to put Dot's letter into her writing desk until she had time to reply.

Chapter Forty Six

Friday, 19th May, 1967

Elinor, Colin and Jeffrey sat on the third front row in Rutherglen Town Hall that evening to watch Fiona's dancing display. 'There she is, second from the right,' Elinor whispered.

Grandma Susan had made 4-year-old Fiona's emerald green skirt which she was wearing over a white leotard, the costume finished with a tall emerald green pointy hat. The dance was an Irish jig and the children on the stage gave it their all. They finished to rapturous applause.

'Did you see Fiona?' Colin asked 6-year-old Jeffrey, who was standing up on his dad's knees to be able to see over the heads of the people in the row in front of them. 'She danced really well, didn't she?'

Jeffrey nodded and waved to Fiona, who saw him and waved back before they were ushered off the stage, to allow the next act to come on. Elinor was grateful to her mum for offering to stay back stage and change Fiona from one costume to another, thus allowing Elinor to sit in the audience and enjoy the performance.

Elinor smiled happily. Both she and Colin were keen to let Fiona lead as normal a life as possible and they'd been so happy when the dance teacher, Miss Houston, had agreed to take Fiona into the class despite her handicap. 'Fiona seems very well-behaved and also has a great sense of rhythm so I can't see any problem about her joining the class,' Miss Houston had told them last year when she'd come to the house to meet Fiona and her parents.

Fiona had quickly fitted into the dancing class and the

fact that the other little girls had accepted her straight away was an added bonus. Although unable to attend Calderwood School, where Jeffrey was due to move into Primary 2 in August, Fiona was looking forward to starting at Parkville House in Blantyre that same month.

Elinor recalled the day that Mrs Chalmers, the Headmistress at Parkville House, had come out to Melrose Avenue to interview them. Elinor had warmed to her straight away; she came across as a very caring, understanding lady and both she and Colin felt certain that Fiona would be safe in her care.

Colin's voice beside her pulled Elinor's wandering thoughts back to the present.

'Here's Fiona again,' Colin whispered to Jeffrey, when Fiona's group walked on to the stage once more. This time she was dressed in a Royal Stuart tartan kilt and a white blouse with a lacy front, to dance the sword dance with some other little girls. Fiona bent to pull up one of her long socks which was slipping down her leg and then she took her stance over her crossed swords waiting for the music to start. Right on time, the girls began to dance, their faces registering concentration as they made their way through the steps.

Jeffrey was asleep on Colin's knee by the time the display was over but it was a very proud mum who went backstage to collect Fiona. 'You were wonderful, darling,' Elinor told her, scooping her daughter up into her arms.

Both children were sound asleep before their heads hit the pillow that night and afterwards the three adults discussed the success of the evening over a cup of tea.

Chapter Forty Seven

Monday, 21st August, 1967

'Bye, darling,' Elinor said to Jeffrey, when she and Fiona were leaving him at Calderwood School for his first day in Primary 2. Elinor was glad that at least most of Jeffrey's classmates would be the same children who'd been with him in Primary 1. He seemed to have grown so tall during the summer holidays and now looked more like a Primary 3 or 4 boy, standing at her side, with his school satchel on his back.

Jeffrey let go of her hand and she restrained her natural urge to kiss him, not wanting to embarrass her son in front of the other children in the playground. 'I'll be here waiting for you when you come out of school at three o'clock,' she told him. 'And have you got your dinner money?'

For answer, Jeffrey jingled the coins in his blazer pocket. Elinor had picked him up and taken him home for lunch when he was in Primary 1 but now that he was going into Primary 2 it was a different story. 'I don't want to come home at lunchtime,' he'd told her, 'it's only babies that do that. Big boys like me eat school dinners.' Unable to talk him out of it, Elinor had finally agreed.

'Jeffrey,' Matthew Brown yelled and ran over to stand beside his best friend.

Matthew's mum followed behind him, puffing her way over to Elinor. 'Hello, Jeffrey,' she said, once she got her breath back. 'Did you enjoy your summer holidays?'

'Yes, thank you, Mrs Brown,' Jeffrey replied, politely.

Mrs Brown smiled at Elinor. 'It's good to know

they'll be back at school and will get into a routine once more, isn't it?'

'Yes, they begin to get bored by the end of the holidays and are keen to see all their pals again. There are two Primary 2 classes so hopefully our two will be in the same group again.'

'Bye, Jeffrey,' Fiona shouted after her brother but he was too busy chatting to Matthew to hear her. The teachers came into the playground to accompany their own pupils into the school for the new session.

When the children had all filed into the building, Mrs Brown walked with Elinor and Fiona out of the school grounds. 'And how are you doing, Fiona?' she asked the little girl.

Fiona beamed at her. 'I'm fine, thank you, Mrs Brown. I'm going to school tomorrow, aren't I, Mum?'

Elinor squeezed her daughter's hand. 'Yes, you are love.' She turned to Mrs Brown. 'Fiona's starting at Parkville House in Blantyre tomorrow, where she'll meet new friends. Not sure how she'll get on as she hasn't been separated from me until now,' she said quietly to the other woman.

'Oh, I'm sure she'll be fine, she's a friendly wee girl.' Mrs Brown dipped into her shopping bag and brought out a packet of jelly babies, which she handed to Fiona. 'Put these into your school bag, Fiona, in case you get hungry.'

'Thank you, Mrs Brown,' Fiona said, clutching the packet of sweets to her chest.

The two women parted company out on the main road and Elinor walked home, with Fiona skipping along at her side, humming contentedly.

Chapter Forty Eight

Tuesday, 22nd August, 1967

After Elinor had taken Jeffrey to school that morning, she and Fiona boarded the bus to Blantyre. Normally, Fiona would be picked up each morning by a special bus and brought home again but, on their first morning at Parkville House, the parents were expected to accompany their child to make sure he or she settled in.

'Look at that lady's lovely hat, mum,' Fiona said, pointing excitedly to a passer-by's bright green beret. She continued to comment on the places they passed during the journey and she and Elinor chatted happily together. Before either of them realised it, the bus was coming into Blantyre and shortly afterwards Elinor spotted the Black Horse bar that she'd been told to watch out for. 'Right, this is our stop,' she said to Fiona, helping her daughter down off the bus.

Hand in hand, Elinor and Fiona walked from the main road where the bus dropped them and followed the path up the hill past a farmer's field to Parkville House, a solid red brick building which stood on the brow of the hill.

As Mrs Chalmers, the headmistress at Parkville House, had requested, Fiona carried a small backpack, containing a change of clothes, soap and a facecloth, toothpaste and a toothbrush, £2 in money and her owl, her favourite soft toy that she'd had since she was tiny.

Mrs Chalmers met them in the entrance hall and showed them into Fiona's classroom. Her teacher, Miss O'Hara, welcomed Fiona to the school and showed her where she could leave her coat, with her name printed above her peg. Fiona and Elinor were introduced to the other children. Elinor noticed that most of the children were Down's syndrome sufferers like Fiona although there were others who seemed to have different disabilities. Fiona was shown to a seat beside another Down's girl. 'This is Theresa,' Miss O'Hara told Fiona, as she sat down next to Theresa. 'I'm sure you two girls will get on splendidly.' The girls immediately took hands and beamed at one another.

Miss O'Hara returned to where Elinor was standing. 'There you are, Mrs Dawson, Fiona is quite at home and has already made her first friend.'

'What time will Fiona be brought home?'

'About half past three, although it can be slightly earlier or later, depending on the driver's route.'

'I pick up my son from school at three o'clock so that should leave me plenty of time to get back home for Fiona arriving.'

'That's fine, Mrs Dawson, but don't worry, even if Fiona was home before you, the driver would wait until you got there,' Miss O'Hara assured Elinor. 'And we have your phone number so, should there be any change of plan, we'd ring you.'

Elinor said her farewells and left the school. She felt relaxed making her way back to the bus stop, sure that both her children were well catered for in a school that suited their individual needs.

Chapter Forty Nine

Thursday, 21st September, 1967

Once Jeffrey was at school and Fiona had been picked up by her school bus, Elinor stripped the beds. Colin now took Jeffrey to school in the morning, giving her more time to get Fiona ready.

Elinor piled the sheets and towels into the twin tub, setting it to a hot wash cycle. She had started on the breakfast dishes when Susan came into the kitchen and began to dry them. 'What can I do to help, love?'

'There isn't much needing done,' Elinor said, but when she saw the disappointment on her mother's face, she added, 'I think the bedroom furniture could do with a polish.'

'Great, I'll do that.' Susan took a yellow duster and furniture polish from the broom cupboard and made her way upstairs, humming to herself..

Elinor smiled as she went off. Mum was fit for her years and mentally alert, but Elinor was aware that she craved the need to be useful in the family. And we do need her, Elinor thought, as she put out the washing rope. She's such a help in amusing the children and taking them on outings when I'm busy with housework and cooking. Elinor made a vow there and then to tell her mum more often just how much the family depended on her help.

She was still in the back garden when she heard the phone ringing and scurried indoors. By the time she got into the hallway, Susan was holding out the phone to her. 'Someone from Parkville House for you, Elinor.'

Elinor screwed up her face and took the receiver. 'Hello, Elinor Dawson speaking.'

'It's Ivy Chalmers here, Mrs Dawson.' The Head's voice was quiet, with an urgency in her tone. 'I'm sorry to have to phone you but it's Fiona, she's disappeared.'

'What do you mean ... disappeared? Where has she gone?'

'Don't worry, Mrs Dawson, I'm sure she can't have gone far. We phoned the police immediately we discovered she was missing but it could be she's trying to get home.'

Elinor gasped, her heart sinking at Mrs Chalmers' words. 'But I don't understand, Fiona is happy at Parkville. How did she disappear?'

'We're very upset as we too thought she'd settled well. The children were all out playing in the back garden, with some members of staff supervising them. Unfortunately the gardener had left the back gate unlocked and Fiona must have slipped out unnoticed into the fields beyond.'

'Oh God, anything could have happened, Fiona's so trusting of people. I'll come up right away.' Elinor's voice rose as she spoke, its pace quickened, and a shudder rippled down her spine.

'No, Mrs Dawson, it would be better if you stayed at home in case Fiona finds her way there. The police are already searching nearby fields and checking at homes in our area. I'm sure she'll be found soon.'

'But how could you let this happen? I sent my daughter to you expecting that she would be protected from harm. I don't think I could trust you and your staff with her after this.'

'Please don't feel like that, Mrs Dawson. Our gardener has been severely chastised for his failure to lock the gate securely. He's very upset and has joined in the search for Fiona.'

'I can't believe this has happened. I can't take it in,'

Elinor said in a choking voice.

'In all my years at Parkville, this has never happened before,' Mrs Chalmers replied, 'and I can only offer you my sincere apologies. But, as I said, I'm sure Fiona won't have wandered far and will be found quickly and returned to us before she reaches Rutherglen.'

'But she has no money to get a bus and she wouldn't know which bus to take anyway. I'll need to let my husband know.' Elinor glanced at her mother, who was standing near her, ashen-faced from hearing the one side of the conversation.

Mrs Chalmers' voice was soft and reassuring. 'Do that, my dear, and I promise I'll phone you the minute we hear anything.'

Elinor replaced the receiver with shaking hands, then lifted it again to ring Colin's work number. 'Colin, oh Colin,' she sobbed into the phone when he answered from his desk.

'What's wrong, love? Hello, Elinor, are you still there?' he said. The silence continued for a few more seconds before Elinor poured out the story of what had happened to Fiona.

'Okay, Elinor, I'll drive up to Blantyre now and help in the search. Try to keep calm, darling, I'm sure we'll find her. The police may already have found her by the time I get there. I'll phone the minute I know anything,' he said, before hanging up.

Replacing the receiver, Elinor walked straight into her mother's open arms and the two women clung to each other, tears streaming down their faces, unable to take in the horrific news.

They sat staring at the clock until, half an hour later, the phone rang again. Elinor got to it first and, with pounding heart, she said 'hello.'

'We've found her.' Mrs Chalmers' relief rang out

over the line. 'Fiona is safe and well.'

'Where was she?' Elinor's voice was barely a whisper.

'The police found her walking alongside the River Calder that flows behind our property. She told them she wanted to see her mum and was walking along the riverbank as she thought it would lead her to Rutherglen.'

Elinor was leaning against the wall and she slid down it and sat on the carpet, cradling the phone. 'Thank you, thank you,' she breathed into the mouthpiece. 'Oh thank God she's safe.'

'We're all so happy to have her back and none the worse of her escapade. We've told her that she must never do that again and always talk to one of us if there is something bothering her.'

'Can I speak to Fiona please?'

'Of course.' Elinor heard Mrs Chalmers speaking to Fiona. 'Will you come and say hello to your mum, Fiona? She's been very worried about you.'

'Hello Mum, sorry Mum.'

'Oh Fiona, what a fright you gave us. Why did you run away, don't you like being at school?'

'I love school, Mum, but I was missing you and wanted to see you. I'm sorry. I didn't mean to make you sad. Do you forgive me?'

'Of course I forgive you, darling, but you must promise me you won't do anything like this again. You know I'll always be here when you get back at half past three.'

'I know Mum and I won't make you sad again.'

'Well Dad's on his way up to the school at the moment so why don't you come back in the car with him and we can talk about things when you get here.'

'But can I come back to school tomorrow?'

'If you want to. Now can you let me speak to Mrs Chalmers again?'

When the Head came back on the line, Elinor explained what she'd arranged with Fiona.

'That sounds like an excellent plan,' Mrs Chalmers agreed, 'and don't worry, Mrs Dawson, Fiona is settling well and gets on with the other children. I think this will just be a one off and she didn't mean to cause such worry. She assures me she won't repeat it and I believe her.'

'I'm sorry if I was rude to you earlier.'

'Of course you weren't rude, Mrs Dawson, you were understandably worried, as we all were too. But thank goodness, she was found quickly and was unharmed.'

Off the phone again, Elinor hugged her mother. 'All's well that ends well. Fiona will come back with Colin for the rest of the day and she'll return to school tomorrow.'

Susan beamed. 'That's great. Now before they come back, let's sit down and have a nice cup of tea.'

Elinor burst out laughing. 'Oh Mum, that's your answer to every problem. But yes, I think I could do with some tea right now.'

Chapter Fifty

Saturday, 12th July, 1969

Being Saturday, the family were having a relaxed breakfast. There were only four of them at the table that morning, as the previous day Susan had gone to St Andrews with Muriel and George to spend the Glasgow Fair holiday weekend.

'Would you like to go to the Art Gallery today, Jeffrey?' Colin moved his empty cup and saucer out of Fiona's reach as he was speaking.

'Is that the place where we saw the polar bears and the elephant?' Jeffrey, his eyes sparkling with anticipation, sat on the edge of his seat.

'That's right. And can you remember the elephant's name?'

'Sir Roger,' the 8-year-old said, giving his dad a smug look. Sir Roger was an Asian elephant who'd previously lived in Glasgow zoo. When he died in 1900 at the age of 27, he was stuffed and presented to the Art Gallery and had brought delight to thousands of visitors, especially children, over the years since.

Elinor smiled at her son's excitement. Jeffrey had always been an easily pleased boy. She collected up the used dishes and carried them over to the sink. 'That's a great idea, Colin. While you're both out, I'll go into town to buy some new school shirts for Jeffrey in Marks and Spencer. He's taken a real stretch recently and his shirts are quite tight on him.'

'Do you want me to take Fiona with us?' Colin tweaked his daughter's pigtails as he said it. She giggled and climbed up on to his knee.

'No, love, you go and spend some time with Jeffrey.

201

You'll both enjoy it. I can take Fiona with me. You'd like to come with Mum on the big red bus, wouldn't you, darling?'

Fiona slid off Colin's knee and jumped up and down, her long pleats swinging around with the motion. 'Yes, let's go Mum,' she chirped, running towards the door.

'Not right now, Fiona. I have to wash the dishes and hoover the carpets first. Why don't you play with your dolly till I'm ready?'

'Okay,' Fiona said in her singsong voice, biddable as ever.

***

'Look, Mum, see that giant umbrella.' Fiona pointed through the bus window when the vehicle stopped at Bridgeton Cross to take on passengers.

Elinor and a woman seated nearby smiled at one another when they caught sight of the giant umbrella. 'That's called a bandstand, darling. The musicians stand or sit inside with their instruments and entertain the public.'

'But there's nobody inside.'

'No, not just now.' Elinor brushed some loose strands of hair away from Fiona's face.

The other woman leaned towards Fiona. 'But you're right, it does look like a giant umbrella, doesn't it?'

Fiona nodded and rewarded the lady with a beaming smile.

'Right, this is where we get off,' Elinor said, when the bus neared Argyle Street. They said their goodbyes to the lady they'd been speaking to and she shepherded Fiona off the vehicle.

Going into Marks and Spencer, Fiona held Elinor's hand as they made their way through the busy store. 'Can you buy me a new party dress?'

'Why would you need a party dress? You aren't going to any parties.'

Fiona, ever the optimist, looked up at her mum, an enchanting smile on her lips. 'One of my friends might ask me to a party.'

Elinor's heart ached for this delightful little girl of hers. She wondered, as she'd often done over the past six years, what the future would hold for Fiona when she and Colin weren't around to look after her. A shiver ran down Elinor's back and she grasped Fiona's hand even tighter. She gave her daughter a reassuring smile, determined to rid herself of any sad thoughts on this bright, sunny day.

It didn't take Elinor long to locate the children's department, where she bought four shirts for Jeffrey to allow for changing. 'Okay,' she said to Fiona, once her purchase had been paid for and the items bagged. 'Let's have a look at something new for you.'

Fiona skipped along at her mum's side on their walk over to the girls' section.

Elinor looked through the rails of dresses, many too fancy to be worn anywhere except a party or a wedding. 'Why don't we get you a summer skirt and a pretty top?' she suggested, and picked out a skirt in Fiona's size, a deep pink tiered cotton one. Nearby she spotted a white frilly top with the same shade of pink flowers embroidered on it. 'Do you like this, darling?'

Fiona clapped her hands. 'It's so pretty. Please buy it for me, Mum.'

They took the clothes to the fitting room where Elinor tried them on Fiona. 'Oh you look beautiful,' she said to her daughter, who twirled around the fitting room, admiring herself in the long mirror. They took their purchase to the check-out and afterwards Elinor led Fiona out on to Argyle

Street. 'We'll go and find a café for an ice cream before we go home.'

Halfway up Buchanan Street they saw a café and Fiona sat on a high stool beside the window to enjoy her ice cream sundae, while her mother relaxed with a cup of tea.

On their return journey, at Fiona's request, they sat upstairs on the double decker. They chose the seat above the driver's cabin and Fiona pretended to drive the bus. They were only in the house about ten minutes when Colin and Jeffrey arrived home.

The normally quiet Jeffrey talked non-stop about what they'd seen and done at the Art Gallery.

Elinor smiled at her husband. 'Your visit to the Gallery seems to have been a success.'

They all adjourned into the back garden where they settled down on the deck chairs, with Jeffrey and Fiona exchanging news of their respective outings.

Chapter Fifty One

Thursday, 23rd March, 1970

'Mum, Mum,' 7-year-old Fiona was calling out as she ran down the path from her yellow school bus that afternoon. 'I need to take £3 with me to school tomorrow because we're going to see where David Livingstone lived when he was a wee boy.' With Parkville House being in Blantyre, it wasn't difficult for staff to transport the kids to the nearby Centre commemorating the life and work of the famous explorer and missionary.

Peggy, the staff member who accompanied the children on the bus home from school, laughed over to Elinor, standing at the open door to welcome her daughter home. It was routine for Peggy to wait at the Dawson's front gate until she knew Fiona was safely in her house. 'We always say there's no need to send a note home with Fiona, as she's perfectly capable of letting you know the message,' Peggy said to Elinor.

Elinor laughed and pulled Fiona into an embrace. 'I know, she remembers everything. Have you had a good day at school, young lady?'

Fiona nodded and brushed her mum aside as she charged into the house. Elinor gave Peggy a wave as she was getting back into the bus so that Ian, the driver, could continue on his round to drop off the other children remaining in the vehicle.

***

'So how did you enjoy your time at the David Livingstone Centre today?' Elinor asked the following afternoon, as she emptied out the contents of Fiona's school bag.

'I enjoyed myself, Mum. It was a sunny day and we had a picnic in the gardens. There are flowers and swings too. And a nice lady showed us round the house where David Livingstone lived when he was at school. And guess what, he lived in one room with his mum and dad and brothers and sisters. There were eleven people living in one room.' Fiona was finally forced to pause for breath.

'Yes, we're very lucky nowadays as we have more rooms to live in and bathrooms in the house too, which people didn't have in David Livingstone's day.'

'And guess what, Mum, he only went to school until he was ten and then he had to work hard in a factory. There's a big bell on the side of his house and it used to ring when it was time for him to get out of bed and go to work.'

'And did the lady also tell you about how, when David Livingstone became a man, he was an explorer and a missionary and worked in Africa?'

Fiona nodded. 'We saw pictures of him in the jungle and healing the sick people. I'm going to play with my dolly,' Fiona said, tired of the conversation by now.

'Okay, darling. I'll bring you through a glass of milk to keep you going until dinner time,' Elinor said, dropping the peeled potatoes into a large pot and covering them with salted water.

PART III

Chapter Fifty Two

Wednesday, 30th June, 1982

'Are you sure you've got time to run us to Wimbledon this morning, Jeffrey?' Elinor asked her son as the four of them were having breakfast in the conservatory of the beautiful home he and Claire owned in Norbury, a twenty minute drive from the centre of London.

Jeffrey reached out for the marmalade and spread some on to his toast. 'Absolutely. I've a meeting scheduled for 11 o'clock but I know you want to be there when the tennis stadium opens at 10. That gives me ample time to get back into the city for my meeting,' he assured her. Jeffrey had his own parking place at the bank, which allowed him to use the car for work.

On leaving school at the age of eighteen, Jeffrey had worked in the Bank of Scotland at Burnside, before taking up a post with Barclay's bank in London a year later. He had done well in London and was promoted six months ago. Elinor hadn't been too happy when she heard that Jeffrey and his girlfriend, Claire, had bought a home together. She knew that many couples these days lived together before marriage but she was old-fashioned enough to prefer that the wedding had come first. However, once she'd met Claire and seen how well suited and happy the couple were, her fears had subsided a little.

'That's really kind of you, Jeffrey,' Joanne said. 'And if we get there early before the matches begin, we can have a look round the museum and also spend some time at the shop. I'd like to buy Dougie a sweater or a t-shirt with the

Wimbledon logo on it.'

Claire smiled at her. 'You'll get that alright, but it'll cost you a pretty penny.'

Joanne shrugged. 'It's a special occasion, so I don't mind too much. After all, it isn't every day that we'll be at Wimbledon.' Dougie had applied for tickets in the Wimbledon ballot, and was lucky enough to get Centre Court tickets for the Quarter Finals. He gave them to her and Elinor, who were both keen tennis fans.

'Yes, please.' Elinor nodded when Claire offered to pour her more tea. 'If you run us to the tennis stadium, Jeffrey, we can make our own way back after the matches. Can you tell us which route on the underground we should take?'

'It's really easy, Mum. You use the Northern Line and get on at South Wimbledon underground station. It's only a short walk from the tennis stadium to the underground. It takes about eight minutes to reach Balham, where you wait on the same platform for the Norbury train. It takes about six minutes to Norbury and you're unlikely to wait more than five minutes at Balham for your transfer. If the trains are running to time, it will only take you about nineteen minutes for the whole journey.'

'I use the Northern Line for work and I think I've got a map I can lend you,' Claire said, as she collected her breakfast dishes and carried them through to the kitchen. A few minutes later she returned, wearing her jacket, and laid the map down beside Elinor's plate. 'There you go, that should keep you right.'

'Thanks, love,' Elinor smiled up at her.

'Right, I'm off to work. See you both tonight and I'll hear about your day at the tennis.' Claire kissed Jeffrey as she passed his chair and they heard the front door close softly behind her.

Jeffrey dropped them off as planned and they showed their tickets as they entered the stadium. 'This is exciting, Joanne, isn't it?

Joanne giggled. 'I know, we're like a couple of schoolgirls setting off on a great adventure. I've always wanted to watch the tennis live.'

'Same here,' Elinor said, as they made their way to the shops. Joanne got her gift for Dougie, and Elinor bought a tea shirt for Fiona and a skip cap for Colin. 'I think I'll get this shopper with the Wimbledon logo on it for Jeffrey and Claire,' she said to Joanne.

'Tell you what,' Joanne suggested, 'let's buy it between us and it'll be a thank you for having us both to stay at their place.' Next they had a look round the Wimbledon museum, which showed lots of old style tennis rackets and outfits.

Their seats in row G afforded them an excellent view of the court and they soaked up the atmosphere as the seats around them began to fill up with excited fans, all laughing and chatting in anticipation of the matches ahead. Joanne nudged Elinor and pointed. 'Look over there in the corner, the Chelsea Pensioners.'

Elinor looked over and there they were, all dressed in their splendid red tunics. 'They must be boiling hot in their uniforms,' she said, as the crowd quietened for a moment while the Duchess of Kent took her seat in the Royal Box. 'I remember watching on TV last year and the Princess of Wales was in the Royal Box,' Elinor whispered to her friend.

'Yes, she was Lady Diana Spencer at that time.'

'And now, eleven months on, she's a wife and mother to baby William.'

A few minutes later the announcement that the first ladies' quarter final was about to begin came over the tannoy system. Joanne and Elinor cheered with the other spectators when Tracy Austin walked on to the court, followed by Billy Jean King. After that match, came another exciting tussle, a fourth round match between Roscoe Tanner and Vitas Gerulaitis.

The two singles matches were followed by two doubles, the first of which included the partnership of John McEnroe and Peter Fleming. In true fashion, McEnroe shouted at the Umpire from time to time, and threw his racket down on the grass, incurring himself a court violation.

'I can't help liking McEnroe despite his behaviour,' Elinor whispered to her friend, during a round of applause in between shots.

Joanne nodded. 'He's a star player, without a doubt.' She fell silent as John raised his racket to serve out his shot at 'Advantage to McEnroe'. By the end of that match Elinor and Joanne felt exhausted, both from the heat of the sun beating down on them and also from nervous tension.

Joanne nudged Elinor. 'What do you say if we go and buy a cool drink and sit in the shade for a while. We can come back later to watch some of the next match?'

Elinor got to her feet at once. 'Great idea, let's do that.'

'These strawberries look gorgeous,' Elinor said, as they were purchasing their drinks at a refreshment stall in the grounds.

'Strawberries and cream for two, please,' Joanne said to the assistant on the stall. 'We can sit over there,' she said to Elinor and they carried their desserts and drinks over to some tables and chairs set out in the fenced off area for the use of customers. They watched the crowds milling around while they ate their dessert.

'These are so lovely,' Elinor said, popping a fat, juicy

strawberry smothered in fresh cream into her mouth.

'Yes, we'll enjoy them and not think of the price. £5 for the two dishes of,' and Joanne counted what was in her dish, 'six strawberries and a couple of spoonfuls of cream.'

'Who cares?' Elinor relished every mouthful.

The mixed doubles match, Tony Roche and Miss Jenny Byrne against Ian Goolagong and Mrs Evonne Goolagong Cawley, was nearing the end of the first set when the two friends got back to their seats in the stadium. Both girls had always enjoyed watching the Australian player, Evonne Goolagong, as she was before she became Mrs Cawley. On this occasion she was partnering her brother, and the sibling team took the second set after losing the fist one six-love. The girls settled down to enjoy the deciding set.

At the completion of play on Centre Court, the two friends made their way out of the stadium in the evening sunshine, happy after their exhilarating day.

'Are you glad you came?' Joanne asked Elinor, when they were sitting on the tube on the way back to Norbury.

'I sure am. I know Colin and Fiona will have got on fine without me.' It was the first time since her daughter was born that Elinor had gone anywhere without Fiona. But Colin had persuaded her to go to London with Joanne, saying he was happy to remain at home with Fiona.

Chapter Fifty Three

Monday, 15th July, 1985

Elinor was out of breath when she walked into the 'Wee Blethers' coffee shop. Joanne was already seated at a table. This café in Union Street was their usual meeting place. They'd chosen it as Glasgow City Centre was convenient for Elinor coming from Rutherglen and also for Joanne travelling from Lenzie. Joanne and Dougie had bought a house there when the car dealership Dougie managed moved to Bishopbriggs from their previous site on the south side of the city.

'Hello, Elinor,' Joanne greeted her long-time friend, 'is this table alright?'

Elinor nodded and exhaled loudly. 'The bus was held up and I didn't want to keep you waiting. By the time I got to Union Street, I was puffing away like an old woman.'

'You shouldn't have rushed. Mind you, I think we're both in good nick for two 47-year-olds. And how are things?'

Elinor hung her jacket over the back of the chair. 'Good thanks. Have you decided what to have?'

Joanne drummed her fingers on the table while she studied the menu. 'Can't make up my mind between steak pie or fish and chips. The soup of the day is either lentil broth or carrot and orange.'

'I like the sound of carrot and orange. I might have a soup and order a slice of gateau with my coffee afterwards.'

'Good idea. Think I'll plump for that myself.'

They gave their order to the waitress and then sat back to enjoy a good gossip.

'So what's been happening?' Joanne asked.

'Well, Colin and I are hoping for good news soon

from Jeffrey. As you know, he and Claire have been together for four years now and we think a wedding is in the offing.'

'Oh, how exciting. My Godson about to be married.'

Elinor held up her hand. 'We don't know for certain but have surmised it from some things Jeffrey has said. Of course, they've lived together for years.'

Joanne shrugged. 'It's the way of the world these days, Elinor. I guess we have to move with the times.'

Elinor nodded. 'But I'm glad my mum didn't live to see it. She'd have been so upset to see her grandson living with his girlfriend before marriage.' Speaking about her mum, reminded Elinor of how distraught Fiona had been when Grandma Susan passed away following a massive stroke just a few months before Jeffrey went to London. Having idolised her grandma, Fiona was devastated over her death. Thankfully, by now she was slowly coming to terms with her loss.

'Who'd have thought how quickly ideas and morals would have changed over the last twenty years,' Joanne said, then stopped speaking when the waitress appeared with their soups.

'How's Lorna doing at Jordanhill?' Elinor asked, as she buttered her bread roll.

'She's loving it. Seems to be a born teacher. Dougie and I are amazed, when we think back on how hard it was pushing her to do her school homework.'

'But she was just a teenager back then.'

The two women tucked into their soup and, when they were finished, Joanne pushed her empty soup bowl aside. 'I brought a photograph taken at Lorna's recent college dance.'

Elinor looked at the picture and smiled. 'Lorna looks gorgeous, her dress is magnificent.'

'Dougie couldn't believe how mature his wee girl looked. The fair-haired lad behind Lorna is Roger and it seems he and Lorna have become an item.'

'What a handsome looking chap.'

'He is, isn't he? You know, of course, that your Jeffrey has always been Lorna's hero. She's been in love with him since she was about 10.'

Elinor chuckled. 'Yes, I guessed that, and Jeffrey adored her, looked on her like another wee sister.'

'Jeffrey's done really well since he went to work down in London. You and Colin must be so proud of him.'

'Yes, we were delighted when he got another promotion in the bank recently.'

'Wasn't it in the bank that he met Claire?'

'Yes, she was a teller in the same branch in Whitechapel.' Elinor stopped speaking for a moment and stared out of the window. 'Although he's only brought Claire up to visit us a couple of times, we do like her.'

Joanne nodded. 'I certainly liked her when we stayed with them on our trip to Wimbledon in '82.'

'Fiona thinks she's wonderful.'

'Fiona loves everyone. She also does you and Colin proud.'

The waitress came over at that moment and cleared away their soup plates.

Joanne smiled at the young girl. 'You're kept busy. Have you worked here long?'

'I'm a student so it's just a summer job. I'll be leaving in a couple of weeks to return to college. Can I get anything else for you, ladies?' she asked, looking from Joanne to Elinor as she spoke.

'I'll have a slice of your delicious Black Forest gateau and a white coffee, please,' Joanne told her.

'Coffee for me too,' Elinor said, 'and I'll have the apple tart.'

'It's good that our kids have found someone to share their lives with, isn't it?' Elinor resumed the conversation once their cakes had arrived. 'Apart from Fiona, of course.'

Seeing the sadness on her friend's face, Joanne brushed her fingers over Elinor's hand. 'Fiona's a very happy young lady and that's thanks to you and Colin. She's well-adjusted and has even managed to get a job.'

Elinor smiled. 'That's true. She likes working in the hairdresser's shop in Hamilton Road. She only washes the hair, of course, as she couldn't cope with handling the money. Colin and I tried to teach her but she can only work out very basic sums.'

'But it's wonderful that she can hold down a job and earn herself a little money. Helps to make her feel independent.'

Elinor's face turned serious once more. 'Yes, and I'm glad of that....'

'But...' her friend put in.

'Colin and I do worry about what will happen to Fiona when we're gone. We don't want Jeffrey to have to take on the responsibility of looking after her.'

'Och, you and Colin have years ahead of you and, knowing Jeffrey, he'd be happy to help Fiona if necessary. And Dougie and I would be here too. Now, before we get too morbid, let's pay the bill and have a look around the shops.'

An hour later, after making some purchases in their favourite store, the two women parted company outside Marks and Spencer. Joanne planned to walk up to Sauchiehall Street to get her bus while Elinor would catch a bus for Rutherglen here on Argyle Street.

'See you in a few weeks' time, Elinor,' Joanne said, embracing her best friend, before the two of them walked off in opposite directions.

Chapter Fifty Four

Thursday, 12ᵗʰ December, 1985

'How many more hours until I can wear my bridesmaid's dress?'

Elinor closed her eyes for an instant and counted to ten when she heard Fiona asking this question for about the sixth time since they'd left Rutherglen that morning. Colin glanced round at his wife from the driver's seat and grinned. She smiled back at him and scratched her head as she calculated the hours until they were due at the registry office.

'Mum, how many hours?' Fiona persisted.

'Hang on, darling, I'm counting them. Okay, it's four o'clock now and the wedding is in two days' time, at two o'clock. So that will be about forty six hours.'

'Forty six hours. That's a long time, isn't it?'

Elinor shook her head. 'Not really, Fiona. There will be lots for you to help with, such as checking that the flowers will be delivered on time and going with Claire to collect the dresses. And tomorrow we will all be going to the Inn for a meal and to check up on last minute things. The time will go by in a flash.'

Colin glanced at Elinor again. 'Can you check the map, love, to see if we need to go through Croydon to get on to the A23? I don't think we did last time we visited Jeffrey so we may be able to by-pass the town and go direct to Norbury.'

Fiona fell silent while Elinor concentrated on directing Colin and soon they were on the right road for Norbury. A short time later they were drawing up outside Jeffrey and Claire's front door.

'Hi there, so you've made it,' Jeffrey's voice came

from the garage, where he'd been checking his tyre pressures.

'Great to see you all,' he said, when he came out of the garage and greeted his family. Claire came out of the house and there were hugs all round. Jeffrey helped Colin get their luggage out of the boot and into the house.

'It's only forty six hours until I can wear my bridesmaid's dress,' Fiona told Claire, jumping up and down in excitement. Claire had asked her friend, Pauline, to be the chief bridesmaid and sign the register, with Fiona as the second one.

Elinor looked at her watch. 'It's only forty four hours now, darling. She's been asking this question constantly,' she mouthed to Claire, as they made their way indoors to be greeted by the delicious smell of cooking coming from the kitchen.

***

'Oh, what a pleasant place, ideal for a wedding,' Elinor said next day, when they all entered the Mallard Inn, a few minutes' walk from Jeffrey and Claire's home. The young waitress smiled in recognition and came over and led them to a large table at the front of the inn, where they had a view from the bay window over the fields facing the building.

'Hello, Amanda.' Jeffrey smiled at the waitress. 'Amanda here is going to look after us at the reception tomorrow.'

'I will indeed.' Amanda gave each of them a lunch menu. 'What would you like to drink?'

Jeffrey looked around the group. 'Is wine alright for everyone?' Getting a positive response, he turned back to Amanda. 'Could you bring us a bottle of house red and one of white?'

'Certainly.' Amanda went to the bar, leaving them to study the menu.

'There are quite a number of hotels and inns in Norbury,' Claire explained, once they'd placed their lunch order, 'but the Mallard was the first place Jeffrey and I came to when we moved into the house so it holds a special place in our hearts.'

Elinor smiled. 'That's a lovely romantic idea. Is the registry office close at hand too?'

'It's only a couple of minutes by car from here,' Jeffrey told her. 'We could easily walk to each venue but decided to do it in style and order some wedding cars.'

'And I should think so too,' his mother said, looking aghast at the thought of them walking, even though she knew he was joking.

'We can go to 'The Flower Basket' on the way home to make sure everything is under control with the flowers for tomorrow,' Claire said.

'And what about the dresses?' Fiona asked.

Claire laughed. 'Don't worry, Fiona, we are also going to the dressmaker's shop, which is next door to the florist. Pauline couldn't make it for lunch today but she's going to meet us for our final fitting of the dresses. You men can make yourself scarce,' she said to Jeffrey and Colin, 'it's supposed to be bad luck for the bridegroom to see the wedding dress in advance.'

'No problem.' Jeffrey looked across the table at his dad. 'You and I can go and have a drink at the golf club, Dad.' He stopped speaking and sat back as Amanda arrived with the wine they'd ordered.

***

'You both look a picture,' Elinor told Fiona and Pauline next day, as they stood in the bedroom wearing their deep rose pink taffeta dresses. Elinor kissed both girls lightly on the cheek, not wanting to spoil the face make-up that had

219

been applied. The hairdresser had come to the house that morning and had set their hair into a page boy style .

Elinor turned to face Claire. 'My dear, you are magnificent, I hope my son appreciates what a beauty he's getting.' Claire's dress was white brocade with pearls sewn on to the front of the bodice and down the full skirt. Her blonde curls framed her face and a tiara secured her long veil on to her head. The veil was patterned with butterflies. The toes of her white satin high-heeled shoes peeped out from under her dress as she walked.

At the registry office Claire walked down the aisle on the arm of her dad, Norman. When she stood beside Jeffrey, in front of the celebrant, Norman, a widower, slid into the front row beside his sister-in-law, Sheila, who was taking the place of the bride's mother for the day. The ceremony over, the bridal party and their guests moved on to the Mallard Inn, where the wedding photographs were taken in the gardens behind the inn. Although mostly greenery at this time of year, some late-flowering bushes gave colour to the pictures.

Inside, the inn was decorated for Christmas with a brightly-bedecked tree in one corner and some sprigs of holly and mistletoe in evidence. A toast was drunk to the happy couple and the cake was cut. Pauline ran over and held a sprig of mistletoe above the newly weds, who gladly obliged and kissed under it. Norman took Elinor and Colin under his wing, introducing them to Sheila. Then he steered them towards a group of people seated at a nearby table. 'Elinor and Colin are Jeffrey's parents,' he told the folk at the table. 'Louise and Derek, Nancy and Clive and Emily and Bob,' he introduced his friends to the Dawsons.

'Have a seat beside me, Elinor,' Louise invited, while Colin sat down between Derek and Nancy. Elinor knew she'd never remember all the names but they were a friendly bunch and she felt relaxed and easy in their company.

Later, at the end of the meal, Matt, one of Jeffrey's bosses in the bank, came over to speak to her and Colin. Matt endeared himself to Elinor by singing the praises of her son.

She and Colin were proud of their son's speech and delighted that the young couple had enjoyed their wedding day so much. Elinor knew it was a day she'd always remember and seeing the joy on Fiona's face at being a bridesmaid added to the happiness of the occasion for her.

Chapter Fifty Five

Saturday, 31st May, 1986

'Right folks, think we better head off if we want to get a good place in the crowd,' Jeffrey said, once the breakfast dishes had been washed and dried.

Fiona, who'd been watching the weather report on television, looked up. 'Are we going in your car, Jeffrey?' This was the family's first visit to Norbury since Jeffrey and Claire's wedding six months ago and she was looking forward to a run in her brother's flash car.

Jeffrey smiled at his sister. 'No, Fi, it's a nightmare trying to park in the city. Best we use the tube.'

'But we can go into your parking place at the bank, can't we?'

'No, the bank's too far from The Mall, Fi,' Claire said, putting bottles of water into a cool box. 'You'll enjoy the journey on the tube.'

Elinor nodded, looking at Fiona. 'That's right, Auntie Joanne and I loved travelling on the underground when we were down at Wimbledon a few years ago. It's great fun watching all the people on the tube and trying to guess where they are going and at which station they'll get off.'

'Oh yes, that sounds fun.' Fiona's disappointment at not getting a run in Jeffrey's car vanished immediately.

Fiona did indeed enjoy her journey and, coming out of Green Park underground station, the family walked to The Mall, where a vast crowd had already assembled.

'Go to the right nearer the palace,' Jeffrey instructed and the five of them squeezed into a space behind the barrier. Metropolitan police officers stood at intervals along The Mall in front of the barriers to ensure people didn't cross over on to the concourse in front of Buckingham Palace.

'We should get a good view of the carriage coming through the palace gates from here,' Colin said to the others.

'You'll need to have the camera at the ready,' Elinor reminded him. She bent down and directed Fiona's gaze towards the palace. 'See that big archway, darling, the coach will come through there.'

'When will it come?'

'Soon, darling.'

The time passed quickly as they watched spectators jockeying for a good position behind the barriers, excitement coursing through the crowd. The police officers were happy to chat to members of the public who'd come to see the spectacle while, at the same time, keeping their alert eyes trained on what was happening around them.

When at last the open carriage, pulled by magnificent horses ridden by members of the Queen's Household Cavalry, came through the archway and passed near where the family were standing, Fiona looked up at her mother. 'But where's the Queen, Mum? The seats are empty.'

'Oh no, the Queen isn't here today, darling. This is a rehearsal for Trooping the Colour in two weeks' time.' Elinor stroked Fiona's arm and bent to kiss the top of her head. 'They need to rehearse today to make sure that everything is perfectly timed so that there will be no hitches in a fortnight's time when the Queen will be present and sitting in her carriage.'

The police officer facing them, with his back to the carriage, smiled at Fiona. 'Your mum's right, this is just a rehearsal. You'll have to come back in two weeks' time if you want to see the Queen.'

Fiona sighed. 'I can't. I live in Rutherglen and it's a

long way to come.'

'Oh well,' the officer replied, 'you'll have to watch it on telly instead. But there's loads to see, plus all this lovely music we're being treated to.' He moved over a little to his right to answer a question posed by another spectator in the crowd.

'Okay, everybody happy to move on now?' Jeffrey asked, when the carriage was almost out of sight at the top of The Mall. 'It'll be ages before the carriage returns to the palace as they still have a full rehearsal to get through on Horse Guards Parade. How about us going up to Kensington High Street to find a nice café.'

'Great,' Elinor replied. 'I could really do with a seat. With this heat, my feet are killing me.'

'Right, follow me,' Jeffrey said and led the way through the crowd. Kensington High Street was also jam packed but the café they went into was cool, with lots of ceiling fans circulating air over the customers.

***

'It's beautiful,' Fiona said, her breath leaving marks on the glass case which held the Crown. 'It sparkles so much.'

Elinor stood behind Fiona, with her hands on her daughter's shoulders. 'Yes, that purple stone came from India. India used to be under the rule of Britain, in fact the country of India was known as the jewel in the crown of the British Empire.'

'Come and see this one, Fiona,' Claire called out, and they moved over to a nearby glass case with a different crown on display. Fiona gazed at the fabulous items in the case.

'Are you glad Jeffrey brought us to the Tower to see all these wonderful things?' Elinor asked, as they were making their way out of the viewing room.

Fiona nodded, unable to put her feelings into words.

They visited a few more places of interest, including St Paul's Cathedral, where Prince Charles and Lady Diana Spencer had been married in 1981. A guide in the cathedral showed them around and gave them some leaflets with the history of the church to take home with them.

***

'Oh, it's so lovely and cool out here.' Elinor voiced all their feelings as they lay back in garden chairs on the patio that evening. 'I loved everything you showed us Jeffrey but my feet were protesting because of the heat.' She stretched out to take another drink of her shandy.

'There's still a lot Claire and I want to show you in the next few days but we'll take things at a slower pace and not try to fit in so much sightseeing in one day. Now what would you all say if we go along to the Mallard shortly for a meal?'

Receiving general assent, he got up out of his deck chair. 'Okay, I'll phone and book a table for eight o'clock. That'll give us time to change into our glad rags.'

Chapter Fifty Six

Sunday, 7th April, 1996

It was on Easter Sunday that Elinor's tranquil family life ended. Being a holiday weekend, Fiona was at Ayr with her friends from Parkville House. Although Fiona had left Parkville when she was eighteen, Mrs Chalmers had kept in touch with her and Elinor. Fiona was often invited to join in any weekends away. She was there in the capacity of carer because she loved looking after the younger children in the group.

With Fiona away, Elinor and Colin went to the Easter service at church and planned a restful day thereafter. When Elinor went to the toilet in the middle of the afternoon, she noticed a smear of blood on the white porcelain. Colin had seemed a bit under the weather lately although he would never admit to being ill. When she returned to the living room, she gently challenged him about the blood.

At first he made no reply but when he looked up the worry etched on his face alarmed her. 'Colin, please tell me what's going on.'

Another silence ensued until Colin finally confided in her that he'd passed blood three times in the past few days. He'd felt scared and hoped it would go away but this obviously wasn't going to happen.

'Why didn't you say? We can make an appointment with Dr Pearson. It will likely be easily remedied.' Elinor tried to sound upbeat for Colin's sake but she felt deeply uneasy. Elinor had been sorry when Dr Orchard retired last year, especially as he'd been so caring of Fiona, but she'd found his younger colleague equally easy to talk to and by now she had great faith in his judgement.

'How many times have you passed blood?' Dr Pearson asked on Tuesday morning, when Colin and Elinor were sitting in his consulting room. Elinor had impressed on the receptionist that Colin needed to be seen urgently and had been given a cancellation.

'Three times.' Colin hesitated for a moment, then added, 'and I passed some more this morning.'

Elinor looked at her husband in surprise; she hadn't realised it had happened again this morning.

Dr Pearson got up from his chair. 'If you could lie on the couch, Mr Dawson, I'll check you over.'

During the examination, Elinor prayed that Dr Pearson wouldn't discover anything nasty. The doctor returned to his desk and wrote something on Colin's notes.

'I can't detect anything untoward, Mr Dawson, but it is important to find the cause of the bleeding. I'll take some blood from you now for testing and I'll refer you to a specialist at the Victoria Infirmary. I'll request an urgent appointment so we can find the cause quickly and begin any necessary treatment.'

'I'm glad you were with me, love,' Colin said, once they'd left the surgery, 'I can't remember half of what Dr Pearson told us.'

'Don't worry, it'll all work out,' she said, as optimistically as she could. 'You'll receive treatment for it. It might be a simple wee cyst which could be cut out and then you'll be as right as rain in no time.'

When they got back home, Colin sank down in his favourite armchair.

'Will I pour you a wee whisky, darling?' Elinor asked him. 'Fiona will be home soon from Ayr and she'll cheer us up with all her tales about the weekend.'

Just then, as if on cue, Fiona came into the hallway, having been dropped off at the house by the Parkville mini bus. 'Mum, Dad, I'm home,' she called, as she came into the living room, where she dropped her case at the side of the settee. 'I've loads to tell you,' she promised, giving each of them a big hug.

Elinor smiled at her daughter. 'I thought you might. Sit down and tell us everything.'

'The hotel was lovely and Mr and Mrs Williamson made us very welcome,' Fiona began, looking from one parent to the other as she spoke. 'Mr Williamson is a chef, who used to work for the Navy. He was made redundant and then they opened the hotel. Mrs Williamson helps him with the cooking and they employ two girls who work as waitresses. Their names are Sandra and Maureen and they both told me they like working in the hotel.' Fiona stopped speaking for a moment to draw breath, then turned to Elinor. 'I'd like to be a waitress, Mum, but I also like my job in the hairdressers'.'

Elinor nodded. 'I know you do and the shop is so near that you don't have any travelling expenses. You got good weather when you were in Ayr, didn't you?'

'It was gorgeous. Some days it got too hot to sit outside and we had to go into a café to keep cool. Mrs Chalmers was worried in case the girls would burn in the hot sun. I helped her put suncream on the girls' faces and arms.'

'I hope you remembered to put cream on your own skin,' Elinor said.

'Yes, I did.'

'Did you go to the beach?' Colin spoke for the first time, trying to keep his voice lighthearted.

'Yes we did, Dad, and I walked along the wall at the prom just like Jeffrey and I used to do when we were little and went to Ayr with you and Mum.'

'That's great, darling,' he replied, smiling at the thought of his diminutive daughter speaking about when she was little.

Elinor got to her feet. 'You tell Dad more about your holiday, Fiona, and I'll go and organise the meal for later.'

Chapter Fifty Seven

Monday, 15th April, 1996

Six days after their visit to the G.P., Elinor sat beside Colin in the hospital waiting room, the walls painted in a soft shade of green. To calm the patients I suppose, Elinor thought; she'd always been told that green was the most calming colour. There were posters on the walls, some advertising clinics to come off smoking or sleeping tablets, and others about diet. She knew Colin's anxiety about the forthcoming appointment matched her own but they both tried to keep their concern at bay by chatting quietly about incidentals.

'Mr Dawson.' A short, stoutly-built nurse, holding a set of casenotes, stood in the doorway. Colin raised his hand and the nurse smiled brightly. 'Can you come with me?' she said, and Colin and Elinor followed her down the corridor to the Consultant's room. The specialist got to his feet as they entered the room and he shook hands with them, introducing himself as Mr Hay. He looked about the same age as Colin and towered above both of them. 'Please take a seat,' he invited.

Once they had done so, he sat at his desk, facing them. He looked over his rimless spectacles at Colin. 'Now, Mr Dawson, I understand you've been referred to me by your G.P., Dr Pearson, because of recent bleeding. Is that right?'

'Yes,' Colin agreed.

'Dr Pearson took some blood for testing,' Elinor put in.

'I have the result of your tests here.' The doctor looked down at the blue and white result forms in front of him. 'No abnormalities have shown up,' he told Colin, looking from him to Elinor. 'But I think it would be worthwhile for us to repeat the blood tests today.'

Mr Hay took off his specs and laid them down on his desk. He clasped his hands and looked at Colin again. 'I would also like to arrange for you to come into hospital over the next few days for a body scan. Are you okay with that?'

Seeing Colin nod, Mr Hay wrote something in his notes. Then he completed another blood request form and handed it to Colin. 'If you and your wife could take a seat in the corridor, Mr Dawson, a nurse will take some blood from you and she will also arrange an appointment for your scan. When we have the results of your scan, I will see you again.' He shook hands with Colin and Elinor once more and they left his consulting room.

They were sitting in the corridor for about ten minutes when a young nurse approached them and ushered them into the treatment room, where she took another lot of blood for testing.

'I'm beginning to feel like a pin cushion,' Colin said, attempting a joke.

The nurse smiled. 'At least you have good veins which makes my job easier.' She put a sticker with his details on the phials of blood and placed them into a wire basket on a shelf near the door. Then she handed Colin a green appointment card. 'I've made an appointment for you to attend for a scan on Tuesday of next week.'

'Thank you.' Colin took the card and handed it to Elinor, who put it into her handbag for safekeeping.

'Will you find your way back to the exit?' the nurse asked, opening the door for them.

'Yes, thanks,' Elinor replied, and both she and Colin smiled at the nurse as they left.

***

'How did Dad get on today?' Jeffrey asked Elinor that

evening on the phone.

'He got on fine. The specialist couldn't find anything wrong with his blood but they're going to do a body scan next Tuesday just to be certain.'

'Well it's good to know they are being thorough. It's always better to check these things. Has he had any further bleeding?'

'No, he hasn't and I think this has helped curb his anxiety a bit.' Elinor didn't say to Jeffrey that she would have preferred they had found some abnormality in the blood samples and been able to treat Colin. 'Do you want a word with Dad?'

'Sure.'

Elinor laid down the receiver and popped her head round the living room door, where Colin was watching a quiz programme. 'Jeffrey's on the phone and wanted to hear how you got on at the appointment today.'

Fiona looked up from the picture she was drawing. 'I want to speak to Jeffrey too.'

'That's fine darling. You can speak to him once Dad is finished on the phone.' Elinor smiled fondly at her daughter, glad that she and Jeffrey were so close.

From her armchair Elinor could hear the one side of Colin's conversation with his son and was pleased that Colin sounded so upbeat. She was worried sick about him but best that not too much of this was conveyed to Jeffrey or Fiona meantime.

***

Elinor picked at her nails and stared at the posters on the wall of the waiting room, just as she'd done at their last appointment with Mr Hay. The waiting room was much busier today and Colin had to sit on the opposite side from her. She could see the tension lining his face and she ached with love and tenderness for this man she'd lived with and loved for so many years. While she sat there, she tried to pray, but the words would not come.

'I have both good and bad news, Mr Dawson,' the specialist started, once they were sitting in his consulting room, 'the bad news is that your tests have revealed a stomach tumour.'

Elinor heard herself gasp and saw Colin's face turn ashen. Noticing his hand tremble, she reached over and grasped it with her own shaking hand.

Dr Hay went on to explain things to them. 'Although an operation isn't appropriate in your case, Mr Dawson, the good news is that a session of chemotherapy, with possible radiotherapy thereafter, gives us a chance of treating and hopefully resolving your condition.'

Neither Elinor nor Colin recalled later how they got home after receiving the devastating news. In bed that night, they held one another tightly, clinging on to the positive way Mr Hay had spoken about Colin's forthcoming treatment.

Chapter Fifty Eight

Thursday, 10th April, 1997

Somehow Elinor got through the day, willing herself to stay strong and comfort her grieving daughter. Fiona had hero-worshipped her dad and his death had torn her world apart. She clung to Elinor and Jeffrey during the funeral service at Linn Crematorium. Later, while they were at the funeral tea in the Kings Park Hotel, Fiona shadowed her mum around the room as Elinor spoke to the mourners and thanked them for coming.

Back at the house, it felt empty and dismal without Colin. During his illness, when it had become obvious that the treatment hadn't worked and that his condition was terminal, Elinor had tried to explain things to Fiona. She told her that, although her dad would soon leave them and go to Heaven, he'd live on in their hearts. But, despite this, both of them were unprepared when the end came.

'When do you need to return to London?' Elinor asked Jeffrey, when the four of them sat around the table that night, playing with their food, no-one having any appetite.

'The day after tomorrow, Mum. I wish we could stay longer but I have some important meetings next week that I need to attend.'

'It's no problem, Jeffrey,' Elinor said to her son, smiling at him. 'Of course you need to get back. Fiona and I were glad of your support today, weren't we, darling?' she said, putting her arm round her daughter's shoulders and cuddling her.

Tears rolled down Fiona's cheeks. 'I wish you'd come here and stay forever,' she said between sobs to her beloved brother and his wife.

'We'll be up again soon.' Claire, tears filling her eyes, stretched out and placed one hand on Fiona's and the other on Elinor's. 'That's a promise.'

Fiona cried herself to sleep that night and, once she finally dropped off and Jeffrey and Claire had retired for the night, Elinor returned to the living room.

She sat on the sofa nursing a mug of cocoa in her hands; she cried when she looked at the words on the mug, 'The Best Wife in the World'. Inside she felt dark, cold and empty. The lamp at her side shed a soft glow over and around her, highlighting the silvery thread that ran through the pattern on the soft green wallpaper.

Elinor stared at a framed photograph sitting on the mantelpiece. It was a picture of her and Colin, taken during their honeymoon in Morecambe. She sighed at how young they looked and so much in love. We couldn't imagine a day when one of us would be left alone, she thought, swallowing hard to get rid of the lump in her throat.

Tears rolled down Elinor's cheeks as she thought back to the harrowing period of chemotherapy. Colin had suffered many side effects, but he struggled on in a desperate attempt to get better. She recalled how well he'd been for the first five months after his treatment had finished. There was a good spell over the Festive season but in the first few days of January his symptoms had returned. It was in early February that they were given the devastating news that there was no hope of a recovery. Things seemed to move rapidly from then on and she'd found it difficult to comprehend what was happening. It was worse for poor Colin and he spent his last couple of weeks in the Prince and Princess of Wales' Hospice in Glasgow. At least there he could be given suitable pain relief.

It hit her forcibly at that moment that her beloved Colin would not be returning, that he was gone from her forever. Although she'd tried to remain calm for Fiona's sake, Elinor's Christian faith had been shaken by Colin's death and she was finding it hard to try to come to terms with his loss after such a cruel illness. Her tears came fast and furiously now and she curled herself into a ball and sobbed and sobbed. During the time she'd been sitting here the heating had gone off and she began to shiver with the cold.

Shortly afterwards, she got up and switched off the lamp. The room was plunged into darkness, like the darkness she felt in her soul, and slowly she made her way into the hall, feeling her way towards the stairs. As she got into her bed, she reached out to the empty space at her side and her tears began afresh. She lay there in the darkness, sobbing, with no hope of sleep taking her away from her misery.

Chapter Fifty Nine

Tuesday, 12ᵗʰ May, 1998

Elinor came indoors from pegging out the washing when she heard the postman pushing the mail through her letterbox. There was an electricity bill, a few pieces of junk mail and a letter from Dot, with something enclosed by the weight of it. She glanced through the electricity bill, which thankfully wasn't as bad as she'd been expecting, and sat down at the kitchen table with a mug of coffee for company while she read Dot's news.

6ᵗʰ May 1998

Dear Elinor

Thank you for your last letter and I'm sorry for taking so long to reply. I've been busy clearing out things of Mum's. There was a lot to go through as she was such a hoarder. As I told you when Mum passed away last July – can't believe it's almost a year ago – I couldn't face going through everything at that stage. It's taken me until now to set to and get on with the task and I feel better now that I have de-cluttered. I came across some nice photos of my parents and yours. I have chosen some to keep and I am enclosing a few for you which I hope you will like. They bring back memories of happy times.

It was good to read that Fiona is well and still enjoying her work in the hairdresser's shop. You said you'd been busy in the garden; I know how much you enjoy your garden, Elinor, and it lets you get out in the fresh air and of course the exercise that is so good for us all. I don't think I get enough exercise although I do still walk with my rambling group from time to time.

Winter has started early here and it's very cold. It probably wouldn't seem cold to you hardy individuals in U.K. but cold for us warm-blooded antipodeans! Hopefully we'll get an early spring this year. I hate the winter and yearn for the warm days to return. Don't think I could exist in your neck of the woods, Elinor!

I was pleased to hear that you feel more positive now and beginning to come to terms with the loss of your beloved Colin, although of course the pain never really heals. I know how hard it has been for me to lose Mum so I can only imagine how much more difficult it was for you to part with your spouse. It's great that you and Fiona are so close and of course I know Jeffrey and Claire are very supportive too.

Since Mum died, I have taken up my golf again and have joined the Eastern Golf Club. The club house is a magnificent building, erected around the late 1800s, when the property was known as Tullimore Mansion. Another plus is that the golf club is quite near Doncaster. Why Doncaster I can hear you ask? The answer is that I decided it was time to move and have bought a unit in Doncaster, at 25 Burgundy Street. That is one of the reasons for the present clear out as I don't want to take too many belongings with me to Doncaster. I sold this house easily, put it up for auction. The Blackwoods, the young couple who bought my house, aren't long married and have been living in rented accommodation up to now. I'm reminded of my parents who bought the house as a new-build shortly after their marriage. The Blackwoods plan to move in here next week and I will take up residence in Burgundy Street on the same day. So it seems to have worked out – fingers crossed no problems arise on the day of the move.

As I am due to retire next month, I will commute between Blackburn and Doncaster until then. I've enjoyed my years of nursing but feel ready now to retire and have more time to myself. I've a week's holiday due to me so will either leave a week prior to my retirement date or be paid for the week. I will keep you posted on that.

Elinor, once I move into my new unit, I wondered if you and Fiona would like to come over to visit me? I know it's still early days since Colin's death but I thought a trip away might be something you'd enjoy. Although the Doncaster unit is smaller than this family house, it is plenty big enough to accommodate us all as it has three bedrooms. I've never met Fiona and would love to do so and, of course, to see your dear self again too. It would be a joy for me to show you and Fiona something of Melbourne and perhaps take you back to some of your old haunts when you lived here in the 1950s.

I know this suggestion will have come like a bolt out of the blue for you. I have been thinking about it for a couple of years now although I shelved the idea when Colin was ill. You don't need to say yes or no right now, Elinor, but please think about it. You can talk it over with Fiona and Jeffrey and let me know later if you'd like to come.

I'll close for now Elinor and you can address your next letter to me at 25 Burgundy Street, Doncaster, 3108. I know you have my phone numbers, both mobile and landline (I am taking my landline number with me to Burgundy Street) but don't think you have my email address, which is dot38@bigpond.au. I don't think you've got yourself on to email yet but you could get Jeffrey to email me on your behalf.

With much love to you both,

Dot.
xx

Elinor read the letter through twice, her thoughts in turmoil about the prospect of a trip to Melbourne. It seemed so long since she'd left Australia with her parents, almost like another world. She'd enjoyed the happy family life she'd led during her years with Colin and she'd never had a desire to return to Melbourne. And yet, it would be wonderful to be with Dot again and chat face to face.

She laid the letter down on the table and carried her empty mug over to the sink, from where she looked out on the garden. Her eyes strayed to the two azalea bushes growing one on either side of the garage. Their heads were huge, or ginormous as her favourite radio presenter, Terry Wogan, would describe them. She'd bought the azaleas as one blue and the other pink but both bushes had flowered in blue. She knew the colour had something to do with the acidity or alkaline of the soil, although she could never remember which was which. The clematis she had trained over the side fence was thriving and the blossom trees had been magnificent this year, their flowers, as ever, reminding her of cotton wool balls. The blossoms by now lay like a pink and white carpet on the grass. She'd need to get herself organised and clear away the blossom; I'll do that tomorrow, she decided.

Elinor marshalled her thoughts and got ready to go to the shops. She'd promised Fiona a steak and kidney pie for dinner so needed to pay a visit to Warnock's for the meat.

Fiona loved a steak pie, so it would be a nice wee treat for her.

That evening, over dinner, Fiona told her mum all about her day in the salon. 'Mrs Martin is going to visit her son in America soon. And guess what, Mum, Mrs Baird's daughter is going to have a baby. Mrs Baird's very excited.'

While they washed the dishes, Elinor almost blurted out the invitation they'd received to visit Australia. But she curbed her desire to do so until she'd given it further thought and talked it over with Jeffrey. Fiona became easily excited about things and was then disappointed if the plans fell through.

Her decision made, Elinor slipped Dot's letter into the bureau drawer for reply later.

Chapter Sixty

Friday, 22nd May, 1998

Elinor felt her excitement mounting as she dialled Jeffrey's number that evening. Over the past ten days, each time they'd spoken on the phone, he'd been telling her about the extension they were having built and she'd become caught up in how the work was going and only remembered about the Australian trip after he'd hung up. Tonight, therefore, she'd phoned Jeffrey with the express purpose of asking his opinion about the trip.

'Hello, darling,' she started, when Jeffrey's voice came on the line.

'What a fantastic idea of Dot's,' he said, once he'd heard about the invitation to visit, 'both you and Fiona would enjoy exploring Melbourne. A wonderful new experience for Fiona and, as you were young when you lived there, Mum, it would be great to see the city again.'

'Everything will be very different.' Elinor sensed a feeling coursing through her body. Was it regret or simply ghosts from the past? She wasn't sure but her feelings frightened her. And yet, was it unkind of her to deny Fiona a trip and to meet Dot who, up to now, had only been a face in a photograph to Fiona? 'Do you think Fiona would be able to handle such a long journey?'

Jeffrey's laugh rang over the line. 'Fiona would take it in her stride. And it isn't as though she couldn't carry her own case. She's sensible too and wouldn't wander away on her own.'

'I think you're right,' Elinor said, in a voice that lacked conviction.

'Are you sure you aren't making Fiona an excuse,

Mum?' Jeffrey's voice was soft and understanding. 'Go for it, you'll have a super time.'

'You're right, Jeffrey. I am using Fiona as an excuse because I'm scared of taking on such a huge prospect. I don't know why I'm hesitating as I'm sure we'd have a wonderful time.'

'Right, Mum, you tell Fiona about the invitation and if she's happy, as I'm sure she will be, then I'll find out about travel arrangements for you both.'

'That's great, Jeffrey, I'd like if you could do that.' Elinor knew how much travelling her son did through his work so she was satisfied that she and Fiona would be in safe hands.

'What time of year would you like to travel?'

'I think around September would be good, if it isn't too soon after Dot moves house. It would be spring over there so not too hot for us to cope with. Once I've told Fiona, I'll write to Dot and suggest we come in September.'

Chapter Sixty One

Tuesday, 1st September, 1998

'Why don't you go home, Joanne, rather than hanging about here until our flight is called?' Elinor said, as she and Fiona were standing with Joanne and Dougie outside a Boots' store in Glasgow Airport.

But Joanne shook her head firmly. 'Definitely not, I'm staying put. I want to make sure you go through that gate and we get rid of you for four weeks,' she joked, in a brave attempt to cover up her emotion at this farewell to her best friend and her daughter. 'Will you manage alright at Heathrow?'

Elinor smiled. 'We'll be fine. Jeffrey and Claire are going to meet us at Heathrow and see us on to the next plane. If I know my son, he'll get Claire there much too early.'

'What's the number of our flight?' Fiona asked her mum.

'It's BA128,' Elinor told her, 'you listen out for the number will you, darling?'

Fiona nodded and yawned. She took her backpack off and stood closer to Dougie, who put his arm around her shoulders and smiled at her. 'We'll miss you both,' he told her, 'will you look after your mum while you're away?'

'Yes, Uncle Dougie, I will.' Next minute Fiona donned her backpack again when Flight BA128 to London was called over the Tannoy.

'Right, have a great time.' Joanne hugged Elinor, struggling to hold back her tears.

Elinor's eyes glistened with unshed tears. 'We'll be back before you know it,' she said in a choked voice.

With hugs all round, Elinor and Fiona moved towards

Gate 7. They turned briefly and waved to Joanne and Dougie, before disappearing from sight.

***

Sure enough, Jeffrey and Claire were waiting for them at Heathrow.

'We don't have to worry about our cases,' Elinor said, 'they'll be transferred to the next plane. It's on the return journey that we have to collect them here at Heathrow.'

'That's because you have to come through customs on that occasion.' Jeffrey looked at his watch. 'Let's get you both to the correct terminal and we'll check you in for your next flight. That'll leave us time to find a café before you get on board.'

'Okay.' Elinor was pleased that Jeffrey was here to guide them as he knew the ropes.

'I'm so glad we're stopping off in Singapore for a couple of days,' Elinor said, when they were in the airport café. She hadn't relished the long journey directly to Melbourne and had gratefully taken up the travel agent's suggestion of having a stop-over en route.

'You'll love Singapore,' Claire assured her, 'and it's such a safe place that you can wander around quite happily.'

'I'm glad you've booked for afternoon tea at Raffles hotel,' Jeffrey added. 'You couldn't be in Singapore and not go to Raffles. It's a must. And don't forget to introduce my wee sister to a Singapore Sling,' he said, cuddling up to Fiona.

Fiona sat at the window on the Qantas flight, with Elinor in the seat next to her. A brief touch down in Bahrain allowed them to have a wash and tidy up in the ladies' room before re-boarding the aircraft.

When they emerged from the plane in Singapore, a smiling hostess directed them to the transit bus waiting to take them to the terminal. Searing hot air hit them on the walk across the tarmac. 'It's like a sauna,' Elinor said to Fiona, hoping their hotel would be cooler.

After an uncomfortable run on the bus, being jostled and crushed by so many bodies squeezed into the vehicle, they arrived at the terminal, dishevelled and exhausted, to collect their luggage.

Elinor was delighted when they entered the air-conditioned foyer of their hotel, the Singapore Orchid. The marble floor was cool under their tired feet and the leaves of the potted plants placed around the foyer were shiny and healthy looking.

The hotel receptionist greeted them with a smile. 'Good afternoon, ladies, and welcome to the Singapore Orchid. Can I have your names, please?'

They sat their cases at their feet and Elinor returned the woman's smile. 'Mrs Elinor Dawson and Miss Fiona Dawson. We have reserved a twin room for two nights.'

The receptionist checked the hotel register. 'Yes, that's correct. May I see your passports, please?'

Elinor took the two passports out of her handbag and laid them on the desk beside the receptionist. The woman glanced at the pictures and wrote the passport numbers in her register. 'Thank you,' she said and handed back the documents.

'Will there be a safe in our room?' Elinor didn't relish the idea of carrying the passports and their travellers' cheques around in her handbag.

'Yes, there is. Your room is 336 on the third floor, Mrs Dawson.' The receptionist handed the key card to Elinor. 'There is a lift over there on your right,' she said, indicating with her dainty hand. 'We will assist you with your luggage,' she added, as a smartly dressed bell boy appeared at Elinor's side.

The lift doors opened noiselessly on to the third floor. They walked along the carpeted corridor to Room 336, where the bell boy sat their cases just inside the door.

Elinor wasn't sure about tipping but she handed him some Singapore coins that she had in her bag and he seemed quite pleased. She was glad Jeffrey had given her the loose change before they'd left Heathrow. She'd find a bank later today to change one of their travellers' cheques into Singapore currency.

Room 336 was enormous, with an en-suite. There were two beds, much larger than a standard single, separated by a table. A lamp sat on the table and there was a standard lamp over in the corner near the sofa. A wicker table and chairs sat on the balcony, with another coffee table and two easy chairs in the room.

Fiona opened the sliding door and went on to the balcony. 'Come and see this, Mum, there's water down below us.'

Elinor stood beside her and put her arm around Fiona's waist. 'Yes,' she said, looking down, 'it's a sort of lagoon I think, or maybe a river? See that little bridge over there,' she said, pointing to her left. On the other side of the water were what looked like blocks of flats or perhaps holiday apartments. The white stonework sparkled in the sunlight and the roofs were of red tiles.

'What are these umbrellas down there?' Fiona looked towards the side of their hotel, which you could just see from the balcony.

Elinor followed her daughter's eyes. 'I don't think they're umbrellas, darling. It looks like a little market. See the stalls set up under the awnings. We could have a walk through the market before dinner. But first, let's unpack.'

Elinor put the passports and their British money into

the safe at the bottom of the wardrobe. She added their travellers' cheques, minus the one they were going to cash today. She set a code that she'd remember easily.

When they got down to the hotel reception once more, Elinor cashed a travellers' cheque there to save having to find a bank. Then they wandered through the market and enjoyed an iced drink from one of the stalls.

After dinner, they joined some other hotel guests for a river cruise, departing from a jetty near the hotel. Darkness had fallen by now and the temperature had also, with a soft breeze keeping them cool while on board. The boat was illuminated with coloured lights, which reflected off the water. Underneath the awning where the passengers sat, red and gold lanterns were suspended from the cane beams holding up the awning.

'Happy?' Elinor whispered, as they listened to the commentary in English about what they were passing.

Fiona nodded, too awestruck to reply.

Fiona slept well that night although Elinor wakened quite frequently, afraid they'd sleep in. After breakfast, they set off for their guided tour. The coach dropped them in Orchard Road, one of Singapore's famous shopping streets, for an hour's spending spree. Later they spent time in the Botanic Gardens, where they viewed the exotic blooms. Elinor's camera clicked constantly, collecting memories to re-live once they were back at home.

The highlight of the day was their visit to the famous Raffles Hotel, which Elinor remembered seeing in the T.V. drama 'Tenko' years earlier. After the heat of the day, it was delightful to feel the cool air wafting down on them from the enormous ceiling fans. They were booked for afternoon tea at 3 pm in the Tiffin room, which was separated from the main lounge by a decorative fence, giving privacy to the diners.

As they were half an hour early, they made themselves comfortable on a luxurious pink and gold upholstered sofa in the lounge. 'Two Singapore Slings please,' Elinor said to the waiter to who came over to check if they wanted something to drink.

'What's in a Singapore Sling, Mum?'

'I don't know the exact ingredients, darling, but I know there is gin and cherry brandy in it and possibly some other alcohol. The main ingredient is I think pineapple juice.'

Their drinks arrived, in tall glasses, and the waiter happily agreed to Elinor's request that he take a picture of them holding up their Singapore Slings. 'We can let Jeffrey and Claire see the picture when we get home,' she said to Fiona, once the waiter had moved away.

Fiona sipped her drink through the straw provided. 'Oh, this is lovely.'

'Don't drink it too quickly, darling. There's a lot of alcohol in it.' Elinor knew it would be potent, especially as neither of them normally consumed much alcohol.

Fiona giggled. 'Will I be drunk?'

'We might both be. Anyway, who cares? We're on holiday.'

Afternoon tea didn't disappoint. The Tiffin room was vast, with windows looking on to the well-tended gardens surrounding the hotel. Magnificent framed pictures, that looked expensive, adorned the walls. White ornamental columns divided the various sections of the room. A waiter, dressed in white, crisply-laundered trousers and jacket, with a white linen serviette folded over his wrist, came to their table. He held a highly-polished silver teapot in one hand and a coffee pot in the other. He laid both pots down on the table and directed Elinor and Fiona towards another table in the far corner, which was weighed down with a wonderful selection of daintily-cut sandwiches, scones, vol au vents, tarts, sponges and fresh fruit.

When they returned to their own table, the waiter poured their drinks for them. As the afternoon tea slot lasted for an hour, they didn't feel under pressure to eat quickly.

It was a very happy and satisfied mother and daughter who returned to Room 336 in the Singapore Orchid. After another repose and an early breakfast next morning, they left the hotel to be driven to the airport for their onward flight to Australia.

Chapter Sixty Two

Friday, 4th September, 1998

Elinor gently nudged Fiona, who was snoozing with her head leaning against the window frame. 'We'll soon be landing in Melbourne, darling.'

Fiona opened her eyes slowly and grimaced when she lifted her head from its awkward position.

Elinor rubbed Fiona's neck. 'You've had a long sleep. And now we're going to see Dot.' She felt her excitement mounting at the thought of being with Dot after so many years.

'Yippee,' Fiona said and clapped her hands. 'I've never met Dot before. Do you think she'll like me?'

Elinor smiled at her daughter. 'Of course, darling. Everyone who meets you, likes you.'

When they arrived in Tullamarine Airport, having gone through passport control and baggage reclaim, the first person Elinor saw in the terminal was Dot. She was standing right at the front of the crowd, holding up a placard which said 'WELCOME TO SUNNY MELBOURNE, ELINOR AND FIONA'.

The two women hugged and hugged, then brought Fiona into their embrace. 'Right,' said Dot, wiping her eyes and becoming business-like. 'You must be very wearied from the flight, so let's get you both home.'

Dot drove her Suzuki Swift along the Tullamarine Freeway towards the Eastern suburbs. 'I usually stay on the Freeway until I get to Bell Street but I've decided to take a different route to let you see some of the suburbs on the way.' Fiona quickly fell asleep on the back seat of the car while

251

Elinor quietly told her friend about their trip so far. From time to time Dot broke into her account, to point out something of interest, while carefully watching the flow of traffic. 'This is Rosanna we're driving through.'

'What beautiful houses,' Elinor said, peering out of the car window. 'And gardens.'

'I bet your garden in Rutherglen is magnificent.' Dot knew how fond Elinor was of gardening.

'I like to keep it in good order. It was good of you to pick us up, Dot. We could have taken a taxi to Doncaster.'

Dot took a hand off the steering wheel and punched her friend playfully on the arm. 'You must be joking. It's about 38 kilometers, that's 23 miles to you, so a taxi would cost you an arm and a leg.'

Elinor smiled at this expression that she'd noticed cropping up at times in Dot's letters. 'Well, thanks anyway. I've been back in Scotland so long that I'd forgotten the vast distances between places in Australia.'

'You'll see lots of changes since you were last here.' Dot took the road through Eaglemont first and then Bulleen, before indicating left and moving into the next lane, to follow the sign marked Doncaster.

Dot turned into her driveway at Burgundy Street and got out of the car. 'Wakey, wakey,' she said, giving Fiona a gentle shake. 'You've arrived at your home for the next four weeks.'

Chapter Sixty Three

Friday, 11th September, 1998

Dot carried the tray out on to the decking, where Elinor and Fiona were sunning themselves, both wearing sunglasses and a large straw hat. Laying the tray with a jug of her homemade lemonade down on to the table, she poured them each a glassful. The ice cubes made a ringing noise as they dropped into the glasses. 'I hope you two have applied plenty of suncream. Our sun is more harmful than what you're used to.'

Elinor took off her sunglasses and looked up at her friend standing over her. 'We're smothered in the stuff,' she said as she took the glass from Dot. Despite the week that had elapsed since she'd arrived, Elinor was still trying to believe that she was back in the country she'd lived in all those years ago; a country which held such bittersweet memories for her. She glanced over at the wattle bush that blanketed the garage roof, its bright yellow flowers glinting in the sunshine. Beside it was the bottle brush, its red blooms reminding Elinor of the little wire brush she used for washing up. Dot had told her the bottle brush was blooming early this year; it didn't usually flower until about October. The two bushes intermingled, forming a thick red and yellow plait.

Fiona gulped down her lemonade. 'Oh, Dot, it's gorgeous. And you made it yourself?'

Dot sat down with her own glass, facing Fiona across the table. 'Yes, I use my lemons from these trees over there.' She pointed to her right where some sturdy looking trees were crowded into the corner beside the fence. 'More?' she asked, lifting the jug and, when Fiona nodded, refilled her glass.

'Now where shall we go tomorrow?' Dot asked her

guests. 'I feel I haven't shown you much of Melbourne yet.'

Fiona put her glass down on the table. 'Oh but you have, Dot. I loved seeing the kangaroos and kookaburras at Healesville. And holding that koala bear was awesome.' Fiona's eyes widened as she spoke of all the animals she'd seen for the first time.

'And don't forget,' Elinor said, pushing a marker into her place and closing her paperback, 'you've taken us into the city for shopping. And the day we spent at Brighton brought back many happy memories for me. I must remember to write up my diary for yesterday.'

Dot beamed at them both. 'I'm glad you're so happy with what we've done so far but tomorrow I thought we might drive up to the Dandenongs. That's the mountain range in Melbourne,' she explained to Fiona. 'You might have seen pictures on your television news of the serious bush fires that can erupt in the Dandnongs.'

Elinor took off her hat and fanned her face with it. 'Have there been any fires recently?'

'None this year, thank goodness. But there was a serious bush fire in the Dandenongs in January 1997. If my memory serves me correctly, I think three people died and over forty houses were destroyed by the blaze.'

Fiona, her eyes enormous, turned to their hostess. 'It must have been very scary.'

'It was. You could smell the burning from miles away. I could see the smoke from here on the deck.' Dot put her empty glass down on the table. 'And the awful thing is that the authorities discovered the fire had been started deliberately.'

Elinor shook her head. 'You wonder what sort of person would do that.'

'A really evil one.' Dot turned her attention back to

Fiona. 'If we do drive into the Dandenongs, Fiona, there are some fantastic forest tracks up there for walking. And we could have lunch in Olinda, where there are some gift shops and tea shops.'

Fiona's eyes sparkled with excitement. 'Yes, Dot, let's do that. I like tea shops. Is Olinda a big town?'

'It's not really big enough to be called a town, more a hamlet, and a picturesque one at that. The only problem with Olinda is that it gets very busy when the schools are on holiday.'

'But the schools aren't on holiday right now, are they?' Elinor played with some strands of her hair as she spoke.

'No, the kids started back recently after their August break so Olinda should be quieter at the moment. We can also drive to Emerald one day. You'll like it there, Fiona. Puffing Billy, the famous steam train, passes through Emerald on its journey from Belgrave to Gembrook, so we can have a ride on that if you'd like.'

Fiona beamed at Dot. 'Oh yes please, let's go on the train.'

They fell silent and sat for a time taking in the scents and sounds of the garden. The silence was broken by Fiona when she pointed towards the large gum tree, positioned to the left of the decking. 'Look at that gorgeous bird.' The blue and red bird sat on an overhanging branch of the silver-barked gum.

'That's a rosella,' Dot told her, 'it's similar to a parrot. We'll see lots of them in the Dandenongs.'

'And they're really tame; they sit on your shoulder or your head when you're having a picnic.' As if to prove Elinor's point, the rosella flew down and sat on the wooden rail around the decking. Putting its head to one side, the bird looked straight at Fiona.

'Hello, little birdie,' Fiona crooned. She clapped her hands and the rosella flew off into the bushes. 'Have you seen rosellas before, Mum?'

'Yes, darling, I saw lots of them when I lived here as a teenager. I saw my very first one when I was staying in the migrants' hostel and I was as excited as you are at their gorgeous colours.'

Soon afterwards, Dot and Elinor went indoors to prepare food for the barbecue they planned to have later and to make up some salad.

'Do you want any help?' Fiona called after them.

'No, you stay where you are, darling, and enjoy the sunshine,' Elinor replied.

***

A couple of days after their trip to the Dandenongs, they set off for Sugarloaf Reservoir, north east of Melbourne and a forty five minute drive from Doncaster. Dot drove up through Eltham and followed the road that goes over Christmas Hills to Yarra Glen. When they reached Sugarloaf, she parked the Suzuki close by the barbecue area.

Elinor stood outside the car, looking across the water to the tree-covered hill on the opposite side. 'What a beautiful view.'

Dot closed the driver's door and came round to Elinor's side of the car, where Fiona had joined her mother. 'Yes, I like it here because it's so peaceful. The water level is low at the moment due to our exceptionally dry winter. We badly need some rain, see how parched and yellow the grass is.' Dot's hand swept out in a circular motion. 'There's a 15 kilometer walk right around the reservoir. Not that I'm suggesting we do the entire walk,' she added, raising her eyebrows as she spoke.

Elinor stood, with her chin cupped in her hand, staring at the scene. The hill opposite them was in the shape of a loaf. 'I don't remember this reservoir. Was it here when I lived in Melbourne?'

Dot shook her head. 'It was only opened in 1981. It's correct name is the Winneke Reservoir, called after a former Governor General, but it's always known as Sugarloaf.'

'I expect there will be other activities here, in addition to walking.'

'Yes, there's sailing and fishing, which are both popular. There's a sailing club near here, around Eltham way, and they run lots of races on the reservoir. Fishermen come here too. We'll likely see a few folk fishing while we're here. Will we walk first and build up an appetite for our barbecue?'

'Sounds good,' Elinor agreed, 'are you alright with that, darling?'

Fiona nodded.

Pulling on their backpacks, they left the barbecue area and walked in a clockwise direction. 'Which fish would you catch here?' Elinor asked, when the path led them closer to the water where a fisherman sat on the bank, patiently holding the end of his rod.

Dot counted the species on her fingers. 'Trout, roach and European carp. And I think there are also some Redfin in there. The reservoir is managed by Melbourne Water.'

For the next hour they walked out in the open and were glad when the path took them into a glade of trees, sheltered at last from the blazing sun.

'This is much better.' Fiona took off her hat and wiped her face and neck with a towel.

Elinor gulped down water from her bottle. 'Yes, it's a relief to escape from the sun for a wee while.'

Dot pointed to a large log further along the track. 'We

can rest our weary bones on that log. Later we'll walk back the way we came.' The view of the reservoir through the trees was lovely and Elinor took her camera out of her backpack. 'Time for another photo shoot,' she murmured, as she clicked the button and captured the scene.

'You'll have a good collection of pictures by the time you get home.' Dot's voice at her side sounded very sleepy.

Elinor yawned in response and before long, one by one, they dozed off. Elinor remained seated on the log, propped up from behind by the trunk of a gum tree, while Dot and Fiona both lay on the ground with their rucksacks for pillows.

When they wakened, their limbs felt a bit stiff. The temperature had dropped slightly while they'd been sleeping, making the walk back to the car more comfortable. By the time they got there, they were ravenous.

Dot took the eski out of the boot and carried it over to the barbecue area. A family of four was using one of the barbecues but the others were free. 'We'll soon get this going and cook our tucker,' Dot assured them, and it seemed no time until they were sitting at the picnic table with laden plates.

'This smells yummy,' Fiona said, using her fork to spear a sausage. She made a contented sound as she bit into the sizzling pork meat inside.

They tucked into the meat they'd brought with them in the cool box and scoffed the bread rolls. Their food was washed down with lots of fruit juice, still chilled from its time in the eski.

'Why is a cool box called an eski over here?' Fiona asked Dot.

Dot shrugged. 'Search me, maybe it's short for Eskimo. Your guess is as good as mine.'

When they'd finished their meal, they put everything

back into the Suzuki's boot. On the drive home, Dot switched on the air conditioner, both to keep the car and its occupants cool and also to ensure that she remained awake behind the wheel.

***

A few days later the trio made another excursion into the city, giving Fiona the thrill once more of travelling on one of Melbourne's single-decker tramcars. The window blind was pulled down to help protect their arms from the scorching sun. They spent time in some of the many air-conditioned shopping malls that had sprung up all over Melbourne and also went to the Victoria Market to buy some more fresh fruit and vegetables. Before returning to Doncaster, they popped into the Scots' Church in Collins Street, where Elinor and Dot had been members of the youth group. Fiona was entranced to see the places where her mum had gone as a teenager, and asked numerous questions.

Back home in Burgundy Street, they spent the afternoon sunbathing out on the deck, coming back into the house only when the evening air turned cooler.

'Your mum and I have some exciting news for you, Fiona,' Dot told her young guest when they were sitting round the dinner table.

Fiona laid her cutlery down and looked up expectantly.

Elinor stretched across the table and touched her daughter's hand. 'I know you're going to be as excited as I am that Dot has arranged a trip for us all to fly up to Queensland and see the Great Barrier Reef.'

Fiona gasped. 'Oh thank you, Dot. When are we going?'

'Tomorrow. We fly to Cairns and will stay in the Palm Court Hotel for three days. During our time in Cairns, we will go to Port Douglas and take a Quicksilver boat out to the reef. We'll have the chance to fly over the reef in a helicopter and, if we want, we can go down in a submersible boat and see all the coral underneath the water. What do you think?'

Fiona's response was to get to her feet, her eyes shining, and clap her hands. She hugged first Dot and then her mum and jumped up and down on the spot.

Dot and Elinor burst out laughing.

'I think that's a yes,' Dot said.

'And as if a trip out to the reef wasn't enough, Dot has also booked for us to travel on the scenic railway train from Cairns to Karunda,' Elinor told Fiona. 'Aren't we lucky?'

'Yes, yes, yes,' Fiona almost screamed with excitement.

Chapter Sixty Four

Friday, 18th September, 1998

They boarded their flight at Tullamarine. On landing in Cairns, they took a taxi to the Palm Court. It was a huge hotel, overlooking the beach, and their luggage was taken up to their room on the sixth floor. They'd booked a room for three and were pleased with the accommodation. There was an enormous double bed, which Elinor and Fiona would share, while Dot would use the single divan near the verandah door.

'Mum, come and see this,' Fiona called, from where she stood on the verandah.

Elinor went out and joined her, throwing an arm around her daughter's shoulder. 'Oh, darling, isn't it wonderful?' From here, they had a panoramic view over the beach.

Fiona pointed down to some trees in the hotel grounds beneath them. 'Look at these gorgeous trees? The ones with the purple flowers?'

'They're jacaranda trees,' Dot, who'd joined them on the verandah, told her. 'They're pretty, aren't they?'

They unpacked and had a stroll through Cairns' many air-conditioned shopping malls, where Elinor and Fiona purchased gifts for friends in Scotland. Back at the Palm Court, they enjoyed a siesta, after which they changed their clothes and went downstairs to the bar before dinner. They settled themselves down on high stools at the bar counter and Dot and Elinor studied the cocktail menu.

'Let's try a Cosmopolitan,' Dot suggested.

Fiona giggled. 'Sounds like an ice cream.'

Elinor nudged her and laughed. 'That's a Neopolitan.'

Fiona giggled again. 'So it is. What's in the cocktail, Dot?'

'Let's see. It says here vodka, Cointreau, cranberry juice and lime juice. Sounds good, what do you say folks?'

'I'll have one,' Fiona said immediately.

'These cocktails are becoming a habit, young lady,' Elinor teased Fiona, thinking of the Singapore Slings they'd enjoyed on the journey to Australia. 'Don't be expecting to drink cocktails once we're back home again. This is just a holiday treat.'

Fiona sighed and shook her head, raising her eyebrows. 'Okay, Mum, anything you say.'

Dot gave their order and the barman mixed the drinks in front of them. He laughed when he saw the rapt expression on Fiona's face as he used the shaker. 'Is this the first time you've tasted a cocktail?'

'No, 'I've had a Singapore Sling.'

'An experienced cocktail drinker then,' he said, and winked at Elinor.

They carried their tray of drinks over to the only vacant seats away from the bar. 'Do you mind if we sit here?' Dot asked a woman sitting on her own at the horseshoe-shaped table.

'Not at all,' the lady said, 'my husband and I were the only people at the table.' She indicated to a tall, bald-headed man standing at the bar with his back to them.

Once the three of them had settled themselves at the table, Dot raised her glass. 'Cheers,' she said and Elinor and Fiona did likewise.

'We're having a cocktail,' Fiona informed the woman opposite.

'So I see. Which one are you having?'

'A Cosmopolitan.'

'Are you here on holiday?' the woman asked, looking over at Dot.

'Yes, we've come up from Melbourne for a few days. What about you?'

'We're having a short break from our home in Noosa. Haven't been in Cairns for years.'

'Noosa is south of here,' Dot explained to Elinor and Fiona, then turned back to the woman. 'You live in a beautiful part of Queensland.'

The woman smiled. 'Yes, we're very lucky to live so near to the beach. I'm originally from Melbourne but my husband's family have all been in Noosa for years. I'm Molly, by the way,' she added and the other three told her their names.

'We're going to the Barrier Reef tomorrow on the Quicksilver boat,' Fiona told Molly.

'Tony and I are doing that trip too, Fiona. It'll be a great day out. Here's Tony now.'

Elinor turned her head as Tony approached the table. A sun-tanned man, he wore cream shorts and a casual open-necked shirt. Around his neck hung a gold Cross on a chain and he had a tattoo on his arm. He laid a glass of brandy and a bottle of ginger ale in front of Molly and sat down with a can of Foster's in his hand.

'Tony, the ladies here are going on the same trip as we are tomorrow,' Molly told him.

'Great,' he said, his smile taking in the three of them. He pulled the ring on the top of the can and it opened with a fizz. Some froth came out and ran down the outside of the can.

'Here,' Molly said, putting some paper tissues down under the can.

Leaving Molly and Tony some peace to themselves, Dot's group chatted quietly about tomorrow's trip to the reef.

Elinor took her mobile phone out of her bag. 'I'll see if I can send a text to Joanne. Don't know if I'll be able to get a signal.'

'Make it brief,' Dot advised. 'Otherwise it will cost a fortune.'

'It's okay. I've got a package and pay a fixed amount each month. It covers me for international texts.'

Hi Joanne, she texted. *Still having a fab time down under. We are in Cairns and going to the Great Barrier Reef tomorrow. Fiona really enjoying her holiday. Will have lots to tell you when we get back. Luv to u and Dougie. xx*

***

Next morning they were the first three people to get on to the coach for Port Douglas. Elinor and Fiona sat on the front seats and Dot was on the other side of the passageway behind the driver.

'Good morning, ladies,' Tony said to them as he boarded the coach, followed by Molly, and the two of them took seats further back in the coach. As Tony walked past Elinor's seat, she had the same feeling as on the previous evening that she'd seen him before. And yet, it wasn't possible, as it was her first time in Queensland. But the feeling continued to nag her.

In Port Douglas they boarded the Quicksilver boat and found seats on the outside deck, sufficiently underneath the awning to screen their faces from the hot sun. Molly and Tony sat in the row behind, Tony's floral shirt making him stand out from his fellow passengers. His bald head was protected from the sun by a digger's hat.

When they got out to the reef, the boat berthed at a pontoon. After listening to the instructions coming over the tannoy system, Dot, Elinor and Fiona joined the lunch queue. Lunch was included in the cost of the trip and as the queue moved quickly they didn't have to wait long to serve themselves from the fabulous selection of dishes set out on the table. With their plates full, they picked up a glass of chilled wine and found a secluded spot on deck. Soon afterwards, Molly and Tony joined them.

'Pretty good tucker,' Tony said, as he polished off the meat and used his last piece of crusty bread to soak up the sauce left on his plate.

Dot, her deckchair facing Tony's, swallowed the last morsel of food on her plate. 'The sea air definitely gives you an appetite.' Her sentiments were echoed by Fiona and Molly, sitting together on the other side of Dot.

'It's nice to feel the motion of the water underneath us.' Elinor said, to no-one in particular. She placed her empty plate at her feet and lay back on the deckchair.

Tony's deckchair was positioned next to Elinor's. 'It can't be,' he said aloud, and when Elinor turned her head, he had removed his hat and was staring at her while he dabbed a handkerchief over his shiny pate.

Taking off her sunglasses, Elinor returned Tony's gaze. The strange thought came back that she had seen him somewhere, but where? Perhaps he had a double back home in Rutherglen.

'The name's Elinor, isn't it?' He saw her nod. He'd been introduced to them in the bar last night but the only name that had stuck in his mind was Elinor. His eyes now stayed on Elinor's face for a moment, before they widened in surprise. 'You're never Elinor Bonnington, are you?'

She nodded slowly and, when he smiled, the penny dropped. 'Michael,' she murmured, 'but you can't be, you're Tony.'

He smiled again. 'My full name is Michael Anthony, but as I had three workmates called Michael, I became known as Tony. I was Tony by the time I met Molly.'

From her seat further along the deck, Molly looked over, mystified. 'What's going on over there?'

'You won't believe it, love,' Tony told her, 'Elinor and I were at school in Melbourne together. Before I moved to Queensland and long before you and I met.'

'Good Lord, it's a small world. Did you recognise Tony, Elinor?'

'No, it was Michael, I mean Tony, who recognised me.'

'Elinor knew me when I was Michael, before I changed to Tony,' he explained to the others. He laughed. 'Of course, I've changed more than Elinor has. For a start, I had hair when she last saw me.'

'And are you and Fiona still living in Melbourne?' Molly asked Elinor.

'No, we live in Scotland. We're staying with Dot in Melbourne at the moment. Dot and I are old friends.' Elinor stopped speaking and looked at Michael again, trying to convince herself it really was him. Her heart was pounding and she felt like a teenager once more. She pulled her hat further over her brow, partly to shield her skin from the blazing sun but also to keep her face hidden from Molly and Dot. She was embarrassed about the excitement that was building up in her at seeing Michael again, a man she'd thought of as belonging to the past. It was a bit scary.

Over the years since she'd last seen Michael Lynch she'd thought she'd got over him, but now she wasn't so sure.

Shortly afterwards, Dot, Fiona and Molly all dozed off, leaving Elinor and Tony to chat quietly about the old days at Symonds High. She couldn't think of him as Tony, to her he would always be Michael. She also had great difficulty believing that he was sitting next to her. After a time Michael also dropped off to sleep, leaving her alone with her thoughts.

'Will we go to the purser's station to book our helicopter and boat trips?' Dot suggested to Elinor and Fiona, once they'd recovered from their huge lunch. 'You can also snorkel and swim with the fish if you want.'

Elinor laughed. 'No thanks, I'll pass on that one but the other two sound good.'

While they were waiting their turn in the purser's station, Elinor checked her mobile. 'Oh, Joanne must have got the text I sent yesterday. I've had a reply,' she said and read it out. *Hello Elinor and Fiona, gr8 2 get your txt. Your weather sounds super, here it is wet, cold and miserable. Missing u both lots. Love from Joanne and Dougie. xx*

They'd decided to go up in the helicopter first and when their turn came, they were asked to stand individually on a scale to be weighed. 'We have to spread the weight out evenly on the helicopter,' the staff member explained.

The helicopter was a bright pink five-seater, with the words HELI ADVENTURES printed in blue lettering on its side. Dot and Fiona sat in the back seat, along with a slim Japanese chap, while Elinor was in front beside the pilot. From her seat in the helicopter, Elinor captured lots of pictures looking down over the reef; from the air it was like a gigantic map spread out before her.

Next came their trip in the submersible. It was shaped like a long canoe with a glass top. The passengers boarded one at a time, with one person sitting on a single bench seat on each side of the vessel, until it was full. Fiona sat behind her mum and in front of Dot. This method of seating afforded all the passengers a clear view of the world beneath the surface.

For the next twenty minutes they experienced the wonders around them. They were cut off from the sounds of the world above in this silent underwater realm. The shapes of the reef were varied and Elinor saw some pieces of coral shaped like human skulls and others that resembled a large cauliflower or cabbage leaves. The colours of the coral were spectacular; one minute they were passing orange trumpet-like pieces of coral and the next some luminous blue star-shapes would glide past the window. All manner of fish swam around in their underground world, twisting and turning in and out of the crevices in the reef. Some of the fish were two-toned, flashing their brilliant hues at the spectators. Elinor turned her eyes to the left and the right, trying not to miss anything. She took what she hoped were good shots on her camera.

'That was spectacular.' Elinor voiced what they all felt when they arrived back at the pontoon. 'I could have stayed down there for hours.'

'I was sure I'd feel claustrophobic,' Dot said, 'but I didn't have any problem after all.'

'It was awesome.' Elinor smiled at this phrase that had recently entered her daughter's vocabulary.

Back at the Palm Court, they had a drink with Molly and Tony in the bar before bed, because Molly had told them they were going home next morning. 'If you give me your email address, Dot, I'll send you copies of our photographs,' Molly said. 'And you too, Elinor.'

'I'm not on email.'

Dot wrote down her email address and gave it to Molly. 'If you email the photos to me, I'll have them copied and send them to Elinor. And remember, if you and Tony are ever in Melbourne, please pay me a visit.'

'We sure will and you'll be welcome in Noosa with us.'

Elinor leaned forward in her seat. 'And of course, should you get to Scotland any time, I'll be pleased to welcome you too.'

'Thanks, Elinor. We might take you up on that offer as Tony and I hope to have a trip to Europe and U.K. next year to celebrate our 30th wedding anniversary.'

They said their farewells at the hotel lift as Molly and Tony had a bedroom on the ground floor. 'It's been great to meet you again, Elinor,' Tony said, 'have a safe journey back to Scotland.'

'Thanks.' She shook hands with him and Molly, then followed Dot and Fiona into the lift.

'Oh, I forgot to give Molly my address in Rutherglen,' Elinor said, as she was turning down the bed sheets in their room.

Dot, who was already in bed, yawned. 'That's no problem. When she emails me, I can give her your address. Night night, sleep tight,' she said, and switched off her bedside lamp.

***

'Here's our train now,' Dot said next morning and ushered Elinor and Fiona on board at Cairns railway station. The scenic train journey took them past stunning waterfalls and deep ravines, and at Barron Gorge they got out of their carriage and joined their fellow passengers on the viewing platform to stare down the gorge that seemed to go on forever. The rugged landscape made it easy to understand why a great many men who worked on the building of the railroad lost their lives during its construction.

They alighted from the train at Kuranda. The little station was clean and well cared for and the platform was decorated by tubs of exotic plants and flowers. On either side of the rail track huge ferns and palms crowded together.

After a barbecue in Kuranda, they climbed into a green and yellow-painted amphibious vehicle for a guided tour of the rainforest, which they were told was millions of years old. Elinor tensed up when they crossed a crocodile-infested lake but she relaxed again when the vehicle reached dry land once more. Later they were treated to an Aboriginal corroboree in the forest.

The rest of the holiday flew by and they were sorry when the trip came to an end. By the time they returned to Melbourne, Elinor had built up a huge photographic record of their stay in Queensland, her diary bursting with information about everything she'd seen and done there. Michael Lynch featured many times in the entries. Sometimes Elinor referred to him as Tony, the name he was using now, but more often the old familiar name of Michael crept into the writing.

Over the years of her life with Colin, she'd never once doubted but that Michael had left her mind completely. The idea that romantic thoughts of him had been lying dormant all that time, and had now resurfaced, frightened her. Because of this, she was glad that he was married to Molly, as that kept her silly notions of rekindling their previous relationship at bay.

Chapter Sixty Five

Monday, 28th September, 1998

On their return from Queensland, they took things easy for a few days, before planning any further outings. Towards the end of the week they did manage to fit in a trip to Emerald for a ride on Puffing Billy, which Fiona described afterwards as 'awesome'.

Today, their last Monday in Australia, they were having morning coffee out on the deck. Elinor lifted her eyes from the postcard she was addressing. 'I can't believe we're on to our last week in Melbourne. The time seems to have whizzed by.'

Dot closed her book and laid it down beside her lounger. 'I'm going to miss you both, I've enjoyed all our days out.'

'I wish you'd come to Scotland and stay at our house, Dot,' Fiona said, from where she stood at the rail of the decking, looking over Dot's extensive garden.

'Well, who knows, Fiona, maybe one day I will. But it would need to be in your summer as I'd freeze in your winter.'

Elinor laughed. 'Sometimes there's very little difference in temperature between summer and winter in Scotland. But, as Fiona says, it would be great to have you over and show you around.'

'Yes, I'd like it too, especially as I've never been in Scotland. Anyway, back to the present, we must do some interesting things over this last week.' Dot glanced over at Fiona. 'Would you like to go panning for gold, Fiona?'

Fiona turned enormous eyes on Dot. 'You mean real gold?'

Dot laughed. 'Well if you found any it would be real. I thought we could go to Sovereign Hill tomorrow, where there used to be a gold mine and you can try your hand at finding some.'

'Sovereign Hill is a conservation place,' she explained to her young guest, 'they've kept the old shops and prospectors' huts as they would have been at the time of the gold rush. The people serving in the shops are dressed in period costume.'

'Will it be like the town in 'Paint Your Wagons'?'

'Yep, I guess it is similar, Fiona, but I don't think you'll bump into Lee Marvin.' Dot got up from her lounger. 'Right, I'll get the map and plan our route for tomorrow.'

They had an early breakfast next morning and, while Elinor and Fiona washed up, Dot prepared a picnic. The morning rush hour was over by the time they set off and, although the traffic was still quite heavy when they left Doncaster, it eased off when they got on to more country roads.

'I think we'll stop here for some coffee,' Dot said, when they drove into Bachus Marsh. To Elinor it looked a pretty country town, with fairly wide streets lined with well-stocked shops. Dot turned off the main road and found some open parkland, where they placed their folding chairs under a canopy of trees. Dot gave each of them a sandwich, a piece of fruit and a cup of coffee. 'We can keep the remains of the picnic for later,' she said, once they'd eaten.

Sovereign Hill proved to be a winner with Elinor and Fiona. They both tried their luck at gold panning but came away empty-handed.

'Don't think anyone ever finds anything,' Dot told them. 'I suppose it's possible although I think the gold has been mined out years ago. Still, it was fun to try, wasn't it?'

'And I've got a picture of me panning for gold,' Fiona boasted, as they headed off to see what the shops had to offer. Fiona bought some old-fashioned candy in the sweet shop. She was served by a lady wearing Victorian costume; a grey serge dress with a white pinafore apron over it and a white dustcap covering most of her hair, the edges of the cap turned up at the side like wings.

Before they left the sweet shop, Fiona insisted that Elinor take a picture of her standing beside the sweet seller, their arms linked around one another.

Elinor purchased a couple of gifts in the craft shop next door to the sweet shop. 'I'd love to buy lots more things, but I have to remember the weight of my case going home.'

As they emerged from the craft shop, Fiona pointed to a group of children coming towards them. 'Look at these children, they're all in fancy dress.'

'They'll be kids from one of the local schools,' Dot told her. 'It'll be a classroom excursion and the children will have been given the clothes to wear while they're here. They might be working on a school project about Sovereign Hill.'

They found a shaded spot where they devoured the remains of their picnic. When they got back to the Suzuki, it was boiling hot inside the vehicle so they had the air conditioning on full blast during their journey back to Burgundy Street.

Chapter Sixty Six

Friday, 2nd October, 1998

'How's your packing going?' Dot used her elbow to push open the bedroom door and came in, carrying a mug of tea in each hand. 'Thought you might like a cuppa while you're working.'

'Thanks, Dot,' Fiona said, taking one of the mugs from her and putting it down on a coaster sitting on the bedside table.

Elinor finished folding her yellow blouse and laid it on top of the clothes already in the case. 'That's great, Dot, I just needed a drink.'

Elinor and Fiona sat on the bed to drink their tea and Dot perched on the dressing table stool.

'I think I'm almost finished,' Elinor told her. 'I've left out something for us to wear tonight and our clothes for the flight home are hanging in the wardrobe. I've got the passports and plane tickets in the handbag I'll be using for the journey.'

'Good, sounds like you're well organised. I'll go into the garden and leave you in peace to get everything finished.' Dot stood up as she was speaking and moved to the door. She stopped, with her hand on the doorknob. 'We'll be leaving about 6.30 as the table is booked for 7.30 and we need to leave time to drive into the city and find a parking place.'

'Why don't we use a taxi tonight?' Elinor suggested. 'That way we can have wine with our meal. I'd like to treat you to a few drinks to thank you for all you've done for Fiona and me.'

'But you're already treating me to the meal. It's going to make it a very expensive night for you with the cost of a taxi too.'

'No, problems, Dot. I've got plenty of Aussie dollars left and I can't spend them once I get on the plane tomorrow.'

'You can have them changed back into sterling when you get home.'

But Elinor shook her head. 'No arguments, Dot, go and relax until it's time to get dressed for our big night out.'

Dot smiled. 'Okay, you win,' she said and slipped out of the room.

The taxi dropped the three of them in the city centre, just beside the bridge that spanned the Yarra. 'What a lovely evening,' Elinor said, blinking in the late sunshine, as they headed for the steps at the side of the bridge, leading down to the riverside, or Southbank as it was known. She held up her long, blue skirt as they went down the stairs, three abreast.

The tables and chairs outside the Southbank restaurants were occupied by customers, their laughter filling the evening air. Fiona, looking lovely in her pink and white spotted dress and white high-heeled sandals, walked ahead of Elinor and Dot, revelling in the excitement of the occasion.

'What's that?' Elinor pointed to a large, brightly-lit establishment they were passing.

'That's the casino,' Dot told her. 'It opened last year. I've only been in once for a meal but a neighbour of mine goes there regularly to the gaming tables and spends a fortune. Here's the restaurant,' she added, directing Elinor and Fiona into 'Bergerac'.

'I love the name,' Elinor whispered to Dot when they went into the entrance foyer. 'Makes me think of John Nettles in his television role.'

'I think the restaurant is called after the town that the owner came from,' Dot replied, before turning to the member of staff who greeted them and showed them to their table. They'd been allocated a table in the upstairs section of the restaurant, overlooking the river.

'This is lovely,' Elinor said, looking around at the pictures of Paris on the walls; the ones she recognised were the Eiffel Tower, the Louvre and Notre Dame.

Dot nodded. 'I've only eaten in here once before, but I remember that the service and food were excellent.' She opened the bag she'd been carrying and brought out two bottles of Australian Chardonnay which she placed on the table.

'I said I'd buy the wine,' Elinor protested.

Dot shook her head. 'There's no way I'm going to have you paying for our food, taxis and also wine. This way you can do the tucker and I'll provide the vino.'

Elinor shrugged and smiled at her friend. 'I'm still getting used to the fact that you Aussies take your own wine to restaurants. I don't think we can do that in the U.K.'

With the help of their friendly waitress, Gabrielle, a most attractive blonde with a figure to die for, they chose their order from the menu. 'How long have you lived in Australia?' Elinor asked Gabrielle. Apart from a slight trace of a French accent, Gabrielle spoke fluent English.

'I came here with my family about fifteen years ago,' she said, taking the menu from Elinor.

Dot handed her menu to Gabrielle with a smile. 'Can you open the wine for us please?'

'Sure,' Gabrielle said. She pushed the menus under her armpit and, carrying a bottle in each hand, she went off in the direction of the kitchen.

'What a super meal,' Elinor said a couple of hours later, when they emerged from the restaurant, and walked along the Southbank towards the bridge once more. It was dark by now and the coloured lanterns strung across the bridge twinkled brightly, as did the lights adorning some of the crafts bobbing up and down along the river.

'Yes, thank you so much, it's been a lovely ending to our four weeks together. I'm going to miss you guys when you leave tomorrow,' Dot told them.

'It makes me want to cry,' Fiona said, walking in the middle between her mum and Dot. 'We've had such a great time here that I want to stay forever.'

'And what about Jeffrey and Claire?' Elinor reminded her. 'It would mean you wouldn't see them very often.'

'Oh yes, I'd forgotten about that.'

Dot gave Fiona's arm a squeeze. 'You'll just have to come again. But don't cry yet, it'll be bad enough tomorrow saying farewell at the airport. Let's try and flag down a taxi,' she said, as they reached the top of the stairs and were standing on the bridge once more.

Chapter Sixty Seven

Saturday, 3rd October, 1998

The chap behind the counter had his long hair pulled back into a pony tail, his hands performing their familiar task with great speed and efficiency. The lady he was serving sat on a high stool at the bar, swinging her legs back and forward as she waited for her drink to be prepared. Watching the barman at work, Elinor wondered idly how many cappuccinos and other drinks he produced in the course of a day.

The coffee bar was well away from the entrance hall and check-in desks, and as a result was a lot quieter. Dot had suggested that they have a drink here, but they all knew it was just to keep their minds off the impending farewell. Scanning the faces of her fellow travellers sitting at the nearby tables, Elinor saw the same tension on their faces that she was feeling. She twisted her coffee mug between her hands, without drinking any of its contents, and the same applied to her companions. Dot drummed her fingers on the table top, while Fiona hummed 'Waltzing Matilda'.

'Will I have time to go to the toilet before we go on to the plane, Mum? The Ladies is over there.' Fiona pointed to the sign.

'Yes, darling, if you're quick and come right back.'

Fiona, wearing a navy and white sleeveless dress and low-heeled, open-toed sandals, scooted off and Elinor smiled after her. Up until Colin's death, her reaction would have been to accompany Fiona but nowadays she resisted, keen to let her daughter have some independence. It had taken her many years to arrive at this stage but seeing how Fiona thrived on her new-found freedom confirmed to Elinor that she'd taken the right course.

She and Dot sat quietly after Fiona left, each with her own thoughts. Elinor stared up at the illuminated sign above the coffee bar and Dot crossed and uncrossed her legs. Elinor looked round to face the windows. 'It looks like it's going to be a lovely day in Melbourne,' she said, her voice wistful.

'Yep, it's forecast to reach 36 today. When I get home, I'm going to spend the afternoon out on the decking as it'll be too hot to do anything else.'

Elinor made a face. 'And we'll be stuck in a plane all day.'

'Fingers crossed you have as smooth a journey home as you had coming here,' Dot went on, trying to keep the conversation on a practical level. Time enough for tears, she reckoned, once Elinor and Fiona were called for boarding.

Elinor played with the strap of her shoulder bag. 'I'm glad we aren't stopping off anywhere on the way back. I think once we get on the plane, we'll just want to get home.' She saw Fiona coming towards them, and gave her a wave.

Arriving back at the table, Fiona threw her arms around Dot. 'I hate having to say cheerio to you, Dot. I wish we could stay here forever, or you could come to live in Rutherglen.'

Dot took Fiona's hands in hers, unable to stop the tears this time. 'Well that's life, love,' she said, choking slightly on the words, 'and we can at least keep in touch by letters and the occasional phone call. Or, better still, we can get that mum of yours on to email. Now, have you both got all you need for the journey, reading material, hankies, lollies?'

'Yes, thank you, Dot, we'll be fine.' Elinor smiled at the word lollies. The first time she'd heard the word back in the fifties, she'd expected the person to hand her a lollipop on a stick instead of sweeties. During the two years she lived in the country, she'd become accustomed to the different Aussie words but she'd forgotten about them until now.

At that moment a call came over the loudspeaker. *'Message for passengers travelling on Qantas TA249. The flight is now boarding at gate 18.'*

'Right, that's us,' Elinor said, getting to her feet.

Dot accompanied them to gate 18, where they had a very tearful but quick farewell, all of them keen not to delay the agony of parting. 'Bye, phone me when you get home,' Dot said, then turned abruptly and hurried towards the escalator taking her back to the exit.

***

Elinor and Fiona came through from the Customs Hall at Heathrow, feeling slightly dishevelled and jaded after the long flight from Melbourne. Elinor pushed the trolley with their cases and Fiona walked at her side.

'There they are,' Fiona shouted above the noise, when she saw Jeffrey and Claire waving to them from the crowd.

'Hi, Mum, hi, Sis,' Jeffrey greeted them, hugging each one in turn.

Claire hugged them too. 'It's fantastic to see you both again. You're looking so tanned and healthy. From your postcards, it sounds like you had a great time.'

'It was wonderful,' Elinor told her. Then she turned to Jeffrey. 'Now, we'll need to check in our cases for the Glasgow flight.'

Jeffrey took the trolley from his mother and pushed it towards the check-in desks. 'You'll be a couple of seasoned travellers by now. We'll move to Terminal 3 and get shot of the luggage and then we can all have a cuppa before your next flight is called. It's good you have almost an hour between flights.'

Over their drink in the Costa coffee bar, Elinor and

Fiona told the other two all about their wonderful experiences in Melbourne. 'Mum has taken lots of photographs so you can see them next time you come up to Rutherglen,' Fiona said.

'Yes,' Jeffrey nodded, 'we'll come up soon for the weekend. But we'll give you time to settle down again after all your travels.'

Claire laughed and punched Fiona playfully on the arm. 'I'm quite jealous at all the places you've been to.'

Fiona beamed at her. 'You and Jeffrey can come with us next time.'

'Oh so there's going to be a next time,' Jeffrey said, winking at Elinor as he spoke.

At that moment, before Fiona could reply, a message came over the tannoy to inform passengers on Flight BA129 to Glasgow to proceed to gate 25 for boarding.

'Looks like we're off then,' Elinor said, picking up her bag, for the final part of their journey. When they got to the departure gate, she and Fiona kissed Jeffrey and Claire goodbye, before joining the queue that had formed outside gate 25.

'Remember to phone us when you get home,' Jeffrey called after them.

Chapter Sixty Eight

Tuesday, 16ᵗʰ February, 1999

After Fiona left for work that morning, Elinor went down to the Mitchell Arcade in Main Street to do some shopping. Like her fellow Ruglonians, she mourned the loss of the family-owned shops that used to line the Main Street. They'd been replaced by shops under the ownership of large companies, with no longer any personal touch for their customers. Sadly this was the way of the modern world, resulting in most towns and cities losing their individuality.

When she got home, the postman had been and she pounced on the airletter from Dot. She picked up her letter opener with the word MELBOURNE on it, a gift one Christmas from Dot. She smiled; it had obviously been sent a long time ago, before the restrictions about sending sharp objects through the post. She pulled the opener out of its leather sheath and slit open the airletter.

Wednesday, 10ᵗʰ February, 1999.

My Dear Elinor,

Thanks for your letter of 6ᵗʰ January and I was pleased to read that you and Fiona are both doing well. I often wish you were on email as I'm sure I'd be a better correspondent if you were. It always takes me ages to sit down and write a letter, as opposed to an email which you can compose and send so swiftly. Still, since letter-writing is becoming a dying art, at least it's good we both care enough to spend the time it takes.

I was interested to hear of all your activities over the

Festive season. Your church fayre seems to have been a success once again and what a great amount of cash the event has raised. I couldn't believe how many Christmas parties Fiona attended – she has a better social life than you or me!

She's a lovely girl and it's good to know she's having such a beaut time. Please give her a hug from me.

Over the past few weeks, I've been staying around the house, doing very little, as it's been too darned hot. The weather stayed reasonably cool after you left here at the beginning of October and it was a bearable temperature up until Christmas. But since New Year the temps have soared and we've been having many days at 42 (in old money I believe that's around 110!). Far too hot for comfort and I just hate it. My air conditioning unit has been going full blast, day and night. I dread to think what the electricity charges will be!

When I have been out, it is in the early morning or later in the evening. My neighbour, Rona, (you'll remember meeting her last year) and I went to the cinema in Camberwell a couple of nights ago. The film was 'American Beauty', starring Kevin Spacey, and we both really enjoyed it. One morning last week I met my ex-colleague, Brenda, in The Pines shopping mall for coffee. You will remember I took you and Fiona to The Pines last September.

As I told you in my last letter, Molly Lynch and I have been keeping in touch by email since we all met in Cairns. You really must get yourself on to email, Elinor! I had an email from Molly in late January to let me know she and Tony were coming to Melbourne – he had some business to do in the city and she was coming with him.

We arranged to meet during their stay. I invited them here for dinner one evening and my neighbours, Rona and John, joined us so that Tony would have another man's conversation. The evening went well and before they returned to Noosa, Molly and I met for lunch in the city. They were both asking for you, Elinor, and hope to meet you when they come to the U.K. at the end of the year. The trip is to celebrate their 30ᵗʰ wedding anniversary. Tony has done a fair amount of travelling with his business but Molly has never been out of Australia before.

I guess that's about it for this time. I hope I'll have more news for you next time, once the weather cools and I get out and about again. My poor garden is suffering from lack of moisture and we have water restrictions in place.

Love to you and Fiona,
Yours ever,
Dot
xx

Elinor sat for a long time, thinking about the proposed visit from Molly and Tony. Her mind was in turmoil. Since their meeting in Cairns, she had exchanged Christmas cards with them, but there had been no further contact. She was sure Molly had written the Christmas card; she'd have recognised Michael's handwriting from the only two letters he'd ever sent her.

It struck her forcibly now that she'd never disposed of his letters and they lay at the bottom of her jewellery box. She remembered putting them there before she and Colin were married, aware that her husband would never have thought of looking into the box. She hadn't wanted to have secrets from Colin, but felt she couldn't part with the letters.

All this now left her with ambivalent thoughts about their visit; she would try to make them feel welcome in her home, despite the scary feelings that had been aroused in Cairns. Thank goodness Molly would be there and stop Elinor's imaginings coming to the fore.

Chapter Sixty Nine

Tuesday, 24th August, 1999

In later years, Elinor would always remember that Dot's letter arrived on the day she was going to Mrs Mullin's funeral. She opened the airletter, little expecting the bombshell it contained.

Thursday, 19th August, 1999.

My Dear Elinor,

Thank you for your letter and photos, telling me about the holiday you and Fiona spent in North Berwick last month. You said it was nostalgic, remembering the family holidays with Colin over the years. But I'm sure you felt close to Colin there and your memories would be bittersweet, sad but laced with happy times too. I hope that's the way it was, anyway. North Berwick looks like a scenic place from the photos. If I ever make it over there, you must take me to North Berwick to see the beauty for myself.

This is a very difficult letter for me to write, Elinor, as it contains sad news. I pondered over phoning you but decided a letter was better to allow you time to take it in slowly. There is no easy way to tell it, so here goes.

I received a phone call from Tony Lynch about a month ago, breaking the news that his dear Molly had died suddenly from a massive stroke. As happens in such situations, I got the impression that poor Tony was in shock. It was almost as though he was telling me about something he'd seen in a film rather than it being in real life. I know you'll understand how he felt, Elinor, as I remember you told me when you were here that you'd experienced the feelings I've described after Colin's death.

I flew up to Queensland for the funeral, which was well attended. It was a lovely service, if you can use that adjective to describe a funeral; personal and caring. Although I've never been married, I do have a fair idea of how devastating the death of a spouse must be. I'm too far away to offer Tony any help but I will keep in touch with him.

Knowing how fond you are of Tony – I think I've already guessed that you still harbour feelings for him, my dear – I'm sure you'll want to send him a card. I think you have his address but in case you've mislaid it, the details are:-

Mr Tony Lynch
8 Eucalyptus Grove
Noosa, 4567
Queensland
Australia

I do hope you won't be annoyed at me for speaking so candidly, Elinor, but I think we've known one another long enough, and well enough, for me to do so.

I'm afraid this airletter seems to contain only doom and gloom. I'm sorry I don't have happier news for you, Elinor.

Love and prayers,
Dot
xx

Elinor composed herself and dressed for Mrs Mullin's funeral. On her way home, she bought a 'Thinking of You' card, preferring that to a 'With Sympathy' one. She addressed the card, not to Tony Lynch but to Michael Lynch – that was the name he'd always be to her.

Once the card was completed, ready for posting, she got an airmail letter out of the bureau drawer and wrote a reply to Dot.

Tuesday, 24ᵗʰ August, 1999.

My Dear Dot,

Thank you for breaking the sad news about Molly so sensitively. Of course I was devastated to read about her sudden death but thanks to your wording of the letter, I was prepared for something sad before I came to that bit.

My heart goes out to Michael (sorry I can't think of him as Tony) as I know only too well what pain and grief he will be suffering. It's almost like losing a limb, after having the person in your life for so long. I can only hope that he will get lots of support from his friends and family members in Noosa.

Your letter arrived this morning, when I was due to attend my neighbour's funeral. Mrs Mullin has been our neighbour since I moved in here with my parents and, being a retired midwife, it was Mrs Mullin who delivered Fiona. She was a wonderful neighbour and friend, and I will miss her greatly.

Please don't worry about being candid in your letter, Dot. You are correct. Although I loved Colin dearly, and couldn't have asked for a better husband, I realise now that I've never lost the love I had for Michael all those years ago. Even though I was distraught when he stopped writing to me, I have never held any bitterness towards him and was glad that we met up again in Cairns. Molly was a lovely woman and I'm sure she made him happy and that thought makes me happy too.

I'm sorry I don't feel able to write any more tonight but will contact you again soon.

Much love from Elinor

x

Chapter Seventy

Hogmanay, 1999

Elinor sang with gusto as she worked in the kitchen that New Year's Eve afternoon.

'You sound happy, Mum. Is it because Jeffrey's coming home?'

Elinor put the steak and kidney pie in the oven and turned to smile at her daughter. 'Yes, darling, I'm so looking forward to seeing Jeffrey and Claire again. Only another two hours and they should be here.'

'Goody, goody.' Fiona grabbed her mum's hands and they jumped up and down in excitement at the prospect of seeing Jeffrey and Claire again. Like her mum, Fiona was in seventh heaven about their visit; she adored her elder brother and had taken Claire into her affections from the word go. This hadn't surprised Elinor as Fiona, like most Down's Syndrome sufferers, was a loving girl, who saw the best in everyone. Although Elinor had to be careful that people didn't take advantage of this, she wouldn't have had Fiona any other way.

In the fourteen years that Jeffrey and Claire had been married, Elinor had grown fond of her daughter-in-law. They came up to Rutherglen regularly and she and Fiona always looked forward to their visits. Although disappointed that so far they hadn't presented her with a grandchild, she would never pry into their business.

As she began to peel the potatoes for later, her thoughts went back to the shock and pain Colin's death had been to her. It was two and a half years ago now and, if it hadn't been for the support of Jeffrey and the knowledge that

Fiona was so dependent on her, Elinor doubted if she'd have survived the loss of her beloved husband. When tears threatened, she tried to pull herself back to the present joy of Jeffrey and Claire being with them soon.

'I'll prepare the veggies so they'll be ready for cooking when Jeffrey and Claire get here,' Elinor said to Fiona, once the potatoes were peeled. The broth would just need heating up and a sherry trifle, Jeffrey's favourite, was in the fridge.

'Can I help, Mum?' Fiona asked, always keen to be of service.

'Yes, darling, you could set the table for our meal.'

A short time later, with the veggies cut, Elinor went into the dining room, where Fiona had spread out the white damask tablecover on the dining table. Elinor loved that table; it was the one she and Colin had bought for their Macdonald Street flat when they were first married. Elinor watched for a few minutes, as Fiona began to lay out the cutlery and place mats, humming as she did so.

As she moved into the sitting room, Elinor recalled Nurse Middleton, the Health Visitor who'd kept in touch for a while after Fiona's birth, telling her that some parents turned their back on a handicapped child. Elinor, who'd bonded with her lovely daughter from the first, couldn't understand how anyone could do that. Fiona had brought nothing but joy over her thirty six years of life.

Elinor picked up a framed photograph sitting on the mantelpiece and smiled down at the faces of her deceased parents. Elinor's dad, Andrew, had never known his granddaughter, having died when Jeffrey was only months old. But 'Grandma Susan', as Fiona had always called her, had been wonderful with her granddaughter, sharing lots of activities with her and taking her for days out to allow Elinor time to get things done at home.

As she plumped up the cushions on the sofa and armchairs, Elinor recalled how distraught Fiona had been when 'Grandma Susan' died. Like many other disabled people, Fiona was a creature of habit and she found it hard to accept any changes in her life. With the help of her family though, and in particular Elinor herself, Fiona had soon returned to the happy and healthy girl she'd been prior to her grandmother's death.

With their chores completed and the meal prepared, Elinor and Fiona settled down in front of the television set to watch 'Coronation Street'. Fiona was a fan of the soap opera, which had started a few years before she was born.

When they heard a car horn sounding, the two of them collided in their rush to get to the front room window. Sure enough, through the gloom that had descended over the last hour, they made out Jeffrey's red BMW M5 turning into the driveway, its tyres crunching their way over the stones on the path.

Jeffrey had just stepped out of the car when Fiona grabbed him into her outstretched arms. She hugged and kissed him, with Elinor behind her watching the affection shared by her two offspring. Elinor and Fiona both greeted Claire. 'Come into the house out of the cold,' Elinor said. Jeffrey took their cases upstairs and Claire joined the others in the front room.

'Dinner is cooking slowly,' Elinor was saying, when Jeffrey came into the front room to join them. 'We'll have time for a glass of sherry before we eat.'

'I'll organise that for you, Mum,' he said and went off to get the sherry glasses from the sideboard. Elinor fetched the sherry from the kitchen cupboard and placed it on the tray beside the glasses for Jeffrey to pour. He poured three glasses of sherry and handed Claire a glass of orange juice. For a second Elinor wondered why she wasn't having sherry but then Jeffrey asked her something and it went out of her mind.

'Can't believe it's only another four hours until we're into the new Millennium,' Claire said. 'I wonder if all the computers will go haywire as they've been predicting.'

Jeffrey shook his head. 'A load of nonsense. It'll be no different from any other new year.'

'I was a New Year present to my mum and dad,' Fiona told her sister-in-law.

Elinor explained. 'Yes, I was in hospital when Jeffrey was born but Fiona here couldn't wait to join the family and she arrived almost four weeks early. So she was born here in this house on New Year's Eve and she gave her first cry at the same moment as the Town Hall clock struck midnight. We always said afterwards that she was our New Year's gift.'

'What a lovely story,' Claire said, her eyes moist. 'I've not heard that before.'

Fiona laid her finger on the side of her nose. 'Mum and I don't tell you all our secrets,' she said, winking at Claire.

It was after ten when they finished their meal. The three young folk insisted on clearing up and washing the dishes to allow Elinor some time to sit with her feet up.

Just before eleven the doorbell rang. 'I'll get it,' Elinor called into the kitchen, on her way to the front door. She opened it and gaped at the figure standing on the doormat, a fur hat covering his head and the collar of his heavy coat turned up over his ears.

Elinor stared, wordless, for a few minutes, her heart turning somersaults. 'Michael,' she finally stammered, and stood back to let him come into the hallway.

'Sorry to arrive unannounced,' he said, crossing his arms over his chest and thumping them with his hands to get some feeling back into them. 'Dot suggested that I turn up at New Year to surprise you. But I'm not so sure that it was a good idea,' he finished, noticing the shocked look on her face.

She realised that she hadn't spoken other than to utter his name. 'Of course you should have come. It's just the shock of seeing you on the doorstep that rendered me speechless.' She smiled. 'Doesn't happen very often as I'm sure you'll remember.'

Jeffrey came out of the kitchen and saw Michael standing in the hallway. 'Hello,' he said to the stranger and looked at his mum with raised eyebrows.

'Jeffrey, this is Michael Lynch, an old school friend of mine from Melbourne,' Elinor explained to her son.

'Oh yes, you met in Queensland last year. Pleased to meet you, Michael,' he said, holding out his hand to their guest. 'Let me take your coat,' Jeffrey offered, after they shook hands.

When Fiona came into the hall, she let out a joyous yell when she saw Michael. She ran over and hugged him.

'You'll stay overnight I hope?' Elinor asked Michael.

'Only if it isn't too much trouble. I've been staying in the Central Hotel in Glasgow for the past two days and haven't cancelled my room there, so I can go back to the hotel later tonight.'

But Elinor shook her head. 'Absolutely no way. The bed in the spare room is already made up, so there's no problem. Jeffrey and Claire are here for the next few days and you're welcome to stay on with us.'

'Thank you, Elinor. I'll be happy to have the company.'

'Would you like something to eat? We've had our dinner but there's plenty left over.'

'No thanks, Elinor, I ate at the hotel before I left.

There are a couple of bottles in my backpack to help celebrate the New Year.' He got out the bottles and handed them to Jeffrey.

Elinor touched Michael's arm. 'Come and get a heat.'

She led the way into the front room, where the fire was switched on and the room was cosy. When Jeffrey saw his mother with Michael, he signalled to Fiona and Claire to come into the living room with him and give the old friends time to chat.

Elinor and Michael sat down together on the settee. 'I was so sorry to hear from Dot that Molly had died,' Elinor said. 'It must have been a tremendous shock to you, Michael. I'm sorry but I can't think of you as Tony.'

He smiled. 'No worries. Both names are mine anyway so you can continue to call me Michael if you prefer.'

'I hope Molly didn't suffer any pain.'

'No, it all happened too quickly. She was waiting at the bus stop to go to work and just dropped dead. The paramedics said she wouldn't have felt a thing.' Tears ran down his face as he was telling her this and Elinor put an arm round his shoulder and held him towards her for a moment.

He moved away again and wiped his face with a handkerchief. 'Molly and I had arranged this trip, spending Christmas and New Year in the U.K., and going over to Europe in January. After Molly died in July, I couldn't face the thought of coming on my own. It was when I was down in Melbourne on business in September and met Dot for lunch that she convinced me that Molly would want me to make the trip. Dot suggested that I pay a surprise call on you. I hope you don't mind.'

'Of course I don't mind. I was so sad to lose touch with you, Michael.'

'I'm sorry about that, Elinor,' he replied, laying his

293

hand over her much smaller one. 'As you knew I wasn't any good at writing letters and a few months after you left Melbourne, I moved with my parents to Queensland to be near my sister and her family. My mother was able to help with child-minding and my dad and I both got jobs up there.'

'It was a good move then?'

'Yep, it proved to be a good move for me as a plasterer because Queensland, being a newer State than Victoria, began to attract more house owners and new migrants. This meant there was plenty of work in my trade and I did eventually start up my own business.'

'Did you meet Molly in Queensland?'

'Yes. I was living there at the time and she came up on holiday from Melbourne. We met on the beach.'

He fell silent for a moment. 'I really did mean to let you know my new address but I got caught up in my new life. I'm sorry, I loved you very much, Elinor, and I shouldn't have let it happen.'

'Well it's all water under the bridge, Michael, and I'm so happy we're in touch again. I didn't expect to ever see you again.'

'Same here.' Then he smiled, that same smile she remembered so well. 'Still, you did alright for yourself with Colin from the sound of it and Jeffrey and Fiona are a credit to you both.' He sighed, and his face clouded over. 'Molly and I had a very happy marriage. A child of our own was the one thing that was missing. It broke Molly's heart and, although we did speak of adoption, we didn't actually go down that line.'

Elinor's first reaction was to tell him about the child he'd almost had with her but, seeing the sadness etched on his face, she decided it would be cruel to mention that. She'd kept it secret for all these years so why bring it up now. It couldn't alter the paths their lives had taken so best to leave things as they were. 'I'm so glad you came tonight.'

He brushed his hand over her arm. 'Same here.'

Neither of them spoke and they simply stared into one another's eyes.

The spell was broken when Jeffrey put his head round the door. 'Sorry to interrupt your reminiscing but it's only fifteen minutes to midnight so how about us getting our drinks ready.'

The others came into the sitting room and Jeffrey produced a bottle of champagne that he'd brought with him from London. He popped open the cork. 'I think we'll have a drink to welcome in the new Millennium and to celebrate two old friends being reunited.'

'I'll get the glasses,' Claire said, jumping to her feet.

'Happy reunion,' Jeffrey said, raising his glass and they all drank a toast to Elinor and Michael. 'And as it's almost midnight, happy birthday, Fiona.' Fiona gave her brother an adoring smile and a second toast was drunk. 'And we have a triple celebration tonight,' he announced, unable to wipe the smile off his face. He held his glass against Claire's and two pairs of shining eyes met. 'I'm happy to tell you all that there is going to be a new addition to the Dawson clan.'

In the stunned silence that followed, Claire clinked her glass of orange juice against her husband's glass. 'The baby's due in May so you better get the knitting needles out, Mum.'

Elinor and Fiona let out a united yell of happiness and danced around the room. 'Does that mean I'm going to be an auntie, Mum?'

'Yes, darling, and a wonderful aunt you'll be. This is our second New Year surprise.'

Michael looked on with a smile lighting up his face,

happy to be part of all the excitement. Getting to his feet, he raised his glass and looked at Elinor. 'To friendship rediscovered.'

'To friendship rediscovered,' she echoed and her glass touched his just as the Town Hall clock chimed midnight, heralding in the 21st century.

The End

About the author

Irene Lebeter worked as a secretary for forty-five years, in industry, Civil Service and latterly the NHS. Her childhood love of story writing has continued throughout her life and has led to professional creative writing in her retirement. She is a member of Strathkelvin Writers' and Kelvingrove Writers', and has completed a two-year creative writing course at Strathclyde University.

Irene has been an award winner in both novel and short story genres at the Annual Conference of the Scottish Association of Writers and she has been published in the Federation of Writers' anthology 'Making Waves'. She has had multiple short stories and non-fiction articles published in a U.K. magazine and is a regular contributor of non-fiction historical articles in The Highlander magazine in USA. She has given talks on writing to church and other groups and more recently was invited to speak to high school pupils about novel writing.

'The Clock Chimed Midnight' is her third novel, following on from 'Vina's Quest' and 'Maddie'.

About Author Way Limited

Author Way provides a broad range of good quality, previously unpublished works and makes them available to the public on multiple formats.

We have a fast growing number of authors who have completed or are in the process of completing their books and preparing them for publication and these will shortly be available.

Please keep checking our website to hear about the latest developments.

Author Way Limited

www.authorway.net

29458379R00170

Printed in Poland
by Amazon Fulfillment
Poland Sp. z o.o., Wrocław